GREEN

•••

OTHER WORK BY TOM BAKER

The Sound of One Horse Dancing
Full Frontal: to make a long story short.
Paperwhite Narcissus

GREEN

•••

a novel

Tom Baker

Tom Baker (signature)

Lethe Press
Maple Shade, New Jersey

5 September 2017 Malibu, CA

GREEN

Published in 2017 by Lethe Press, Inc.
118 Heritage Avenue • Maple Shade, NJ 08052-3018 USA
www.lethepressbooks.com • lethepress@aol.com
ISBN: 978-1-59021-672-9 / 1-59021-672-5

This novel is a work of fiction. Names, characters, places, and incidents are either products of the author's imagination or are used fictitiously. Any resemblance to actual persons, living or dead, organizations, events, or locales is entirely coincidental.

Set in Minion, Stencil, and Steelfish.
Cover and interior design: Alex Jeffers.
Cover image: Steve Jakobson.

LIBRARY OF CONGRESS CATALOGING-IN-PUBLICATION DATA
Names: Baker, Tom, 1944- author.
Title: Green : a novel / Tom Baker.
Description: Maple Shade, New Jersey : Lethe Press, 2017.
Identifiers: LCCN 2017015206 | ISBN 9781590216729 (pbk. : alk. paper)
Subjects: LCSH: Gay military personnel--Fiction. | United States. Army--Fiction. | Homophobia--Fiction. | Vietnam War, 1961-1975--Fiction |
GSAFD: War stories. | Bildungsromans.
Classification: LCC PS3602.A5882 G74 2017 | DDC 813/.6--dc23
LC record available at https://lccn.loc.gov/2017015206

for

DTAB

PROLOGUE

● ● ●

The year is 1967. I had just graduated from William & Mary and was scheduled to enter Yale Drama School in September to get my masters in theatre arts. Meanwhile young men were burning draft cards and refusing to cut their long hair, using the excuse they were in a rock band, some thinking about moving to Canada, ready to embrace a maple leaf before dying for stars and stripes. Straight men were "checking the box," choosing to lie about sucking cock rather than die in a war they didn't give a shit about. Their homes, moms, and girlfriends were not being threatened by men with slanty eyes, so why did they have to go halfway around the world to kill these people? I know it's probably hard for you to imagine, but that's the way it was. The Vietnam War—in media terms a "police action" or "conflict"—was wiping my friends off the street—guys I went to school with. Images of a naked girl running down a dirt road with other children, her arms open and burned, looking like maple syrup had been poured over her body, would be plastered across the front page of the *Daily News*, winning Associated Press photographer Nick Ut a Pulitzer prize in 1973—proof that the napalm sprayed into the palm-tree jungles was effective. You've probably seen that photo in the anniversary issues of *LIFE* magazine that come out every few years. Hell, I even saw a vendor in Times Square selling T-shirts with the little girl's image on it. How fucked up is that?

The United States was fighting an unpopular war halfway around the world and making little progress. The need to beef up our military presence in Southeast Asia created a false wave of hysteria in the country, and I got my draft notice from the Army in mid-June, two weeks after I graduated from college. My deferment request for graduate studies was conveniently ignored. Instead of going to New

Haven in September to register for Yale Drama School on Chapel Street, I would be checking into the U.S. Army Induction Center at 129 Church Street on July 10, 1967. For a few minutes I laughed at the irony of ending up in church rather than chapel, but my sense of humor quickly wore thin.

If you really want to hear my story, I'll dispense with the Holden Caulfield background stuff and get right to it. I had no idea what lay ahead of me when I entered the Army. Somehow I got through eight weeks of basic training, being singled out and humiliated as the only college graduate in my unit. My nickname was "college boy," a moniker that stuck with me throughout my military service. Trust me, that's not a label you want plastered on your back. After basic training I was transferred to MOS training at Fort Eustis in Virginia. I should probably explain that MOS stands for Military Occupational Specialty. I'd later figure out that the Army selects the field that you are least qualified for and assigns that to you as your MOS.

It was about six weeks after I arrived at Fort Eustis when the base was put on lockdown because hurricane Edith, a Category 4 storm was heading up the Atlantic Coast for the Tidewater area and predicted to make landfall in nearby Virginia Beach. While everyone was hunkering down, nailing plywood over windows and filling sandbags to redirect expected floodwaters away from strategic buildings, I was summoned to Captain Oliver's office. The power had gone out, so when I arrived at the administration building, it looked like a chapel inside with vigil lights the only illumination. The spec 4 sitting at the desk I usually occupied motioned me into Oliver's office. I entered to face the captain and an Air Force lieutenant I'd never seen before.

The inquisition that followed changed my life forever.

"I think we're done here," the Air Force officer said, sliding a manila folder across Oliver's desk. "I'm going back to Langley."

"No one's going anywhere. We're on lockdown," Oliver said pulling a bottle of Jack Daniels out of the bottom drawer of his desk.

"You're dismissed, Halladay. We can take up this matter in the morning."

"Take up what?" I said. "There's nothing to take up because this is all bullshit."

"We'll discuss this in the morning."

"There's nothing to discuss because nothing happened."

"Halladay, you're dismissed," Oliver repeated. "Return to your barracks and wait for instructions."

"Yes, sir," I said, saluting and turning my back on the two officers drinking shots of Jack Daniels. I charged out of the administration building cursing, "Fuck this shit."

Edith spat out rain, pelting my face as I sprinted past rows of housing units where windows were boarded up with sheets of plywood. I stumbled and hugged myself against the grabbing wind, running toward the rifle range where waves exploded over banks of the James River. The hulls of mothball fleet ships were tethered in the heaving waters, slamming against each other.

I staggered to my knees in the mud and embraced the wide girth of the elm where I had spent off hours reading Faulkner and Salinger. The old tree was swaying defiantly in the raging wind as I wrapped my arms around its coarse bark. I opened the belt on my fatigues and pushed them below my knees, letting the rain beat on my bare ass. I sank facedown in the mud, tightening the leather belt, securing myself to a gnarled root of the old tree, holding on as Edith slammed down. The relentless rain cascaded with tears running down my cheeks as I sank into the muck, sobbing.

CHAPTER ONE
(July 9–10, 1967)

● ● ●

I guess I should start at the beginning; it was the night before I was to report to New Haven for my induction into the Army, and I needed someone to talk to when I called Karen.

"You're crazy," she laughed the way she always did. "Shouldn't you be packing?"

"We're going to Vahsan's," I said, not letting her speak. "I'll pick you up in ten minutes."

"This is insane," Karen smiled as we drove down I-95 toward Port Chester.

"Of course. That's why we're going."

"But we're of age now and could go anywhere in Westport or Norwalk to have a drink."

"And run into all our parents' friends?"

"Right," she said placing her hand on the back of my neck.

I should clue you in that Vahsan's was the saloon in Port Chester we all went to with our fake IDs back in high school. It was just over the state line in New York where the drinking age was eighteen, and we could all pass. The owners didn't care. They gladly served rich kids from Fairfield County who came on weekends to order Singapore Slings and pepperoni pizzas, humoring us until one of our dates threw up on the jukebox while trying to put a quarter in to play "Chances Are" by Johnny Mathis.

"Why did you want to come here?" Karen asked as we sipped the sweet cocktails.

"Just trying to hold onto some of the past," I said, twirling the little umbrella stick in my drink. "We used to have a lot of fun here."

"You know, you don't have to go through with this," Karen said, getting serious, placing her hand on mine.

"Yes, I do." I pulled back, chugging my drink.

"Why?" she asked simply.

"You wouldn't understand," I shot back, annoyed. I threw a ten-dollar bill on the table and got up. "Let's get out of here."

"Whatever." Karen sipped the last of her drink and followed me to the parking lot.

We didn't speak on the drive back to Westport. We ended up in the parking lot at Compo Beach, overlooking stone barbecue pits, waves lapping quietly on the pebble shore of Long Island Sound. This is where we had come to make out and explore each other's bodies as young horny teenagers, fueled by the sweet Singapore Slings from Vahsan's Tavern and the romantic sounds of *Music till Dawn* from the car radio.

"You could just tell them you're gay, and that would be the end of it," Karen broke the silence as we sat in my dad's Lincoln.

"I can't."

"Why not?" Karen looked at me, lighting a cigarette.

"You think I have a canned answer for that? It's just something I have to do."

"For your parents?" She sat up in the front seat.

"Fuck, no."

"Then for who? And for what?" she said, wheezing a long puff of smoke into the car.

"You wouldn't understand."

"I guess not, if you don't tell me," Karen said in the way that always made her seem superior.

I was frustrated by my inability to tell her how I felt. I was frustrated that I couldn't even tell myself why I was throwing away an opportunity to go to Yale Drama School, choosing instead to pick up a gun and risk getting my ass shot off in some jungle halfway around the world. *For what?* To prove something…that I was as good as the next guy…that always getting selected last in the lineup for basketball with the Shirts against the Skins wasn't the end of the world. I was so fucking confused. The one thing I did know was I would never "check the box" to get out of serving in the military.

This was not how I had pictured my last civilian night, getting into a confrontation with my girlfriend parked in the make-out section of Compo Beach. Funny, I thought, nothing seemed to be working as it was supposed to be written in this romance novel. I turned on the ignition, ending *Music till Dawn*, and dropped Karen off at her mother's house.

"Take care of yourself, Timmy." She kissed me on the cheek, opened the car door and walked up the driveway to the front door without looking back. "You know I love you."

• • •

I have to bring you into a Norman Rockwell setting here. My mom was in the velvet-upholstered wingback chair in our living room, a canvas tote bag filled with yarn and pattern books at her feet. She was always busy knitting something—Afghans, scarves, sweaters, baby booties—whatever the occasion—birthday, anniversary, shower. I jokingly called her Madame Defarge. Recently she'd elevated her craft to needlepoint, according to her a more ambitious endeavor than knitting. She had made floral seat covers for our eight dining room chairs, and turned out several intricate throw pillows that now adorned the sofa.

On summer weekends Mom sat in her folding aluminum chair at Compo Beach, her tote bag of yarn and patterns propped up in the sand beside her. She'd sent away for a needlepoint catalogue offering plastic cutouts of Christmas ornaments. She stitched intricate candy canes, snowmen, Santa Clauses, angels, even a whole nativity scene, as the gentle waves of Long Island Sound licked the beach. The group of ladies she sat with thumbed through dog-eared copies of *Peyton Place*, looking over sunglasses to eye other women on the beach who might fit roles of incest, abortion, adultery, lust and murder from the small New England town depicted in the Grace Metalious novel—never considering for a moment they might be models for the characters in the salacious book.

Evenings while sitting in front of the black and white Zenith television set, sipping the last of a whiskey sour from her pre-dinner cocktail, Mom would knit, crochet, or needlepoint as she watched canned-laughter sitcoms. At half-hour commercial breaks, she'd go to the kitchen to pack fresh ice cubes into her melted drink, top it off with a touch of bourbon, according to her, to give it a little color. By the eleven o'clock news she had dozed off, the gingerbread man or angel she'd been working on limp and unfinished in her lap. Exactly at 11:30 when the *Tonight Show* with Jack Paar came on NBC, she would wake up, sip the last remains of her drink and go up to bed.

When I was thirteen, Mom knitted a white Irish wool ski sweater for me with two reindeer on the front. I loved it, but there was one problem: the sleeves were about a foot too long. When I first pulled on the sweater and folded back the extra sleeve length, it looked like I was carrying a hand muff on each arm. When I left for college, I packed the sweater into the my clothes trunk, where it stayed the four years I was at William & Mary.

"Breakfast's on the kitchen counter," Mom called out as she heard me coming down the carpeted stairway to the living room. "I made scrambled eggs with chopped chicken livers. They're warming in the electric frying pan." Mom pretended to busy herself with knitting, but her hands were shaking and she kept missing stitches.

The kitchen radio was turned to the morning talk station, WNLK from Norwalk. The announcer was forecasting a hot, humid day in Fairfield County with showers likely in the afternoon; there was a minor traffic accident on the Merritt Parkway at the Weston Road Exit 42, causing ten- to fifteen-minute delays. The electric frying pan was on "warm" as I picked up the lid to inspect the egg and chicken liver mixture. Mom knew it was my favorite. I split open an English muffin with a fork, popped the two half circles in the toaster and poured a glass of orange juice from the carton on the refrigerator door. I wanted this to be just an ordinary day, like all the ones we'd sat down to breakfast before. But today was different—very different.

"Kay Bankhead will be coming up at seven," the radio announcer promised. "She'll be speaking with lifeguards from Sherwood Island and Compo Beach who made a number of courageous rescues this past Fourth of July."

I have to give some background here because you probably never heard of the local radio programs in Fairfield County. Kay Bankhead was a popular socialite in Westport. She was married to Seth Bankhead, a business associate of my dad. They played golf at Longshore Country Club, and spent many afternoons at the Nineteenth Hole bar. Kay hosted *Talk Around Town*, a weekly program on WNLK that covered the social scene in Fairfield County. During the summer season at the Westport Country Playhouse, Kay interviewed actors appearing at the theatre. Most plays ran for a week; many were pre-Broadway tryouts. This created a rotating pool of celebrities for Kay to interview: Eli Wallach and Anne Jackson, Betsy Palmer, Mike Nichols and Elaine May, Imogene Coca, Cesar Romero, and a young

Jane Fonda, who at eighteen had created a stir on Compo Beach by wearing a revealing polka-dot bikini. The photo of Miss Fonda on the beach was the lead item on the front page of *The Town Crier*.

"Next week Kay will be talking to four of our local boys who've just returned from service in Vietnam," the radio announcer continued. "Be sure to tune in and hear their stories. You won't want to miss that." A commercial jingle for *Chock full o' Nuts, that heavenly coffee, a better coffee a billionaire's money can't buy,* sang out from the radio.

I knew Kay's only son, Seth Ronald Bankhead III, who had received his commission from West Point and was a second lieutenant serving in Vietnam. Ronnie, as everyone called him, used to babysit for my sister Kathy and me during summers whenever he was home from Lawrenceville Academy. I have to admit that I thought Ronnie was sexy. He was just over six feet tall, with a thick mane of dark brown hair that fell over his large, almond-colored eyes. He was captain of the Lawrenceville swim team and a lacrosse player. Ronnie let me stay up late watching TV, while Kathy was in her room listening to 45s of the Everly Brothers and Bobby Darin, talking on the phone for hours with her girlfriends.

Sometimes Ronnie and I would play cards, usually go fish or hearts. But one night, while Ronnie was teaching me the basics of poker, we got into a discussion of his injuries as a lacrosse player. Ronnie rolled up his pant leg to reveal a long scar on his lower calf. The card lesson progressed to a version of strip poker that ended abruptly when we were both down to our Jockey shorts. Ronnie quickly shuffled the cards and put the deck back into the plastic tray container. The game was over for the night.

When I was in fifth grade, I was invited along with six other students from Assumption School to go on Kay Bankhead's radio program to talk about our upcoming Christmas pageant. It was a loose adaptation of *Amahl and the Night Visitors*, the Gian Carlo Menotti opera that had become a tradition in school and community theatre programs since its premiere in 1951. I was cast in the lead role of young Amahl.

"What is special about the part you play?" Kay asked me.

"I get to carry a stick around for a crutch and limp a lot," I volunteered.

"And..."

"I see things that other people don't. Like this big star in the sky, but no one believes me."

●●●

The English muffins, blackened around the edges, popped out of the toaster. I scooped a helping of eggs onto a plate and sat down at the kitchen table. Mom had abandoned her knitting and was sitting across from me.

The radio announcer came on reminding listeners that a freshly-brewed cup of Chock full o' Nuts was available at the coffee company's stand in Grand Central for only twenty-five cents—a perfect way to start your day in the city. He then gave times for high and low tide, and confirmed that all commuter trains on the New Haven Railroad line were running on schedule.

Dad entered the kitchen and poured coffee in his mug with the *Number 1 Dad* inscription.

"You'd better finish up. We should get going before seven to be safe."

"I'm all packed." I said scraping the remains of my breakfast into the sink. I bounded upstairs to get my duffel bag, as my parents sat at the kitchen table, frozen like a tableau on a *Saturday Evening Post* cover.

CHAPTER TWO
(July 10, 1967)

● ● ●

Dad eased the Lincoln onto the curving Weston Road entrance ramp to Merritt Parkway with a sign indicating "Eastbound New Haven." It was just past seven a.m. He stopped the car behind a line of brake lights, as a tow truck from Izzo Brothers Texaco station slipped clamps under the bumper of a battered VW that had been rear-ended by a Ford Country Squire station wagon. Both cars were damaged, but the owner of the station wagon was able to drive away. No one appeared to be hurt, but the inconvenience would domino down through the snarl of frustrated drivers waiting to move ahead onto the parkway.

"Mind if I change the station?"

Dad waved his hand indifferently as he lit a cigarette. I turned the dial to WICC, the Bridgeport station that played music in the morning between traffic and weather reports. Lulu was singing "To Sir With Love"—something about crayons and perfume and writing in the sky. The Izzo tow truck horn was beeping as it pulled the crumpled Beetle off the shoulder of the road where it had been pushed, dragging it unceremoniously to a repair shop on Post Road. The on-ramp was now clear, and the Connecticut State trooper directing traffic waved cars ahead.

We picked up speed as Dad merged into the right hand lane. The Merritt was one of the most beautiful roadways in America, opened in 1940 and designated an historic, limited-access, highway. I knew this because in sixth grade I had submitted a report on the Merritt Parkway, responding to an assignment from Sister Claire to write about trips we had taken during our summer vacation. My classmates boasted about cross-country adventures on Route 66, the Seven Mile Bridge to the Florida Keys, a drive through the Blue Ridge Mountains and one report on the hazards of driving on the other side of the road through the English countryside. I chose to write about the Merritt Parkway in our backyard, and I spent hours in the Westport Public Library researching its history. No trucks, commercial vehicles, bicycles, or pedestrians were allowed. The overhead bridges along the thirty-seven miles of roadway were designed by the architect, George L. Dunkelberger, in an Art Deco style with touches of neoclassic and modern design. The five-mile expanse between Westport and Fairfield was unofficially known as "No Man's Land" because there were no exits or entrances along that long stretch of road.

I looked out the car window at dogwood trees and mountain laurel bushes now past flowering and sleepy in verdant foliage, gracing the grassy areas along the shoulders of the parkway. As Dad pressed the accelerator of the Lincoln to mount the steep rise outside Westport, I remembered the times Aunt Emily drove her 1949 Ford—a tan shoebox with slab-sided pontoon design, sleepy cat-eye tail lights and goldfish oval mouth grill: Aunt Em calling out "Here we go!" as she pressed the accelerator to surmount the steep hill ahead, Kathy and I pushing our feet against the floorboards to help the climb, shrieking in delight as the Ford conquered the ascent and coasted down the steep road toward Fairfield. Today the Lincoln effortlessly forged over the same pavement heading toward New Haven.

"I think we'll be okay for time." Dad flicked the stub of his Camel out the window and lit another cigarette with the lighter mounted in the dashboard. I hated riding in his car. The sun visors were stained yellow from hours of him smoking on long thruway trips with air-conditioning on and windows rolled up, stale nicotine air recycled through the car's vent system. I looked out at the leafy forest along the parkway, passing Exit 44, the off-ramp for Fairfield University and the Jesuit prep school I had attended; it all seemed so long ago. We passed Bridgeport and Stratford, crossing the Housatonic River Bridge, to connect with the Wilbur Cross Parkway that would take us to New Haven.

"Looks like it's up there on the right." Dad pointed as he stopped the Lincoln a block away from a drab brick building—the Army Induction Center at 129 Church Street. A few guys lingered outside, smoking and laughing, as though in line for a rock 'n' roll concert.

Dad turned off the ignition and we sat without speaking, the only sound pumping softly from the car radio speakers—"All You Need Is Love," the Beatles' latest hit.

"Guess this is it," I said, opening the car door and grabbing my duffel bag from the back seat.

"Good luck, son. Be careful."

"Sure, Dad," I said, gripping his handshake. It felt awkward, like making physical contact with a stranger.

You might be thinking there should be some conversation here—a few words between my dad and me. But our family wasn't like that.

The Lincoln edged away from the curb—the lingering sounds of the Beatles fading into the humid July air as Dad lit another cigarette and headed back to Westport.

I approached the group lined up outside the Army Induction Center. The guys stopped talking and looked at me suspiciously.

"Couldn't buy your way out?"

"Guess not," I joked nervously, addressing a boy in a black T-shirt, sleeves rolled up with a pack of cigarettes tucked under his left arm. "Just along for the ride. Like the rest of you."

"Wrong, white bread," he looked at me menacingly. "None of us arrived here in a fuckin' Lincoln limousine."

"That was my dad. He just dropped me off."

"Fuckin' A," he snickered.

The door of the brick building opened and a soldier wearing pressed khakis, a clipboard in hand, called, "You faggots get in here now. Take seats in the room on the right."

"Where, man?" a lanky black guy, chewing gum and bouncing a basketball, laughed, looking around at the others waiting in line.

"In there, you dickhead," the soldier barked, grabbing the basketball and hurling it down Chapel Street. "This isn't your goddamn high school PE class. Just sit down and shut the fuck up."

The kid looked around, but seeing no one was coming to his defense, shrugged and moved into the classroom with other recruits. "Fuckin' A," he mumbled under his breath.

"I said shut the fuck up," the soldier shouted, slamming the door.

The walls of the room were tiled in chipped, dirty yellow blocks. Fluorescent lighting troughs hung from a ceiling with exposed coils of electrical wiring and sooty heating ducts. A row of horizontal hinged, wire-glass windows ran along the top of the far wall, letting in the only natural light. A cracked blackboard hung on the wall up front, and an American flag on a pole stood askew in the corner. Dilapidated metal folding chairs with writing tablet arms were scattered around the room.

The soldier opened the door and yelled, "You fuckheads take a seat and fill out those forms on the chairs. That is if you can read and write. Donna," he pointed to a handsome Italian boy sitting in the front row, "will pick them up when you're finished. Won't you, darling?"

The kid looked confused.

"I see your name is Donathon Cretella," he said referring to the roster on the clipboard. "Mind if we just call you Donna for short, since you're such a pretty thing?"

"Yeah, sure," he said embarrassed.

"Okay, sweetheart," the soldier said. "When these dickheads are finished filling out the forms, move your sweet ass, pick up the papers and bring them over here to Mother. Think you can handle that?"

The door opened and Sergeant Murphy entered the room. He was a short, pudgy man, fine red hair thinning over his scalp with a shiny bald spot at the back of his head. His beer belly pressed tightly against the brass buckle sagging below his waist.

"Everything in order here?" Murphy asked.

"So far, so good," the arrogant soldier reported. "Donna, here," he pointed to the young Italian boy, "is going to collect the forms."

"You can go back to your desk and I'll take over."

"They're all yours." He turned and exited the room.

"Gentlemen, be seated." The paunchy sergeant motioned us to sit down. "I know this is difficult," he said as the clattering of metal chairs squeaked across the linoleum floor. "Just as it is for all of us in the service of our country."

Coughing and suppressed chuckles rumbled through the room as we waited for the pep talk.

"You think this is funny?" The sergeant pointed to a Puerto Rican boy sitting behind Donna. "Stand up, young man," he ordered. "Tell us your name."

"You mean me?" he asked.

"Do you see me talking to your mother? Yes, you fuckhead."

The kid shrugged indifferently, standing up.

"Ricky. Ricky Rodriguez," he said smugly, thumbs tucked in the top of his jeans. The slam of the sergeant's fist against his face came without warning, sending the kid reeling back into the metal folding chair, blood drooling from his lip.

"Get up, Rodriguez. The only one with attitude in here is me. Got that?" Murphy shouted.

"Yeah," Ricky mumbled, struggling to get up.

"Yes, sir," the sergeant corrected. "Now, tell me your name, you dumb fuck."

"Ricky Rodriguez," he repeated.

"You mean Richard Rodriguez," he looked at the roster on the clipboard. "Now sit your ass down."

"What the fuck?" Ricky mumbled, dabbing the blood dripping from his lip and sliding back into his chair.

"Good," Murphy said after a short silence. "Any of you other fucks have something to say?" He looked around the room. "All right... now let's get on with the business of the day."

I started to fill out the form, basic information required on any job application: name, address, education. Then there were questions about religious affiliation, blood type, allergies, broken bones, homosexual tendencies. The question was wedged in there between religion and medical history. This was the chance to "check-the-box" and get an automatic 4-F. I heard some guys snickering, but I wasn't going there.

I penciled in the X next to "Roman Catholic" even though I didn't feel I belonged. I'd endured eight years at Assumption School under the Sisters of Notre Dame. They terrified me by preaching an eternity of burning in hell for unnatural behavior. Even at eight years old, I questioned how long it would take a body to burn up. Maybe what they really meant was that I'd end up like one of those fake coals glowing twenty-four hours a day in a gas-fueled fireplace in the lobby of a Holiday Inn. I didn't believe any of the nuns' shit, despite all those Hail Mary's doled out in Confession for my impure thoughts, while the priest behind the lattice screen in that dark cubicle at the back of the church stroked himself under his cassock as I described my secret desires. Deep down I knew I was a good person, bringing home stray cats and taking care never to step on a ladybug or crush a firefly. I don't recall ever helping a little old lady across the street, but I would have if the opportunity had ever presented itself.

Sergeant Murphy stood in front of the blackboard, arms folded, knowing what the whispering was about, and matter-of-factly cautioned, "Any of you pussy eaters who are thinking about pretending you like to suck cock just to get out of this…" he paused, "well you better be prepared to prove it."

The door opened and the khaki soldier reentered the room, nodding to the sergeant. "Time's up," he announced. "Donna, pick up the forms from these losers and bring them here. Move it."

The boy collected the papers and delivered them to the waiting soldier, who then handed Donna a bunch of plastic garbage bags. "Everybody gets one. Start passing them out. C'mon. Move your pretty ass."

"All right, gentlemen," the sergeant said, sounding civil. "Listen up. Strip down to shorts. Put your shit into the bag and hold onto to it. Got that?" he asked not waiting for a response. "Not too hard now, is it?"

We started to undress, self-conscious and awkward, looking around as we shed our civilian clothes.

"Hurry up, ladies. We don't have all day!"

I folded my jeans and jersey shirt, placing everything into the plastic bag with my socks and sneakers. I tucked my wallet, driver's license and two twenty-dollar bills into the toe of my sneaker, and stood next to the metal folding chair in my Jockey shorts. Ricky Rodriguez was next to me, rolling his clothes into a ball and stuffing them into the bag. His briefs clung tightly, hugging his moon ass cheeks and the bulging hump in his crotch. Ricky's right hand slid past the elastic band on his underwear, adjusting a semi-erect cock.

"So how come you didn't get out of all this shit?" he said as he withdrew his hand from his shorts. "I thought you rich white boys could buy your way out."

"Yeah, right." I shrugged, offended by the suggestion.

"Aw shit," Murphy shouted, looking around the room, pointing to a muscular black guy standing buck naked in the back of the room. "There's one in every barrel. Commando, right? I know. Here, you stupid fuck," he threw him a towel. "Wrap this around yourself so the rest of us don't have to look at that fat Lincoln Log."

"Hey, man…whatever," the naked guy laughed, grabbing the towel and draping it around his shoulders.

"That's Dildo."

"Something funny there, Miss Rodriguez?" Murphy yelled.

"No, it's just…"

"Well, you better shut up, dumb ass, unless you want another fat lip."

"This place really sucks," Ricky muttered as we stood in line. "Razor…that's what everybody calls me. Not Ricky."

"Tim…Tim Halladay." We did not shake hands. "Why Razor?" I asked as the line inched forward.

"Because I'm a sharp ass."

The process continued as we waited for our interview with the Army doctor. The overhead fluorescent lights glared, casting an impersonal chill over the depressing surroundings. I was next, and stepped forward to lower my shorts when instructed, coughing as the doctor grabbed my balls. An indifferent look from the inspector, a quick nod and some brief scribbling on the form in front of him, and I was waved through and back into the classroom.

I slipped into my clothes and took a seat in the front row of metal chairs, waiting for instructions. The other guys followed, while Dildo, still naked, waved his giant black cock for everyone to see and paraded around the room laughing.

"Hey, King Kong," Sergeant Murphy bellowed, throwing his clipboard across the room, striking Dildo directly on the head. "Put that black schlong in your pants before I shove this pretty white boy's face up your ass," he sneered looking at me. "Sit the fuck down 'cause nobody here wants to see that tired old thing."

Dildo, stunned by the blow to his ego, looked blankly at the sergeant, fumbled with his pants and sank into the nearest chair.

At that point the door opened and a second lieutenant in perfectly pressed uniform entered the room. Sergeant Murphy and the khaki soldier stood at attention, saluting the officer. Murphy bellowed, "Men! On your feet!"

We all stood up clumsily, pushing back the metal chairs. The lieutenant looked around the room and suppressed a smile. "Everything in order here, sergeant?"

"Yes, sir. So far…so good," Murphy responded.

"Fine," the officer nodded as he pulled down a scroll above the blackboard. It looked like a tattered blackout window shade from previous wars, the edges chipped and frayed. The heading was—*THE ARMY CODE OF VALUES*—sub-titles of *Loyalty, Duty, Respect, Self-*

less Service, Honor, Integrity and *Personal Courage* printed on the discolored paper.

"Gentlemen, take notice. This is why we are here." He paused, peering out at us. "Listen up. This is the *Army Code of Values.* This is why we are here," he repeated. "You will follow theses principles. You will eat, sleep, and breathe them every day. Don't ever forget that." Some yawns rolled though the room as we stood waiting for the pep talk.

"Duty. Respect. Selfless Service. Honor. Integrity. Personal Courage." The officer pointed to the words slowly and deliberately. "Things you may not have thought much about before. But, gentlemen, you will embrace these principles and respect them before you leave here. I can promise you that."

The khaki soldier brought the American flag on the stand from the corner of the room, positioning it to the right of the lieutenant.

"Gentlemen, stand up straight," the officer instructed. "Try to act like you have respect for yourself and your country. Pay close attention. You are about to take the oath of enlistment. Raise your right hand, and repeat after me. I'll go slowly because this is serious."

We stood at attention, looking forward.

"Now, repeat after me." He looked around the room and began. *"I..."* he paused. "State your name." We responded with a litany of names.

"Good," the officer commented. "Now continue, and speak clearly."

"...do solemnly swear that I will support and defend the Constitution of the United States," the officer paused as most of us stumbled with the words, then continued, *"against all enemies, foreign and domestic, that I will bear true faith and allegiance to the same; and that I will obey the orders of the President of the United States and the orders of the officers appointed over me, according to the regulations and the Uniform Code of Military Justice. So help me God."*

No one joked or snickered; this was fucking real.

"Gentlemen, you are now soldiers in the U.S. Army," the officer proclaimed. "Act accordingly."

The khaki soldier moved the flag back into the corner and picked up the clipboard thrown at Dildo, handing it to Murphy. "Now listen up," the sergeant said. "As I call your name, line up in the hallway outside." He started shouting, checking off each one on the roster: "Cretella, Utsinger, Rodriguez, Halladay, Brown, Lapinski, Rivera, Diaz, Murphy, Stein, Johnson, Umberto," as he went down the list.

"You men are in Charlie Company. Remember that," the sergeant announced as he finished reading names. "Line up in the hall and wait for instructions."

"Halladay. Step forward," the lieutenant called out.

I looked around, then went to the front of the line.

"You're the college boy here and look like you might have a brain, so I'm putting you in charge," the officer directed, handing me a stack of manila envelopes. "It's your job to see that you and these men—all twenty-four of you—get to your final destination. Nobody gets lost along the way. Understand?" the officer asked not waiting for an answer. "Here's the manifest." The officer handed me a roster with names of the twenty-four recruits in alphabetical order. "Just make sure everyone's accounted for along the way. If anybody's missing, mark him AWOL, and we'll take care of it. Think you can handle that?"

"I guess so," I answered.

"Yes, sir," he corrected.

"Yes, sir," I repeated.

"Listen up," the officer addressed us. "You are being transported by bus to LaGuardia Airport where you will be getting on a plane to your final destination to report for basic training. Halladay here will be taking roll call to make sure nobody gets lost. Now move out. Halladay, they're all yours."

I read off the names and checked each one off as the recruits got on the bus idling on Chapel Street. When everyone was accounted for, I boarded, taking the front seat across the aisle from the driver. The accordion door thumped shut and the elephantine coach sagged away from the curb. The air brakes hissed and grabbed as the lumbering vehicle lurched through stop-and-go downtown New Haven traffic heading for the Connecticut Turnpike.

Razor was in the seat behind me. He unfolded a pack of Camels from the sleeve of his T-shirt, tapped a cigarette on his forearm, and lit up.

"Sorry, kid." The driver spotted Razor in the rearview mirror. "No smoking allowed. Not my rule. Uncle Sam's."

"Fuck," Razor said disgustedly, squashing the cigarette with the heel of his sneaker into the dirty black rubber aisle mat.

"I know," the beefy driver muttered, looking ahead out the large fishbowl windshield. "It sucks, knowing what you guys are headed for."

The bus lumbered up the westbound Woodward Avenue onramp of I-95 heading toward New York, jerking as gears shifted until it slowly reached cruising speed with the merging traffic. It was just after eleven o'clock, a muggy New England July morning. The air conditioning on the bus wasn't working, so the only ventilation came from two-inch slits of the retracted windows, emitting noxious fumes from passing cars and trucks traveling on the throughway.

I looked out as abandoned factory buildings with broken windows and dangling air ducts slipped by, looking like black and white clips from a TV documentary on urban blight. Rows of wooden tenement houses sagged forlornly on streets littered with garbage—two-, three- and four-family units, some with laundry hanging out from windows to dry in the polluted air. These were the same New Haven and Bridgeport neighborhoods where most of the boys on the bus had grown up.

We moved on through Fairfield, Southport, Greens Farms and then passed Westport, the terrain changing to lush landscapes of maple and sumac trees, an opulence of overgrown vegetation dotted with neat single-family suburban homes framed by Queen Anne's lace. The houses looked like red plastic cottages from a Monopoly board game, placed alongside the throughway, inhabited by the lucky ones who had "Passed Go" and collected money more times than other players rolling the dice.

The I-95 throughway ran parallel to the tracks of the New Haven Railroad commuter line, where every weekday morning, wives dropped husbands at the station to board trains headed into the city for high-paying jobs on Madison Avenue and Wall Street. These dutiful women returned to *Better Homes & Gardens* split-levels, stacking coffee mugs and sticky juice glasses into the dishwasher, scraping remains of half-eaten English muffins into the garbage disposal, filling time and watching the clock on the built-in oven waiting for the acceptable hour to have a gin and tonic before lunch.

The bus passed the Sherwood Island exit and continued over the high vaulting concrete bridge spanning Saugatuck River, passing Route 136, the exit onto Riverside Avenue continuing past our house on Main Street. I drew circles on the dirty bus window with my finger, not wanting to let go where I grew up. At the Westport train station, Mario's, a favorite watering hole for Westport commuters, was opening for lunch. My dad took me there whenever I was home from college. He was a regular, always ordering the same thing: a medium-rare hamburger patty with Tommy's secret sauce, and a martini bucket—a full cocktail shaker of vodka crammed with ice cubes and a drop of vermouth with a small plate of olives on the side. Tommy was the owner's son, and he held court at the bar, occasionally getting up to seat customers. He was a stubby, overweight Italian boy, with black hair slicked over his large head. Unlike his brothers who also worked at the restaurant, Tommy never married. Early on I figured out that Tommy's "secret sauce" was nothing more than Heinz pickle relish mixed with mayonnaise, but I never told my dad, who believed Tommy's sauce was a family recipe from the Old Country.

I looked out the window, watching my past life falling by the concrete highway, the grassy shoulders overgrown with poison ivy. I always wanted to make my parents proud of me. I mean I never got arrested or smashed up my dad's '55 T-Bird. I guess I could go on and list the "nevers" to convince myself I was a good son, but maybe this new crazy chapter in my life would finally prove that to Mom and Dad.

I suspected Dad was right now at the nineteenth-hole bar at Longshore Country Club, having lunch with Seth Bankhead. It was Monday and the golf course would be closed for maintenance, but the bar was open for members. I wondered what Dad was saying about dropping me off at the Army Induction Center in New Haven.

Westport slipped by, each mile fading further into the distance, separating me from the past. The bus moved on through Norwalk, Darien, Stamford and finally across the Mianus River Bridge in Old Greenwich before leaving Connecticut and entering New York State. The throughway signs changed abruptly from green to white, signaling the cross into a different state. The exit sign for Playland at Rye Beach loomed as the bus slowed in heavy traffic.

Whenever Aunt Blade visited from Georgetown, she insisted on taking my sister and me there. I remember the rush I felt when Mom would pull the Lincoln into the gravel parking lot. The giant Ferris wheel with its suspended passenger baskets turned in slow graceful circles above leafy maple trees surrounding the park. The fearsome wooden scaffolding of the Dragon Coaster rose skyward, swaying ominously as train cars filled with terrified passengers inched up the sharp incline, descending in a thunderous roar down steep tracks with riders shrieking, arms thrust over their heads.

I was not allowed to ride the Dragon Coaster. Mom thought I was too timid to endure a scary pass through the dragon's dark mouth tunnel with the monster's eyes lighting up and steam gushing from its nostrils—followed by stomach-turning drops and jerks along the ride's steep tracks. Mom and Kathy faced the terror of Dragon Coaster, leaving Blade and me to ride Grand Carousel across the arcade. The attraction was a magnificent merry-go-round with forty-eight wooden horses that galloped gracefully up and down to music pumped from an ornate Italian organ. Two sculpted male figures struck bells as a lady mannequin conductor lead music with an ivory baton.

Aunt Blade rode one of the outside horses, trying to catch the brass ring. As the carousel slowly started to turn and the organ music pumped, an attendant fed a handful of rings, all iron except for a single brass one, into a wooden arm extended toward the turning carousel. Riders stretched out to grab the rings as the horses whirled past. Blade had perfected a technique of standing gracefully on her right leg, her foot still strapped in the stirrup, leaning out like a ballerina to the wooden hand. Most of the other riders fumbled as they held tightly onto the bobbing horses, but Blade gingerly extracted a metal ring on each turn until she eventually captured the prized brass one, earning a free ride. I loved the game because Blade insisted I stay with her on the next turn. The attendant never charged an extra fare for me, even if a long line of patrons was cued up waiting to ride.

Blade and I spent hours on the Grand Carousel, never tiring or getting dizzy from the repetitive rotations. Eventually Mom and Kathy came looking for us. We regrouped outside the Grand Carousel once Blade abandoned her quest for another brass ring. Mom bought us hot dogs smothered with sauerkraut from the Sabrett pushcart under a blue and yellow umbrella, and we sat on a bench along the boardwalk. In the distance, upon the sparkling blue water of Long Island Sound, a fleet of Blue Jay sail boats tacked in from afternoon races, headed for the Rye Yacht Club.

"This is so much nicer than that awful Savin Rock," Blade commented as she delicately wiped a trace of mustard off her lower lip with a paper napkin.

"It's much cleaner here, but they don't have the soft-shell crab sandwiches," Mom said, commenting on a local delicacy made famous at Nicola's Crab Shack on Front Street at the New Haven seaside amusement park.

"You don't get the riffraff here at Rye that you run into there," Blade added, referring to people from poor neighborhoods in Bridgeport and New Haven that swarmed the amusement park on summer weekends.

After hot dogs, Kathy and I were treated to cardboard sticks of pink cotton candy, the sugary angel hair froth sticking to our lips and fingers as we crawled into the back seat of the Lincoln for the ride back to Westport. Before the car reached the I-95 toll booth in Greenwich, just over the state border, I was asleep, curled up on the back seat, my fingers clutching the iron rings I'd hidden in the pocket of my shorts, the iron rings Blade had plucked from the outstretched wooden arm on the Grand Carousel and had given me to return to the attendant after she cashed in the brass one for a free ride.

• • •

The mud-splattered bus, with mosquitoes and fireflies squashed against the front windshield, crept toward LaGuardia Airport. The arches of Whitestone Bridge, laced with necklace-like bands of suspension cables, stretched over the East River. Gray storm clouds rolled in over the bridge, darkening murky river waters below. The air sagged like a wet washcloth with omens of afternoon thunderstorms. Rounded Quonset huts of airline hangers loomed as the bus navigated a circular off-ramp to the airport before coming to a stop with a loud hissing sound at Eastern Air Lines check-in curb.

"We're here, guys," the bus driver announced as he opened the squeaking, hinged front door.

Two Army MPs were waiting outside. I got off first, clutching the stack of envelopes.

"You in charge of this group?"

"Yes, I guess so."

"Give me a roll call," the MP instructed. "Let me know everyone's here."

I called off names as recruits exited the bus. After each guy gestured or grunted, I reported, "Everybody is here."

"You did good, kid. So far nobody's AWOL. Now, gentlemen, line up over there." He pointed to the check-in area inside sliding glass doors. "You'll each get a food voucher good at any of the airport concessions. I encourage you to eat something; it will be late by the time you get to Ft. Jackson."

This was the first indication where we were headed for basic training.

The MP gave me a stack of vouchers. "It's now fourteen hundred twenty-five hours," he announced looking at his watch. "Your flight leaves at seventeen hundred thirty hours, so you have time to eat, take a shit or whatever. Halladay has your plane tickets," the MP said handing me another envelope. "So make sure you're in the boarding area at least one hour before your flight's scheduled departure. Good luck, gentlemen, and remember you are in the Army now, so act accordingly."

As soon as I finished handing out food vouchers, the guys disappeared into the crowded terminal. *Fuck this shit,* I thought. *How am I supposed to keep track of this mob?* I opened the envelope containing airline tickets, noting the flight number—Eastern Air Lines 392. I looked up at the departure board to find the flight listed: scheduled departure time 5:30 p.m.—destination West Palm Beach. There was a notation in the remarks column—"Unscheduled Stop—See Agent." Looking at the tickets in the envelope, I realized that we were going to Columbia, South Carolina for basic training. I approached the ticket counter where an agent was on the phone. The young man looked up and nodded, cradling the receiver between his cheek and shoulder, while writing notes on a yellow pad.

As I stood in line, I remembered it was five years ago when I was at the same Eastern Air Lines counter checking in for a flight to West Palm Beach. It was spring break of my senior year at Fairfield Prep, and Mom and Dad had offered to pay for a plane ticket to Florida so I could visit my grandparents who were employed by Mrs. Pembroke, the wealthy heiress of the Pitney-Bowes fortune. My grandmother was head housekeeper, overseeing a staff of domestic workers and kitchen help at the villa on Chilean Avenue. Mrs. Pembroke refused to fly and wouldn't consider taking the train, so Pop drove her to Florida in her gray Oldsmobile 98 Holiday sedan. They left Westport the day after Thanksgiving, stopping at luxurious hotels in Richmond, Charleston, Savannah and St. Augustine, eventually arriving in Palm Beach. Nan took the train from Penn Station for the long trip to Florida, arriving ahead to make sure everything was in order.

My grandparents rented a small house in West Palm Beach across the Inland Waterway, preferring not to live in the servants' quarters of Mrs. Pembroke's mansion.

I remembered that flight, only the second time I'd been on an airplane. The woman sitting next to me in the aisle seat had lit a cigarette as soon as the "no smoking" sign was turned off and the Eastern Constellation reached cruising altitude.

"I get so nervous flying," she'd said putting her hand on my arm. "I just don't understand how these big heavy things get in the air and stay up in the sky."

"I'm sure it's safe," I reassured the woman, trying to exude the confidence of a seasoned air traveler.

"What's your name?" the woman asked tapping my arm.

"Tim," I answered. "Tim Halladay."

"Hello, Tim Halladay," she smiled. "I'm Gloria."

My friendly travel companion was well dressed in a tailored cream-colored suit, several expensive-looking rings gracing her fingers, but no wedding band. Her blondish hair, domed in a tight beehive, was resistant to movement, secured in place by large amounts of hair spray. The aroma of bath powder and Shalimar vanilla-sweet perfume was overpowering when combined with the cigarette smoke she blew in deep puffs.

"You going to Palm Beach?" she asked as the plane leveled off.

"Yes, to visit my grandparents."

"Must be nice," Gloria observed, exhaling a long stream of smoke, then crushing the cigarette butt in the armrest ashtray.

"It's not like that. My grandparents work for a wealthy woman who spends the winter in Florida, and then sometimes they do things for her in Westport the rest of the year."

"Westport," the woman hummed, lighting another cigarette. "Is that where you're from?"

"Yes," I answered.

"Old New England Yankee," she smiled. "I know. I was married to one for fifteen years." Gloria purred as she exhaled a long stream of smoke into the aisle of the airplane cabin.

A stewardess spread white cloth napkins on the fold-down tables in front of us, then brought trays of small quarter-cut sandwiches of ham spread, cheese and tuna, pickles and potato salad, accompanied by a cup of vanilla custard and Pepperidge Farm cookies.

"I'm sorry there's no warm food service this evening," the stewardess apologized. "We were late arriving at the gate and the ground crew didn't have time to fully stock the plane for our first-class passengers. This is all we have on board."

"No problem, honey," Gloria replied. "Just as long as they were able to pack the booze on board?"

"Would you care for something to drink?" the stewardess smiled.

"I'll have a gin martini. No fruit or olives. Just gin and lots of ice."

"Of course. And for you, sir?" she asked.

"A Coke would be great, if you have it."

"Certainly." She returned to the forward galley.

"You always fly first class?" Gloria probed.

"My dad's office made the reservation," I deflected the question.

"Of course, for you Westport boys," Gloria hummed. She reclined into the leather seat and blew a smoke ring into the air.

I finished the small sandwiches and was skimming pages of *The New Yorker* I'd brought on board as Gloria swirled ice cubes in her glass, now empty, when she suggested, "Let's move to the lounge where we can have room to stretch out."

The stewardess cleared trays and napkins from the fold-down tables as we left our seats and moved to the lounge in the tail of the plane. Gloria navigated the aisle in front of me, picking her way along seats, disturbing some sleeping passengers; she was a bit tipsy from the martinis and the gentle vibrations of the plane.

We settled into seats in the semicircular lounge, where Gloria leaned back, lit another cigarette and snapped her lighter shut. She picked a small speck of tobacco off her lip with a pinky finger. "It's nice to meet such a polite young man," she smiled.

"Thanks," I replied. "Nice to meet you too."

The stewardess had followed us and graciously asked, "Can I bring you something?"

"Another martini with lots of ice for me, and a gin and tonic for my bodyguard here," she gestured toward me.

Gloria leaned forward after the cocktails were placed discreetly on the armrest between our seats. She'd crossed her legs, running the pointed tip of her beige high-heel shoe along the seam of her nylon stocking. "I hate flying," she said wistfully, peering over the rim of her cocktail glass. "But you've made this a very pleasant trip." A slight turbulence bumped and shook the plane, causing ice cubes to clink in the gin and tonic and martini glasses.

•••

"I was tied up with last minute flight changes," the agent behind the counter explained. "Can I help you?"

"I hope so," I said stepping forward. "I have tickets for the Army group, we're supposed…"

"I know," he interrupted. "You're on 392 with an unscheduled stop in Columbia. The Army just comes in and takes over our whole operations system. Forget trying to run an airline and keep the paying passengers happy."

"Sorry," I returned, taken back by the agent's attitude.

"Hey, I know. Just following orders. That's what they all say."

"Here are the tickets," I said pushing the envelope across the counter. "Is there anything I have to do?"

The agent examined the documents, checking off names on a manifest sheet on the counter in front of him. He pulled out a stack of boarding passes from the drawer pressing just below his belt buckle and peeled off twenty-four cards, pounding each one with a rubber ink stamp labeled "Military."

"Your boarding passes. All set," he said sliding the stack across the counter. "Just make sure the guys are here when we begin boarding."

"Thanks," I said.

"You're too nice to be putting up with this shit," the agent stopped.

"What?" I started.

"I just checked the box and said *screw you*. They didn't want me anyway. No faggots in the fox hole."

"That didn't work for me."

"Whatever…" the agent dismissed officiously. "But you're just too pretty to get your ass shot off in Vietnam."

"Hey, man," the familiar voice came from behind. "Everything in order here, sir?" Razor joked, jabbing me on the shoulder. He was standing behind me grinning. "We all accounted for?"

"Not funny," I said. "I don't know how I got stuck with this anyway."

"Because you're the rich white kid," Razor said. "That's what you guys do. Right, Dildo?" he turned to his friend standing next to him.

"Yeah, man. Rich white dude from Westport. They ain't gonna put any of us nigger or spic dicks in charge," Dildo spat out a wad of chewed bubblegum.

"He can't help being white. Maybe rich. But not white," Razor dismissed.

"Come on, guys. I got drafted just like you. I had no choice."

Razor gave me a long hard look. "He's okay...not one of us, but he's okay." That was the beginning of a bond that would grow and strengthen and change in the days to come.

CHAPTER THREE
(July 10, 1967)

● ● ●

The boarding announcement for Eastern Flight 392 blared across the busy terminal. I looked around trying to get a head count—only twenty of the twenty-four recruits were present.

"Hold on." Razor stepped in. "I know where these fucks are. Wait here." With that, he ran off into the crowded terminal. I moved down the concourse, distributing boarding passes to the recruits. Minutes later Razor, accompanied by Dildo, lugged four drunk, unruly guys, singing "God Bless America," into the departure area.

"You sure you want these douche bags to come with us?" Razor asked annoyed, nodding to the stumbling men he and Dildo had rounded up at the Wings bar.

I looked at the clipboard and checked off names of the last four guys. "As long as we all get there," I said relieved. "After that I want no more of this."

We took open seats on the plane, dodging disapproving looks from passengers on board who'd been advised there was an unscheduled stop due to a military emergency. The door to the dolphin-shaped fuselage of the Constellation thumped shut as Razor, Dildo and I sat down in the empty row behind the galley.

"All present and accounted for, Halladay?" Razor mimicked, elbowing me with a thumbs-up.

The stewardess strode down the aisle in her high heels, making sure everyone's seat belt was fastened. She then pulled out a plastic card and read emergency evacuation instructions while standing like a fashion model in the aisle.

The propellers of the Constellation turned as the engines kicked in one at a time and revved up, until the plane was rocking from the vibrations and puffs of smoke coughed out behind each engine. The graceful aircraft with its elegant three-tiered tail pushed away from the gangway and lumbered onto the taxiway preparing for takeoff. The plane suddenly lurched, coming to an abrupt stop, as the captain's baritone voice came over the intercom.

"Good evening, ladies and gentlemen. This is Captain Sullivan. Welcome aboard Eastern Air Lines Flight 392 headed down to West Palm Beach." The plane idled on the tarmac, wobbling in anticipation of takeoff, as the captain continued his announcement. "We're going to hold here for a while until this weather system moves out, and then we'll be on our way." Rain pelted the metal frame of the aircraft, as rivulets of dirty water streamed down the TV-monitor size windows. A loud clap of thunder followed five seconds after a flash of lightning lit up the horizon. The plane shook in the gusty wind; the cabin was eerily quiet as we sat strapped into our seats, looking forward. The four recruits who'd been pushed onto the plane at the last minute by Razor and Dildo were asleep in their seats; the rest of the boys who'd been so brazen and cocky at the Induction Center in New Haven sat wide-eyed and silent.

Twenty minutes passed before the pilot's voice came over the intercom. "Well, ladies and gentlemen, it looks like this nasty thunderstorm is moving out, and we can be on our way." The aircraft vibrated as the pilot periodically revved the engines. The gleaming plane hesitated, holding back as if on a leash. The captain returned. "We've been cleared for takeoff," he announced calmly as the aircraft inched ahead. "Please make sure your seats belts are securely fastened. I'll be getting back to you with an update on our flight shortly after we're airborne."

Razor and Dildo sat across the aisle as I stashed envelopes and the clipboard under my seat. Razor leaned over, "You ever been on an airplane before?"

"A couple of times," I answered.

"This is Dildo and me's first time flying," Razor confided, grabbing my arm, "and we're just kind of wondering…well…"

"Nothing to it."

The engines raced in a high-pitched roar; the plane jerked as the pilot tested brakes before the aircraft sped down the runway for takeoff. Razor made the sign of the cross, his eyes closed as the plane became airborne.

When the aircraft leveled off at cruising altitude, I looked across
the aisle where Razor and Dildo were seated. Their eyes were closed,
but I could tell they were not asleep. Occasionally the plane bounced
and jerked, passing through a cloud, as Razor and Dildo tightly
gripped the armrests. The stewardess brought cocktails to the paying
passengers, bypassing recruits scattered throughout the cabin. She
delivered plastic trays of what looked like TV dinners, adjusting her
tight uniform skirt and slinking down the aisle to ask if she could re-
fresh cocktails. Returning to the galley, she smashed a plastic bag of
frozen ice cubes with a wooden mallet in the small aluminum sink.

"The Sky-Chefs didn't put on meals for you guys," she looked over
at me. "We didn't know you were going to be on board until the last
minute," as if explaining everything.

"Whatever." I unbuckled my seat belt and got up to go to the restroom. Even though this was the same Eastern Air Lines flight I'd tak-
en a few years earlier to visit my grandparents, I noticed there were
no first-class seats and no circular lounge in the tail section. Both had
been replaced with conventional rows of seats to accommodate more
passengers. There was no Gloria exuding clouds of Shalimar, smoking a cigarette and ordering me a gin and tonic.

I had finally dozed off, letting the events of the day slip by into the
darkness outside the aircraft, when I was jolted back to reality by the
captain's voice announcing over the intercom that we were beginning
our descent into Columbia, South Carolina. The plane wobbled and
swayed left to right as rough sounds of the landing gear being lowered thumped throughout the cabin.

"Ladies and gentlemen, we will be on the ground shortly. Please
remain seated and allow our young men to disembark. We will be
airborne again shortly and on our way down to West Palm Beach."

It was just after nine o'clock when the Constellation touched down
on the tarmac. The captain slowed the engines without turning them
off completely. The propellers still churned as the graceful Constellation came to a lurching halt on the taxiway. A stair ramp was pushed
up and banged against the forward exit of the aircraft as the stewardess unlatched the door, pushing it open. Two MPs were waiting at the
foot of the stairs.

The captain's voice came over the intercom, "Gentlemen, this is
your destination. Please disembark quickly and make sure you take
all your belongings. And good luck to you." Then after a pause he re-

turned. "Ladies and gentlemen, we will be on our way shortly for the trip down to West Palm Beach. We apologize for any inconvenience, and thank you for your patience."

The words smarted. The pilot was apologizing to a planeload of people with golf clubs packed in the cargo hold, their suitcases filled with Bermuda shorts and black-tie accessories for elegant charity events, while we were going off involuntarily to fight in a war that nobody gave a shit about.

"You in charge of this group?" the MP asked as I descended the stairway.

"Yes," I answered handing the soldier the large yellow envelope I'd been carrying from New Haven. "I think this is for you."

"Everyone here?" the MP asked.

"Yes, I think so."

"You think so?" the MP spat out, whacking me on the arm with the envelope. "You're in the Army, kid. You don't think! Now, is everyone here?"

"Yes," I answered as the guys behind me got off the plane.

"Now listen up," the MP called out. "Through that door to the terminal," he pointed, "there's a bus outside by the curb waiting to transfer you to Ft. Jackson. Get a move on, men. We don't have all night."

The airplane engines revved up as the portable stairway was moved back and the cabin door closed. The dolphin-shaped aircraft wobbled as its engines whirred to a screech and the plane inched back onto the runway to continue on to its final destination in Florida.

We moved through the deserted terminal illuminated by bright fluorescent lights. A janitor pushed a humming buffer machine across the scuffed tiled floor, watching this new breed of recruits pass through. He rolled his large, basset-hound eyes as he continued his work.

The MP, clipboard in hand, called off names as we boarded the military bus waiting at the curb: "Rivera, Izzo, Rodriguez, Brown, Stein, Cretella, Murphy, Halladay."

The door slammed closed, and the bus pulled away from the terminal. The Eastern Air Lines Constellation, its engines emitting glowing green and yellow sparks, took off and headed on toward Palm Beach.

Razor and Dildo sat behind me. The bus headed out to a two-lane highway, and lights from downtown Columbia glowed in the distance, becoming fainter as we drove into the dark countryside. We passed an occasional gas station and shacks with harsh neon light spilling onto dirt yards in front, where men sat on folding lawn chairs, playing cards on wooden milk crates. A scrawny dog, momentarily distracted from biting fleas on his hind leg, got up to chase and bark at our passing bus, but soon became disinterested and flopped back down in the dusty driveway by the side of the road. A blinking Krispy Kreme doughnut shop light announced a new batch of hot glazed had just popped out of the oven, but the bus moved forward without stopping. The drain ditches along the side of the highway were over-grown with tangled masses of kudzu vine creeping up to light poles and telephone wires.

"Where the fuck are we?" Razor leaned toward me over the seat.

"I think this is what they call the Deep South."

A half hour later the bus lurched to a stop. I wiped steam off the grimy window to see a white wooden billboard: "United States Army Training Center—Fort Jackson, South Carolina." A large red, blue and yellow insignia was painted on the sign, emblazoned with a fig-ure I would later learn was Andrew Jackson. The words *Victory Starts Here* framed the logo.

The bus door opened and the MP disembarked and saluted a sol-dier at the gatehouse.

"Recruits from New Haven, transported by commercial flight and picked up at Columbia Airport at twenty-one hundred hours. Re-porting here for basic training."

The guard glanced at the roster, then boarded the bus to take a quick head count.

"Twenty-four accounted," he reported to the MP. "God help us. We're really scraping the bottom of the barrel." He waved the bus on, raising the security arm at the entrance to the military installation. The bus moved slowly through rows of small dark wooden build-ings, stopping at a cul-de-sac in front of a four-story brick building whose rooms were illuminated on all floors by fluorescent lights. An American flag and State of South Carolina flag curled around metal poles by the entrance of the building, hanging limply in the humid July night air.

"All right, gentlemen, we're going to make a formation," the MP directed as we got off the bus. "That is, we're going to form two lines. Taller guys in the back; you in front," he said pointing to me. "Try to act like you've got a brain. Sergeant Washington will be out momentarily to give you instructions."

Razor stood next to me in the first row—Dildo in line directly behind us.

"You squirts want me to squirt something on you?"

"Hey, you black fuck." The MP grabbed Dildo by his T-shirt. "You won't think this is so funny when Washington gets through with you."

"Well, well, well…" came the thundering voice of Sergeant Raymond Washington as he strode out the doorway of the administration building. At six feet four, the DI was an imposing figure. He crossed his arms and looked out over us with steely dark gray eyes. "Do we have any problems, here?" he asked the MP.

"I don't think so, Sergeant. Just some attitude adjustment."

"Well, now. That's my specialty," the sergeant beamed. "So this is the best we can expect from the slums of New Haven?" he derided, tucking on the brim of his Smokey Bear drill instructor's hat. "What a bunch of sorry-assed pussies." Ray Washington wore the green and yellow drill sergeant's identification badge emblazoned with thirteen stars and a snake grasping a scroll inscribed *This We'll Defend*.

"Well, gentlemen, you're all mine." The sergeant chose his words slowly, pacing up and down. "Now stand up like you have a stick up your ass. Put those feet together and look forward. Understand?"

When only a few unintelligible mumbles came forward, Washington bellowed, "The correct response is 'Yes, sir!' Do you hear me?"

When we returned a feeble chorus of responses, the DI screamed, "I can't hear you!" He grabbed me by the shoulder, pulling me out of the front row and ordered, "Give me ten, college boy."

"What?" I asked confused.

"I said give me ten," Washington repeated. "Can't you count, college boy? Ten push-ups, you sorry pussy."

I fell to the ground, looking around at the guys lined up, then dug my toes into the sand. *What did I do?* I thought as I pumped myself up and down, my face touching the ground at each thrust. *And what's with this "college boy" shit?*

"Well, that's downright pathetic," the sergeant said, kicking my right arm, forcing my face into the sand. "Is that what they teach you in those fancy schools?" Washington snickered. "Don't worry, kid. You'll get it right before you leave here. I promise you."

I got up, brushed myself off and went back in the lineup.

"Listen up, men," Washington announced. "You're gonna march into that building behind me and take seats in the classroom on the right. You think you dickheads can manage that?"

"What's with this asshole?" Dildo leaned forward mumbling to Razor.

"You got some kind of problem, Sambo?" Washington pushed forward, coming within inches of Dildo's face. "Because if you do, I need to know about it now."

Dildo shrunk back in line, wiping the DI's spit off his face.

"Good," Washington said, stepping back. "We got that straight."

We moved into the building, taking seats in the first room off the hallway, a room eerily similar to the one at the Induction Center in New Haven. The two MPs who'd escorted our bus from the airport were standing in the hallway, smoking cigarettes and laughing with Sergeant Washington. One of them squashed his cigarette on the tiled floor and entered the room where he lowered a torn silver screen.

"You guys watch this. It's important," he said indifferently, walking to the back of the room to flip on the projector. He switched off the overhead lights, leaving us to watch a film: *The Army Code of Values— loyalty, duty, respect, etc.*, narrated by Farley Granger. A long beam of light emitted from the clicking projector, streaming over our heads. At the end of the film the harsh fluorescent lights abruptly came back on and the MP shouted, "Gentlemen…on your feet."

We stumbled up, prompted by Sergeant Washington repeatedly slapping a riding crop into his palm. The MPs and Sergeant Washington stood at attention as Colonel John Knight entered the classroom.

"At ease, soldiers," the officer addressed the trio who saluted him. His uniform was impeccably pressed and the rows of ribbons on his left lapel were impressive. "Gentlemen, be seated," he nodded.

"I'm Colonel Knight, Commanding Officer at Fort Jackson, and it is my privilege to welcome you here tonight." He paused and stared out over the assembly. "Fort Jackson is the largest basic training facility in the United States, and every year we train and prepare young men, just like you, for their service and careers in the Army. I realize that we may do things different around here, but if you keep your nose clean, listen up and follow instructions, you'll do just fine. Isn't that right, Sergeant Washington?" The officer shot a glance at the DI standing behind him.

"Yes, sir," Washington returned.

"Gentlemen, I know you were sworn in this morning in New Haven," the colonel began, "but this is important, and I can't assume my Yankee friends up North got it right." He paused smiling. "So I'm going to ask you to repeat the oath of enlistment."

The colonel gestured to the MP behind him who came forward and shouted, "Attention."

We stood rigidly in front of the commanding officer who read from a handbook. "Now repeat after me," the colonel said. The familiar words came out as if on a recording: "...*solemnly swear that I will support and defend the Constitution of the United States...against all enemies foreign and domestic...*"

"Welcome to the United States Army, gentlemen." Colonel Knight saluted when we completed the oath. "You are expected to act accordingly." With that the officer strode toward the door, turning to the DI. "Proceed, Washington."

"Yes, sir," the sergeant saluted.

I looked up at the round clock with large black numbers hanging on the wall in the back of the classroom. It was just before midnight.

"Gentlemen, be seated," Sergeant Washington instructed. "I know it's been a long day, so let's get through this process with no problems so we can all move on."

The MPs re-entered the room, each carrying a stack of large yellow envelopes. As our names were called, an envelope with our name printed on it was tossed to us.

"These are your orders, " Washington began. "Open up, and inside you'll find the most important thing you'll be issued the whole time you're in the Army—your dog tags." He paused to dramatize his point. "Do it," he instructed. "You'll find your Army ID number. Memorize it and never forget it. If there's one thing in your dumb-fuck head you have to know, it's your Army ID number. You will be asked repeatedly during basic training to recite your ID, and if you don't know it, or can't remember it, you will be one sorry fuck."

I sifted through the papers in the envelope and found the chain with my metal dog tags.

"Check them out to make sure your name is spelled right, your blood type and religious affiliation, if any, correct." The chains jingled as the recruits inspected them, and before anyone could ask a question, Washington ordered, "Now put them on over your head, and never, I repeat NEVER, take them off. Do I make myself clear?" the DI bellowed.

A few mumbles drifted from the rows of recruits fumbling with their dog tags.

"Did I make myself clear?" the sergeant shouted again. "I can't hear you."

"Yes, sir," came a more audible response.

"Good," Washington said. "Now let me repeat myself, just in case any of you fuckheads weren't listening. When I say never take them off, I mean exactly that. You wear them when you're eating, sleeping, showering, shaving, shitting, fucking and jerking off. Do I make myself clear?"

"What the fuck," Dildo laughed nudging Razor. "Even when jerking off."

"You heard me," the DI shot back at Dildo. "Especially when you're jerking off. And now the moment you've all been waiting for," he grinned. "You're about to start looking like real soldiers."

"On your feet, men," the first MP ordered. "Form a single line out the doorway and down the hall. Make sure you have your orders and anything else you brought with you because you won't be coming back to this room." We got up and shuffled into a ragged line. "When you get to the end of the hall, remove your shirt and anything else you're wearing above your waist. You're about to get your first military haircut."

I winced at the thought of having my head shaved, but this was no surprise; the ritual was well known. Two soldiers in fatigues, electric clippers in hand, stood beside execution-style chairs in the harshly lit room. One by one we took a seat, and in less than two minutes we were stripped of any individuality we might have brought to the military base. Feeling self-conscious, I exited the room, brushing my newly shaved scalp. I looked at my fellow recruits with the same uneasy embarrassment I'd felt when taking a group shower after eighth-grade gym class, glancing secretly around the locker room to see who had pubic hair.

We were herded into another stark, fluorescent-lit room where long tables and folding chairs were set up like a makeshift cafeteria. "There's one for each of you," the MP pointed to brown paper bags on the tables. "Just one. So don't take more." I grabbed a bag and opened it to find a dry ham and cheese sandwich, green apple, hard oatmeal cookie and a carton of warm orange juice.

"I know it's not the fancy meal you were expecting, but it'll tide you over until you get a hot breakfast tomorrow morning in the mess hall."

In less than five minutes the MPs were back. "Okay. We're finished here. There are no maids here to clean up your shit so don't leave anything on the tables—not even a fucking crumb. Put your trash in the garbage bin by the door and follow me down to the dispensary."

I rolled up the remains of the snack and stuffed the crumpled bag into an overflowing trash container by the door, then followed in line down the corridor, where a soldier distributed pre-assembled bundles containing two sets of olive-green fatigues, four pairs of white boxers, T-shirts and wool socks. For the lace-up black boots, we could select a size ranging from eight to sixteen.

"These are to get you through the first few days of basic," the private advised. "You'll have time to make adjustments when your regulation uniforms are issued in a few days. For now, just make these work."

"Yeah, sure," Razor groused, asking for a size ten from the soldier issuing boots. "My friend behind me is gonna need something a lot bigger," Razor joked nodding to Dildo.

"This isn't fucking Thom McAn's. But I think we can find something that fits Chocolate Cinderella."

Dildo recoiled and lunged forward, but Razor held him back. "Ease up. We don't need any shit here."

"Listen to your buddy. You don't want to get fucked here in the boot department. Now what size do you want?"

"Fourteen," Dildo mumbled.

"Here," the soldier replied producing a large pair of black boots. "See if you can squeeze your jungle-bunny feet into these."

We were directed out of the administration building onto a waiting bus to the barracks. As the bus door was closing, Sergeant Washington stepped aboard, announcing, "Gentlemen, I will be escorting you to your living quarters here at Fort Jackson." The bus wound slowly past rows of one-story wooden buildings with white paint peeling off the sidings. An occasional dim light seeped out from half-closed blinds, suggesting life inside.

"Gentlemen, we're here," Washington announced as the bus stopped and the driver opened the front door. "Disembark and get into formation in two rows. Line up according to height," he ordered, pulling me, Razor and four other guys about the same size to make up the front row. "You other knuckleheads line up behind."

"What a sorry sight," Washington said disgusted. "Now look around and see who's standing next to you and behind you. This is the position you will take whenever we make formations—everybody in the same place every time. Understand?"

A few mumbles and snickers trickled from the group when Washington bellowed, "I can't hear you?"

"Yes, sir," came a more audible, if not enthusiastic, response.

"That's pathetic," Washington said slapping the horse crop in the palm of his hand. "Halladay, step out here," he said. "Come on, college boy, show these dumb fucks how to respond."

I edged out of the line, pissed that I was being singled out. "Yes, sir," I responded.

"Shit, man. You sound like a pansy in the church choir. Let me hear you like you mean it."

I glanced at the guys behind me, getting only blank stares. I told you that being the only college graduate in my unit was not an advantage, and every minute into this ordeal confirmed it. I straightened up and shouted, "Yes, sir!"

"Better, Halladay. But next time I want to hear it from your balls. Got that, college boy, from your balls. You talk to me from your balls when I ask you something." The sergeant's dark eyes glistened like steel marbles bulging out from his weathered brown skin. He surveyed the new group of recruits, making mental notes and judgments about each man. The DI paced back and forth in front of us, slapping the riding crop repeatedly in the palm of his hand. He pivoted on his polished black boots that he dug into the sand.

"You men are assigned to *C Company—Charlie Company*. That's my division, men, and I'm responsible for you for the next eight weeks. During that time I will know every breath you take, every bite you eat, every shit you take. Don't think you can fool me. I've seen it all and I've done it all. You can't fuck with me. Don't even think about it, not even in your sleep, because I will come in there in the night and rip your fucking balls off if you try to fuck with me. My platoon comes in number one. Always keep that in mind. And you fuckers aren't going to break that record," he glared ominously. "Charlie Company is going to be NUMBER ONE! You understand me?"

"Yes, sir," came the tepid response.

Infuriated by the lack of enthusiasm, Washing grabbed me by the collar and pulled me out of line, shouting, "Maybe they didn't get it the first time, college boy."

I stood stiffly at attention, looking straight ahead, shouting, "Yes, sir."

"Better, college boy. But it's still not from the balls…unless you don't have any."

We were ushered into the one-story wooden building; the screen door hanging by rusted hinges creaked as the MP pulled it open. Two rows of cots, bunk beds with an upper and lower birth, lined the room, six on each side. Bare light bulbs hung from exposed sockets in the ceiling, strung together by coiled wire stapled to raw wood crossbeams. The room smelled of disinfectant, but globs of hair, dust and dead insects clung to the metal feet of the beds on the bare wooden floor.

"You men take bunks in order of formation," Washington instructed. "So when you're called to line up, you won't have to think. Work it out who gets top or bottom." The sergeant turned to the two MPs waiting at the door. "See to it that these knuckleheads bunk down. Lights out in fifteen minutes." Washington looked back, slapped the riding crop against the screen door, and left.

"There's showers, sinks and urinals down there," the MP pointed to the end of the barracks. "The crap house is outside, a hundred feet down the hill," he directed, pointing his flashlight to a shack that looked like a chicken coop. "That's where you go take a shit."

I placed my duffel bag and fatigues on the top mattress of the first bunk inside the door. Razor threw himself on the lower bed, immediately taking claim to it. Dildo was setting up directly across the aisle.

I unpacked and put the few clothes I'd brought in one of the two lockers.

"Two minutes to lights out," the MP announced.

I slipped out of my jeans and shirt, and still in socks and Jockey shorts, I went to take a piss in the communal urinal, a long slimy metal trough along the wall. I was not alone. Several guys hung out their dicks, self-conscious and averting looks as we took part in this new group ritual. The lights were out as I picked my way back to the bunk, stubbing my toe on the metal shaft of the bed frame where Razor was sprawled out lightly snoring.

"Reveille is at zero five hundred hours," the MP shouted from the darkened doorway. "Be up and in formation, dressed in your fatigues, by five hundred thirty hours. Trust me, you don't want to be late."

I lifted myself onto the bunk above Razor, stretched out on the thin mattress and pulled up the itchy brown wool blanket. The lumpy pillow smelled of mildew. I stared at the wood beams overhead with paint peeling like opened gum wrappers. The wheezing and snoring of guys around me was interspersed by buzzing mosquitos looking for a raw arm or leg.

I tried to sleep, pretending I was curled up on the back seat of Pop Halladay's Ford, riding up to our farm in Vermont. Before we'd started the long drive, he had taken me clamming on Long Island Sound in a rowboat he moored in the marina at Compo Beach. Pop fastened the Seagull outboard engine onto the stern, pulled a rope starter-cord several times until the engine sputtered and kicked in, chugging the small vessel out of the harbor until we eventually anchored off Cockenoe Island. Pop pulled out a set of long crossbow clam rakes that he plunged into the shallow waters and dug into the sandy mudflats below. He scooped up a load of seaweed, sand and clams and deposited the catch into a net tied up alongside the boat. I picked through the salty mess and scooped out clams with my hands, depositing the mollusks into a bucket. The ritual was repeated until the bushel basket was full, the one-day quota allowed by the Fairfield County Fish and Game Commissioner. Pop withdrew the clam rakes from the shallow salty waters, placed them in the boat, and started the Seagull outboard engine to power us back to the marina.

I lugged the heavy bucket of clams up the wooden gangplank to the parking lot while Pop fetched a hose and doused off the day's haul with fresh water. He stopped at the Texaco station in Saugatuck to fill the gas tank and buy a bag of ice that he packed over the clams in the trunk.

"This should get us to Wilmington," he announced as he started the car. "Stretch out on the back seat and go to sleep."

The telephone poles clipped by outside the rear window as my grandfather drove up Route 7, past Orem's Diner in Wilton where Aunt Em used to take me for pancakes on Sunday morning drives. I wished we could stop, but I knew Pop did not approve of spending money for food in restaurants. I clutched my growling and gurgling stomach, having only eaten the peanut butter and jelly sandwich Mom had made that morning before Pop picked me up.

In the dark Army barracks, lying under the itchy wool blanket, I wrapped my arms around my stomach, pretending I was on the back seat of Pop Halladay's Ford, heading up to Vermont. Only this time there was no one shaking my shoulder to wake me up after the long ride to tell me, "Tim...we're here."

CHAPTER FOUR

(July 11, 1967)

● ● ●

Somehow I had survived the first day. The recorded blast of reveille blared across the base as the sun rose over Fort Jackson. A corporal, not one of the soldiers from the night before, pushed open the screen door of the barracks and switched on the lights.

"Rise and shine, men," he announced. "Be out in formation, dressed in uniform at zero five hundred thirty hours—exactly one half hour from now. That's five-thirty in case you haven't figured out how we tell time here. Sergeant Washington will be giving you instructions. Don't be late. Trust me," he said emphatically. "You don't want to be late."

I slipped down from the upper bunk. Razor was still asleep. "Hey, guy. Wake up," I tapped him on the shoulder. He groaned and rolled over as I grabbed a towel at the foot of the bed and retrieved a toothbrush from my toilet kit. "I'm hitting the shower."

The sound of running water came from the end of the barracks and clouds of misty steam puffed into the hallway. I slipped out of my shorts, tossing them on a wooden bench, and hung the towel on a hook. There were eight shower stations, four on each side of the tiled room, all pouring into a central drain. Guys were lathering up in front of spigots shooting streams of hot water when I stepped in front of the only unoccupied one. I closed my eyes, trying to ignore the naked bodies around me. With newly shaved heads, we all looked like department store mannequins, impersonal, nameless and sexless.

"Mind if I butt in?" came a deep voice.

I opened my eyes, soap streaming down across my forehead, to face Dildo standing next to me grinning, his enormous penis semi-erect.

"No problem. I'm just finishing up."

Dildo stepped under the running water as I withdrew and grabbed my towel, brushing close to his dark brown body. I patted myself dry, wrapping the towel and tying it in a tight knot around my waist. I returned to my bunk where I changed into my newly issued fatigues.

"All right, men," the corporal announced from the doorway. "Outside and into formation," he ordered as guys fumbled with laces on their boots.

"This is one fucking sorry mess," Sergeant Washington observed as we fell in outside the barracks. "This is one fucking sorry mess," he repeated, slapping the riding crop into his palm, pacing back and forth. "Look at you fuckheads," he snarled. "What a bunch of limp-dick pussies," he said spitting into the sand.

"Halladay," he shouted pointing the riding crop at me. "Yes, you, college boy. Step forward and show these other knuckleheads how to get dressed. I'm sure your mommy taught you how to tie your shoes before sending you off to those fancy schools."

I moved forward, suppressing my hostility and contempt for the drill instructor.

"Okay, college boy, drop trou," Washington instructed.

"What?"

"Did I not make myself clear," the sergeant barked. "I said drop trou. Didn't they teach you that in college?"

I released my belt buckle, undid the buttons on the fly front of my fatigues and lowered them around my ankles.

"Well that's just fine," Washington purred. "Just fine, college boy. I see you have your new tidy whities on," Washington slapped me on the butt with the leather crop. "And such a pretty white ass."

"Now observe, men, how college boy has his pants tucked neatly into his boots. Think you can do that?" Washington continued to pace back and forth checking out each man. "Okay, college boy, we've seen enough."

I pulled up my fatigues and tucked in my shirt.

"That's how you men are to report to formation every morning. Looking just like college boy here. Got it?"

"Yes, sir," came a few feeble responses.

"I can't hear you motherfuckers," Washington screamed.

"Yes, sir," the chorus of boys' voices echoed back.

"Now drop and give me twenty," the DI ordered me.

"Sir?"

"Twenty! Can't you count college boy?" the DI laughed, kicking me in the shins, forcing my facedown in the sand. I spat out grit from my lips, cursing Washington under my breath, pushing up and down in front of the platoon.

Sergeant Washington then led all twenty-four of us, the new Charlie Company, on a jog around the track circling the athletic filed, dropping back after the first cycle.

The corporal took over. "Four more laps and one turn up drag-ass hill," he called out. "Now listen up and repeat after me," he shouted, leading us in a cadence as we ran in rhythm:

Your left, your left
Your left, your right, your left
Sound off!—One! Two!
Sound off!—Three! Four!
One! Two! Three! Four! One! Two!—Three! Four!

Sweating and out of breath, we shuffled into formation in front of the barracks where we had started out.

"God help us," Washington commented to the corporal. "You think there's any hope?"

We were led into the mess hall, located in a large, two-story brick building housing the commissary, rec room with pool tables, TV and vending machines, and the laundry. The NCOs' lounge was in the basement. This drab red building, two magnolia bushes hugging the entrance, overgrown ivy vines clinging to the windows, was the hub of the basic training center.

The mess hall was crammed with recruits from four units: Alpha, Bravo, Charlie and Echo Companies. We assembled in a long snaking line, sliding our plastic trays down the aluminum-tube railing in front of the glass case with heated metal containers of food: steaming mounds of brownish scrambled eggs, globs of colorless grits soaked in butter, bacon strips that looked like scraps of shoe leather, and toast with small packets of grape jelly. It was the morning hot breakfast. Individual boxes of dry cereal—Rice Krispies, Corn Flakes and Cheerios—were stacked on the counter next to small cartons of orange juice and milk that no one had bothered to put in the refrigerator the night before—a large canister of coffee at the end of the line.

"Anything for you?" a heavy black woman behind the counter asked as I slid my empty tray along the aluminum bars.

"I'll pass." I moved down the line, picking up a carton of orange juice and two pieces of toast. After drawing a mug of black coffee, I took a seat at one of the benches lining the tables in the brightly lit cafeteria. The cramps in my stomach hurt; I'd not had a bowel movement since leaving Westport early yesterday. I sipped the bitter coffee, then pushed it aside, afraid it might accelerate my urge to take a shit. Last night I'd checked out the latrine, the chicken coop located a hundred yards beyond the barracks. The stench of shit and vomit blasted into my face as I pushed open the creaking door of the shack. There were four filthy toilets lined up inside, no partitions for privacy. Bundles of brown paper towels stacked along the wall served as toilet paper, and swarms of flies and mosquitoes buzzed around the single light bulb hanging on a wire from the ceiling. The humiliation of having my head shaved to look like an alien was one thing, but the prospect of taking a shit while squatting in the open next to other guys in the stinking outhouse was more than I could fucking bear.

"This place taken?" asked a familiar voice. I turned to see Razor standing behind me, holding a tray heaped with food.

"Sit down," I said sliding down the bench to make room.

"That all you eatin', man?" Razor asked as he climbed over the bench and pulled up next to me.

"Not hungry," I dismissed, sipping warm orange juice through a straw poking out of the cardboard carton.

"I know it ain't the fancy breakfast your mom used to make," Razor said, shoving a heaping forkful of eggs into his mouth.

"You don't know about my mom."

Razor looked at me coolly. "I bet she was pretty comfy in your house in Westport."

"My mom worked."

"Bet she didn't carry you in her belly on a boat from Puerto Rico and end up popping you out in the emergency room at Bridgeport Hospital."

"It wasn't quite like that," I admitted.

"My mom probably cleaned your toilets and did your laundry," Razor continued as he shoved more food into his mouth.

"We never had maids. Besides, no one could ever clean the way Mom did."

"You mean with all that money you never had maids?"

"What are you talking about?"

"I saw you get out of that fucking Lincoln."

"That was my dad's company car."

"And my mom rides the bus on the Post Road every day from Bridgeport to clean toilets in fancy houses behind white fences."

"We live in a small place on Main Street that my grandfather built in the Depression."

"And we live in a tenement on Broad Street with three other families sharing one fucking bathroom," Razor said, spreading a wad of grape jelly on a slice of toast and chomping down on it, his lips now purple with the sticky jam.

"Guess we come from different places, but we're all here now," I said, squashing the cardboard juice carton in my hand.

"That DI, Washington, sure has a bug up his ass for you," Razor changed the subject. "What the fuck is that all about?" he asked, wiping a wad of grape jelly off his mouth.

"I don't know. Maybe just the way he is."

Two corporals marched into the mess hall. The one who'd led our group on laps around the track yelled out, "Finish up here, men, and be outside in formation in five minutes. There are four different staging areas. Remember what company you're assigned to: Alpha, Bravo, Charlie and Echo. Don't screw up."

The corporal standing next to him continued, "Clean your shit off the tables. Put dirty dishes, cups, glasses and silverware on the stand next to the front entrance—trays stacked underneath. Leave nothing, and I mean NOTHING, on the tables. We don't have maid service here at Fort Jackson."

"Just like home, Halladay." Razor picked up his tray.

The mess hall rumbled with the sound of benches pushing back and trays being scraped off tables. We wolfed down the rest of our breakfast, stacked dirty dishes in the plastic bins by the exit and headed to get into formation.

Sergeant Washington was waiting outside, pacing back and forth on the grass in staging area number three. We figured out where Charlie Company was supposed to assemble and hustled to line up in our assigned positions.

"This morning will be easy," Washington announced. "Most of the time in classrooms for orientation and other necessary crap. But don't get comfortable because your real training starts this afternoon.

Corporal, take these men where they need to go, and have them report back here at thirteen hundred hours."

"Yes, Sergeant," the corporal replied. Then turning to us, he ordered, "Follow in formation. We're going back to the admin building where you checked in last night. When we get there, form a line
single file. All right, let's move out—and try to look like soldiers."

The twenty-four of us in Charlie Company broke into a cadenced
trot behind the corporal, jogging several blocks down paved streets
to the four-story brick building. We broke formation and filed up a
steel stairway to a second floor classroom.

"Be seated, gentlemen," the corporal instructed. "Lieutenant Crawley will be here shortly to talk to you." A few minutes later the corporal returned shouting, "On your feet, men. Attention!"

"Thank you, Corporal." The young lieutenant returned the salute
as he entered the classroom. "At ease, gentlemen," he addressed us.
"Take a seat and listen up. I promise, this won't be like going to the
dentist," he smiled.

Second Lieutenant Brian Crawley could have been a model off
an Army recruitment poster. His blond crew cut, peach-colored skin,
blue eyes, Pepsodent smile and tight-fitting khakis made him the perfect spokesman for poor kids who aspired to be like him but who'd
had none of his advantages. The officer leaned back on the wooden
desk. He folded his arms and looked out over our shaved heads.

"I know what you're thinking—another pep talk," he said, sitting
down squarely on the desktop, his feet in shiny black boots hovering
a few inches above the floor. "That's not why I'm here. You've all seen
the loyalty movie, haven't you?"

"Yeah," Dildo mumbled under his breath. "Two times."

"So I guess you don't need to see it again?" Crawley said. "Stand up,
young man," the officer directed in a non-threatening manner.

Dildo stood up awkwardly, looking out the corners of his eyes at
the rest of us around him.

"What's your name, soldier?"

"Dillon," he answered, shifting back and forth. "Dillon Brown," he
said more confidently. "But my friends call me Dildo."

A few snickers rolled through the room, and even the lieutenant
couldn't help smiling.

"I see, Mr. Brown." The officer emphasized his name in a slow, deliberate tone. "Where are you from?"

"Bridgeport," he answered. "Bridgeport, Connecticut."

"And the rest of you men," the officer said, looking around the classroom, "are most of you from Connecticut? Shipped down from New Haven last night?"

A few guys mumbled "yeah" and others nodded.

"You can take your seat now, Brown," Lieutenant Crawley directed, slipping off the desktop. "I grew up in Danbury," the officer looked around the room for a reaction. "Like you guys, I was drafted. Next thing I knew I was down here in basic training at Fort Jackson." The officer was looking out at blank stares. "I'm telling you this because I know what it's like to be in your shoes. I didn't want to be here, and I had no idea what to expect." He paused but there was still no reaction. "I thought I'd just go through the motions. Do my time, get out and then move on with my life, hoping I didn't get my ass shot off in the process. Probably what a lot of you men are thinking right now. I was sitting in this same classroom, right where you are now, when some tight-ass lieutenant came in to give the pep talk. I didn't want to hear it, and I didn't give a shit about what he was saying. But you know something…as I sat there, it started making sense." Crawley paused.

"You men are not here by choice. I get it. As draftees you're the lowest notch on the totem pole. You take what comes along and hope for the best. Two years, you're in and you're out. But…" The lieutenant stopped. "But you have a choice. If you sign up for a three-year enrollment, you get options. Like what training you want after basic where you might learn skills that'll help you later on. Sure, it's another year of service, but trust me, gentlemen, it's well worth it."

Lieutenant Crawley looked around the room. "And for those of you who qualify," the lieutenant made eye contact with me, "you should consider OCS. That's what I did, and it made all the difference in the world. Becoming an officer opened opportunities that I never in my life imagined possible," Crawley said. "If in the next few days any of you men want to talk to me personally about your future in the Army, whether it be signing up for another year or applying for OCS, I will be available. Just check with Sergeant Washington to schedule a time outside your training exercises. I'll be glad to meet one-on-one, no obligation, to discuss opportunities. Trust me, gentlemen; it will be time well spent." With that the officer stepped briskly toward the door, returned the salute from the corporal, and left the room.

"All right, men, be seated," the corporal said. "Listen up and pay attention. Sergeant Dolan will be coming in to brief you. For the next few hours we'll be reviewing maneuvers you will be required to complete during the next eight weeks. Now is the time to ask questions if you don't understand."

Sergeant Dennis Dolan scuffed into the classroom. He looked like a rumpled Mickey Rooney character out of a World War II movie. His puffy red freckled cheeks and labored breath suggested a previous night of heavy drinking. He spat into a paper towel that he stuffed into the pocket of his khakis, wrinkled and hanging loose off his hips.

"Good morning, men," he coughed. "I'm Sergeant Dolan, here to give you a preview of some of the exercises you'll be going through. I'm gonna show you some slides so listen up and pay attention. You might find this helpful if you stay awake. If not, I don't give a shit. It's your ass."

The corporal pulled down a screen in front of the blackboard, then moved to the rear of the classroom to turn on the projector. He flipped a switch that sent a dusty stream of light across our heads, and then clicked to the first slide with the words Pugil Stick. The following slides showed soldiers holding heavily padded pole-like weapons, confronting each other while wearing helmets, gloves, shin guards and groin protectors. They looked like hockey players in full gear.

"Don't worry, men. You'll get the hang of it once we suit you up and you have a go at it." Dolan motioned to the corporal to advance the slides in the plastic carousel tray while the projector fan whirred and each new slide clicked into place. For the next two hours Sergeant Dolan briefed us on a wide range of exercises, maneuvers and equipment: hand-to-hand combat; rope climb; night crawl; grenade throw; firing range; M-14 rifle.

"Each of you men will be issued an M-14. You will be taught how to use it, how to clean it, disassemble it and put it back together. The M-14 will become your best friend…a better friend than your dick," Dolan advised.

The class concluded just before noon, and we were then led in formation to the mess hall. I picked up a tray and moved down the line, surprised to find the lunch selection more appealing than breakfast. There was a choice of soup: tomato or chicken noodle, followed by fried chicken, meatloaf and gravy with mashed potatoes, tuna and ham sandwiches, potato salad and coleslaw. Jell-O, vanilla custard and pound cake for desert. Large pitchers of iced tea and lemonade were positioned at the end of the line, next to a stainless steel coffee urn and cartons of milk.

"Glad to see you're eatin' something," the woman behind the counter smiled, noting the chicken leg and serving of mashed potatoes on my plate. "Want some gravy on there?" she asked.

"Sure," I answered as she ladled a spoon of milky sauce over my food.

"You can have all you want at lunch."

The afternoon started with laps around the athletic field and a sprint up drag-ass hill. We were all panting and sweating by the time we fell into formation in front of Sergeant Washington.

"Get used to it, men. This is July in South Carolina—but nothing compared to Nam. You're gonna be doing a lot of running at Jackson. By the time you men leave here you'll be fucking track stars," Washington predicted.

The rest of the day was a drill of basic exercises: push-ups, sit-ups, jumping jacks, knee-bends, squats—the basic high school calisthenics routine—only with relentless repetitions. We were subjected to tedious drills on the proper way to stand at attention, salute, how to move left, right, forward and backward in formation. The drills were repeated and repeated, with Washington calling on me to demonstrate every maneuver.

After four hours without a break Washington ordered, "All right men, fall out. Take five minutes to cool off. Get some water over there," he said, pointing to two large aluminum canisters packed in ice. Long boxes of white paper cups lay on the grass below. "Don't get dehydrated."

"Yeah, sure," Razor muttered to Dildo as we lined up to get a drink.

"Fuck right, man," Dildo agreed, splashing a cup of water over his face.

"You men got a problem over there?" Washington shouted.

"No, sir. We just fine," Razor mocked him.

"Good..." Washington sneered. "We don't need no problems around here."

The break was over when Washington snapped the riding crop in his palm and ordered, "Fall back in, men." He waited while we scrambled back into formation, then pointed to me. "Halladay, if there's any trash or paper cups left here after we move out, it's your ass."

Before I could respond the DI said, "Pick one man to help you police the area. Then get your butts back into formation with the rest of the company doing laps around the track. Understand?"

"Yes, sir," I answered, shooting a glance at Razor, who nodded back.

"All right, you sorry fuckheads, we're going to do some laps before we break for chow. Now move out and try to look like you're in the Army and not in some sissy kindergarten."

Charlie Company moved out in cadence, chanting, *Sound off!— One! Two! Three! Four!* as Razor and I hustled to pick up crumpled paper cups, gum wrappers, cigarette butts and any other litter left behind. We cleared the grass of all visible debris and stuffed trash into a large barrel next to the water canisters.

"I think that does it," I said, looking around to make sure we'd picked up everything.

"Looks good to me," Razor agreed.

"Better move and catch up with the others," I said, starting to break into a jog.

"Anything you say, college boy," Razor laughed as we fell in to join the other members of Charlie Company around the track.

CHAPTER FIVE
(July 12, 1967)

● ● ●

Day two of basic training started the same with reveille blasting across the base and a corporal banging the barracks door open, switching on lights. No cheerful greeting this morning, just a terse, "Formation outside at zero five hundred thirty hours." The screen door slammed as we rolled out of bed and suited up in fatigues. I had showered after lights out the night before to avoid the morning crush down the hall. My stomach winced with cramps from not having taken a shit for the last forty-eight hours, but I held out hoping for some alternative to the open, disgusting chicken-coop.

We fell into formation on the grass outside, taking our places from the day before. The sky was colorless and overcast, a damp drizzle misting through the warm oppressive air. Sergeant Raymond Washington was not present, so the corporal who'd given the unceremonious wake-up call took charge.

"Because the weather is cooperating this morning," he announced, "we're going to take a longer run. To make it fun, we'll be reciting some new chants along the way. You guys follow me and shout out as we move ahead. You'll get the feel of it and in no time you'll be singing like the fucking Mormon Tabernacle Choir. Just fall in and get with the program," the corporal directed as he led us on a moderately paced jog. He looked over his shoulder, and then called out:

You had a good home but you left / Your right
You had a good home but you left / Your right
Jody was there when you left / Your right
Your baby was there when you left / Your right
Sound off!—One! Two!
Sound off!—Three! Four!
One! Two! Three! Four! One! Two!—Three! Four!

We caught on and were soon jogging and chanting like bellowing bears, louder at every *Sound off!* For the first time since leaving New Haven, I felt there might be a purpose to all this shit.

I actually looked forward to running. It was one activity I was really good at. My feet floated gracefully in rhythm to the cadence, touching down lightly on the ash surface of the track and on the dry red clay of drag-ass hill. My long hours training in dance class had prepared me well for the endurance jogging drills.

I had first started taking lessons at the Michael Richards School of Dance when I was fourteen—too late to think about a career as a dancer, but I thought the training would help my movement and control onstage as an actor. My parents fucking flipped out when I told them I wanted to take a modern dance class. They were never supportive of my theatrical ambitions, but the dance thing pushed them over the edge. My dad refused to speak to me for a week, but I didn't care. I was going to pursue my dream despite my parents' objections.

Every Monday afternoon I boarded a bus in front of the library on the Post Road in downtown Westport for the twenty-minute ride to Norwalk where I transferred to a local bus that took me to South Norwalk. From there I'd walk down Washington Street, cross the bridge over the boat harbor, eventually arriving at the dance school— located on the top floor of a rundown brick building with a liquor store on the ground floor. It didn't bother me that I was the youngest person in the class and the only guy, except for Michael Richards, the instructor. The other students were women ranging in age from early twenties to late forties. They seemed happy to have me in the class, and I was always in demand as a partner for combinations.

One day after class, a woman who'd always aggressively sought me out to be her partner, pulled me aside.

"You know," she said patting my sweaty forehead with a towel, "you have a lot of potential."

"But I've started kind of late."

"You're a quick learner," she said suggestively. "I can tell. You should audition for the Westport Community Theatre spring musical."

"I don't know."

"Next Thursday at 7:00 p.m. Congregational Church auditorium on Post Road. Open call. We could use some new blood."

I was sixteen when cast in my first dance role, in the chorus of the local theatre production of *Annie Get Your Gun*—just two years after I'd started classes at the Michael Richards School of Dance. The choreographer was Janine Van der Meer, a well-known Westport socialite. She had studied dance in Holland under Olga Preobafluska, a famous Russian prima ballerina. Miss Van der Meer toured Europe before the outbreak of the war, and in 1946 she was brought to Hollywood by Twentieth Century Fox to appear opposite Jimmy Stewart in the noir film *Call Northside 777*. When her movie career floundered because producers found her too "foreign" for leading roles, she left California to settle in Westport with her second husband, a wealthy businessman who was a frequent guest at the Kennedy compound in Hyannis.

Janine Van der Meer taught classical ballet from a studio in her home, a sprawling stucco mansion overlooking the Saugatuck River at the end of a private dirt road.

One evening after rehearsals, Miss Van der Meer pulled me aside and asked if I had ever considered studying ballet. I was startled at the suggestion. At best I thought I might be able to do chorus work in musical comedies but never had aspirations of becoming a ballet dancer.

"Think about it," Van der Meer urged. "I give lessons in my studio, and I'd be willing to work with you. With the right training, I think you could become a good dancer."

As rehearsals for *Annie Get Your Gun* progressed, I developed a keen respect for Miss Van der Meer, especially for her discipline and patience working with a group of amateurs. My nonspeaking part required that I sing and dance in chorus numbers, but my big break came when Miss Van der Meer positioned me as the lead dancer, Big Chief Hole-in-the-Ground, in the Indian warriors dance sequence. The other guys in the number were buff jocks from the Staples High School track team. I didn't realize until the first dress rehearsal that the costume for the Indian dancers was a flesh-colored leotard and a burlap loincloth. Our chests, arms and faces were coated in clay colored body make-up, projecting an image of eight naked young men on stage. The response from the audience on opening night was a combination of gasps, whistles and loud hollering followed by a standing ovation at the end of the number.

My mom attended the opening performance and waited for me in the parking lot behind the auditorium.

"How'd you like the show?" I asked brightly, hopping into the front passenger seat of the Lincoln.

"It was something," she responded coolly. "I'm just glad your father wasn't here to see it."

Deflated by her reaction, I decided right then to accept Janine Van der Meer's invitation to study ballet. I dropped out of the Michael Richards modern jazz class and started going to Miss Van der Meer's studio every Saturday morning. It was a small group of four students: three teenage girls who were serious dancers, and me. The class began with stretching exercises and basic positions, nothing too complicated. I think Miss Van der Meer went out of her way not to overwhelm me. The girls seemed pleased to have me there, even though I was an inexperienced dancer. Miss Van der Meer worked individually with each student, giving the girls advanced exercises on the barre while suggesting basic positions and simple combinations for me.

One day after class as the girls were unlacing their ballet slippers and pulling sweat pants over their rehearsal tights, Miss Van der Meer asked if I could stay for a while. When the girls had left, she turned to me and instructed, "Now I want you to let yourself go, Timmy. I want you to explore yourself and let yourself go."

I wasn't quite sure what she wanted me to do, but I was eager to comply.

She pulled a record album off the shelf and placed it on the turntable, gently dropping the diamond needle onto the vinyl disc. Her studio filled with haunting sounds of the *Carousel Waltz*, prologue to the famous Rodgers and Hammerstein musical. She turned the volume up and the music soared. "Move freely. Don't think about dancing. Fly with the music. Let it take you wherever you want to go."

I was clumsy and self-conscious at first, but as I gained confidence and surrendered to the majestic music, I found myself soaring around the studio.

"Jump," she shouted. "Jump into the air and fly. Let your arms carry you."

As the music increased in tempo, I leaped and flew into the sunlight streaming through the studio windows.

"Good, Tim, good," she encouraged until the finale where I did one high leap and landed on my knees with my arms thrust up into the air.

"Excellent, Timmy," she said as she lifted the needle off the record. "You have a natural feel for rhythm, even if your technique is a bit primitive," she added with a smile.

"Thank you, Miss Van der Meer," I gasped, out of breath.

"You are a special young man," she said wistfully, gazing out the arched window overlooking the Saugatuck River. She withdrew a cigarette from a slim silver case, and said, "I've been contracted by the Westport Community Theatre to do choreography for *Carousel* this fall." She exhaled a white wisp of smoke from the cigarette she'd lit, turned toward me and tapped the hard tip of her toe shoe on the polished wooden floor. "My main concern was casting the role of the Carnival Boy in the dream sequence. None of the young men from the high school seemed right," she confided, taking another long puff. "But you, Tim…you could be perfect. You have the sensitivity." She squashed her cigarette into the crystal ashtray on the table next to the record turntable. "That is, if you're willing to work hard and learn to partner."

"You think I could?"

"Only if you want to. We have the summer to work on it…if you are willing to put in the time and effort. It won't be easy, because you have a lot to learn. And of course, it will take more than one Saturday morning class."

I was flattered by the prospect of taking on a leading dance role, but aware that the fee for the weekly Saturday morning class was already stretching money from my caddying job, money I was supposed to be saving for college.

"I'd like to, Miss Van der Meer, but I don't think I could afford more lessons…"

"Nonsense," she cut me off. "You don't think I would charge you for rehearsals, do you? We'll need to work three days a week, in addition to the Saturday morning class. My daughter, Stina, who you know from class, will be your partner."

"Yes, I want to. I really want to do it."

"Then it's settled," the imposing ballerina announced definitively as she lit another cigarette.

The summer flew by. I caddied every day except Monday, often carrying two bags of golf clubs around the eighteen-hole course until my shoulders ached and were pinched from the heavy load. Afterward, I'd ride my bike to Miss Van der Meer's studio where I changed into dance tights in the small bathroom off the entryway. For the next two hours Stina and I would practice the intricate moves of the dream ballet. As the weeks wore on and I became more confident, I lifted Stina high over my head and caught her as she slipped into my arms. The rehearsals went on relentlessly, the haunting music filling the studio, salt air breezes from Long Island Sound drifting in from the open windows, gently brushing our perspiring cheeks. Stina repeated the movements, silently holding back tears; she would never ask her mother for a break. Finally at the end of the session, Stina withered into my arms and expired onto the wooden bench at the side of the studio, opposite the wall of mirrors, where she unlaced her bloody toe shoes, waiting for corrections from her mother.

• • •

The cadence changed to a more raucous Jody as the boys in Charlie Company started the last jog around the track:

Your left, Your left
Your left, Your right, Your left
My back aches
My belt's too tight
I don't know but I've been told
Eskimo pussy is mighty cold
Sound off!—One! Two!
Sound off!—Three! Four!

I was invigorated by the challenging run, my body gliding freely as we trotted around the track chanting the ribald Jody cadence call. I looked behind to see Razor and Dildo lagging with the other recruits, all of them huffing out of breath. I smiled, thinking Miss Van der Meer would be proud of me, although horrified at the circumstances. I was no longer a sissy in black tights, flitting around a dance studio, someone my father would have derided, but instead I was sprinting around the fucking track at Fort Jackson, out in front of the other recruits.

The afternoon session began with hand-to-hand combat. Sergeant Washington described a situation where a soldier was stranded in the jungle without a weapon, when he came face-to-face with Charlie—also unarmed.

"If you're fucking lucky, you may have a sharp stick. But basically it's your hands and your ability to defend yourself."

Washington and the corporal locked eyes, raised arms in a defensive position, and proceeded to exchange blows with their lower arms and fists, bouncing back and forth like boxers in a ring. Washington grabbed the corporal in a headlock and wrestled him to the ground, breaking off cleanly.

"I had him and could have slit his fucking throat with a stick," the DI boasted, wiping sand off his fatigues.

"Okay, college boy," Washington pointed to me. "Show us how you're gonna take Charlie out."

Resigned to another humiliation, I advanced toward the corporal, arms poised in a protective position, only to be immediately thrown down to the ground on my back.

"Great, college boy," the DI laughed. "You're dead. You're fucking dead."

I got up, brushed myself off, hoping to disappear back into the formation.

"Maybe you'll do better with one of your buddies," Washington snickered. "Rodriguez," he shouted pointing to Razor. "Get over here and show college boy how to protect himself in the jungle."

"What...?"

"Move your fucking spic ass over here and show this pussy college boy how to fight."

Razor moved out in front of me, and we locked eyes.

"All right men, you're in the jungle and you hate each other...and only one of you is getting out alive. Now fight like you mean it!" Washington goaded us on.

Razor and I dug our boots into the sand, raised arms and faced each other in a standoff, each of us reluctant to make a move.

"C'mon, you pussies. This isn't the fucking senior prom. You want to kill each other," Washington screamed as he slapped the riding crop in his palm.

Razor made the first move, jabbing me on the left arm. Instinctively, I withdrew, tightening my stomach muscles and pulling my arms in close.

"College boy, you're gonna fucking die if you don't fight back," Washington provoked.

Determined not to suffer further humiliation, I thrust my right arm out hitting Razor bluntly on the cheek. The impact startled both of us, and Razor recoiled, stepping backward, spitting on his sleeve. He was pissed that I had caught him off guard.

"Whoa," the DI laughed. "You gonna let your girlfriend get away with that, spic boy?"

The boys in Charlie Company started to snicker, which infuriated Razor. His Latino pride was being challenged, and he wasn't about to have some white kid get the best of him—not in front of the entire company.

What followed was an uncontrolled frenzy of fists and punches, kicking and grappling, as we rolled entwined struggling in the sand. I felt Razor's face locked next to mine, saliva dripping from the his mouth down onto my cheek.

We broke free, stood up and stepped back, breathing heavily, eyes burning in bewilderment, all sense of reality obliterated. Razor charged unexpectedly, smashing his head into my face. Blood shot from my nose and I staggered unbalanced, my arms flailing as I crumpled to the ground on my back. Razor charged like a carnivorous animal and threw his full body on top of me, pinning me to the ground with his weight. I gave up all resistance and let the sweating and panting boy pummel my limp body.

The corporal came over and pulled Razor off. "All right, men. That's enough. Demonstration's over."

I pushed back on my elbows to get up, wiping blood dripping from my nose on the sleeve of my fatigues, when Washington slapped me across the face with the riding crop.

"You're dead, college boy," the DI sneered. "Give me twenty if you ever want to get up. Otherwise, you can just stay there feeling sorry for yourself."

I turned over and stretched out my battered arms to begin the slow, torturous process of push-ups. My lips brushed the dirt as I cursed, "Fuck you, Washington. Fuck you, Razor, and fuck the whole fucking Army." Blood had caked on my upper lip; my body ached and trembled as I forced myself up and down, trying to recall the melodic strains of the *Carousel Waltz*.

CHAPTER SIX
(July 13, 1967)

● ● ●

Lights were out in the barracks. It was two days into basic training; I had a shaved head, aching muscles, a bloodied nose and little self-esteem. My battle buddy had beaten the shit out of me in a training exercise. The cramps in my stomach from not having taken a dump since leaving Connecticut were excruciating. I was convinced I was dying of shit poisoning. I stretched out on the coarse wool blanket and stared at the raw wooden beams in the ceiling. Snores of labored breathing through half-open, blubbering lips and incoherent mumblings of guys having bad dreams echoed up and down the row of bunk beds.

I tried to will myself to sleep, hoping that would ease the pains in my lower belly. I pressed hard into the flesh of my bloated abdomen, slipping a few fingers below the elastic band of my boxer shorts. I thought of the long hours in Miss Van der Meer's studio, the endless repetitions of the *Carousel Waltz* floating from the record player, as Stina and I worked to perfect the technical movements of the difficult ballet. We watched ourselves in the wall of mirrors, looking like two lovers whose movements became increasingly seductive and sensuous with each rehearsal. As I gained confidence, I'd lift Stina up over my head, then let her slide down along my body, gently wrapping my arms around her; she was like a frail bird in my extended hands.

On opening night, we were oblivious to other cast members and the audience as we entered the stage. Stina wore a wispy pink sundress and I was in tight jeans and a red and white striped T-shirt. Losing ourselves in the music, we became the doomed lovers: Stina the innocent local schoolgirl and I the transient carnival boy.

Backstage I had to beg Stina to go out with me for the curtain call. She was in tears. She'd unlaced her blood stained toe shoes, and was rubbing her bruised feet. Her mother had passed Stina a page of notes on a yellow pad, pointing out flaws in her performance. Miss Van der Meer had a different message for me: a business card from Mr. Harry Engler, Vice President of the William Morris talent agency in New York. Engler had written on the back of the card in ballpoint pen, "Call me for an interview."

• • •

I rolled on my side, trying to get comfortable, hoping to drift off to sleep; Razor was purring like a contented cat on the bunk below. I thought of our encounter that afternoon during hand-to-hand combat training. It had been a humiliating yet strangely exciting experience. As we locked arms and scraped faces, I gave in and let the strong Puerto Rican boy pound me into the sand.

I felt myself getting hard as I relived the encounter. I clutched the lumpy pillow and buried my face in it. The pain in my belly was agonizing and my hard-on only made it worse. I looked at my watch hidden beneath the pillow, and saw that it was just past two a.m., three hours before reveille. I sat up clutching my stomach, then silently lowered myself down from the upper bunk, careful not to disturb Razor, as my feet touched the cold floor.

Wearing only white boxer shorts and slapping my dick to get it flaccid, I crept past the row of bunk beds and slipped out into the night air. The damp grass squished between my toes as I headed toward the outhouse. I pushed open the creaky wooden door and entered the squalid shack. As I had calculated, there was no one there. The single dangling light bulb cast a dim glow as flies and mosquitoes buzzed around hungrily. I quickly lowered my shorts and squatted on a dirty toilet nearest the door, exploding in a massive discharge of relief. I felt like I was giving birth, scrunched over, my head lowered between my knees. I sat there silently as the cramps slowly receded.

The outhouse door thumped open, and I sat up startled. It was Dildo standing like a ghost in the doorway, his large leopard green eyes peering at me, sizing me up like cornered prey. I fumbled with a clump of brown paper towels, wiped myself and stood abruptly, pulling up my white boxers.

"Hey, it's you, college boy," Dildo grinned, his right hand gently dangling over the large bulge in his fatigues. "Guess we both had the same idea...not into group shits, huh?"

"Not my thing." I tried to make a joke as I flushed the toilet. "It's all yours," I said, brushing by Dildo and jogging up the hill to the barracks.

I stretched out on the bunk, hoping to get some sleep before reveille. My thoughts drifted back to the Eastern Air Lines flight when Gloria had ordered drinks as we sat in the circular lounge in the back of the plane. She lit a cigarette, sipping her martini as she stared at me with glazed eyes. The plane bounced gently as the engines slowly changed RPMs, indicating a gradual descent. The stewardess picked up the cocktail glasses and requested we return to our seats.

"I hate flying," Gloria said as the plane banked and circled on its final approach for landing in West Palm Beach. I gazed out the window at the long string of lights dotting the coastline, the blackness of the Atlantic Ocean disappearing into the horizon, white lips of waves kissing the sandy beaches below. I felt Gloria's hand cupping my right knee as the plane touched down on the tarmac and the pilot abruptly thrust the engines into reverse to slow the plane. The graceful Golden-Falcon Constellation lurched and bobbed down the runway, turning onto the taxiway before coming to a jerky stop as the four propeller engines exhaled a hiss and slowly stopped rotating.

Two men in overalls rolled a metal stairway to the front exit of the plane as the stewardess released a hatch, opening the door to let in a blast of tropical night air. The sounds of slapping palm fronds, like leather belts being snapped, filled the gusty evening breeze as passengers disembarked down the steep, portable metal stairs.

"Thank you," Gloria said pressing her palm down on my knee as she rose unsteadily out of her seat.

My grandparents were waiting behind the chain-link fence in the baggage claim area outside the one-story terminal building. Nan was wearing a simple flower-patterned housedress. A white wicker pocketbook the size of a small birdhouse dangled from her right arm. Bluish-gray ringlets of curls framed her sweet face, beaming with a Shirley-Temple smile. Pop stood by, wearing an open-collar, tan, short-sleeved shirt, his pleated linen slacks neatly pressed.

"Timmy," my grandmother squealed, waving her hand franticly above her head. "Over here!"

"The boy can see us, Catherine."

I bounded off the metal staircase, darting past other passengers walking toward the terminal.

"Oh. Timmy, I'm so glad you're here," Nan gushed.

"How was your flight, son?"

"Fine, Pop. It was fine," I answered hoping the two Life Savers I'd popped into my mouth before getting off the plane would cover any trace of the gin and tonics I'd downed with Gloria. My grandfather did not approve of alcohol and would have had a heart attack if he knew his sixteen-year-old grandson had been drinking on an airplane, let alone at the invitation of a divorced, middle-aged woman.

We drove from the airport in an elegant Oldsmobile Super 98 four-door sedan, the car my grandfather had driven Mrs. Pembroke to Florida from Westport.

It was after midnight when we pulled into the driveway of the simple stucco cottage at 1008 Sunset Road in West Palm Beach. I was amazed to see bush-size poinsettias in bloom on either side of the front door and a large grapefruit tree dripping with pale yellow balls of citrus in the side yard.

"We'd better turn in," Pop announced as he brought my Samsonite suitcase in from the car. "Your grandmother and I have to work tomorrow, but you'll come with us. Mrs. Pembroke knows you are here visiting."

The next morning I awoke to hear my grandmother humming in the kitchen, the aroma of coffee wafting into my room.

"Tim, are you up?" she called out.

"Yes, Nan," I answered, getting up from the rollaway bed I'd slept on.

"Coffee, dear?"

"Sure," I answered, joining her in the kitchen.

"There's grapefruit on the table," she said handing me a mug of steaming coffee. "I picked it this morning from the tree outside your room. Once you've had fresh picked, you'll never want to eat citrus from the grocery store." She had sliced the grapefruit sections away from the rind and placed a mint leaf in the center of the glistening pink fruit.

"I'll fix us breakfast when we get to Chilean Avenue," she said, referring to Mrs. Pembroke's villa in Palm Beach.

"You were right about the citrus," I said slurping a luscious warm wedge into my mouth.

"When you finish your coffee, dear, you should pack your bathing suit and a change of clothes. Shorts will be fine, because you'll probably want to walk on the beach."

My grandfather was in the driveway, wiping down the sleek Oldsmobile with a chamois cloth, folding it in squares to avoid smudging the surface of the car. He cleaned the windows with a wad of paper towels that he crumpled and stuffed into a garbage can by the side of the house.

"We're ready to leave," he announced, starting the ignition and checking his watch. It was seven-ten, their regular departure time for the drive across Lake Worth Lagoon to Palm Beach Island.

Mrs. Pembroke's home on Chilean Avenue was a sprawling Spanish-style villa built in the 1920s, hidden behind tall hibiscus. My grandfather pulled the Olds up to the iron gates of the driveway. He got out and unlatched the metal bolt, returning to the car and driving up to the porte cochere. A row of spindly palms lined the brick drive leading to the formal front entrance of the main house that faced a courtyard with a bubbling, three-tiered fountain in the center.

A young Cuban gardener was snipping dead blooms out of the hedges and raking palm fronds that had blown out of the trees during the night. He waved to us and shut the gate.

As soon as the car came to a stop, Mrs. Pembroke's two dachshunds, Hansel and Gretel, bounded out of the open front door and raced toward me, yapping and jumping up and down, licking my face as I stooped to pet the two wagging sausage-dogs.

"They remember you from Westport," my grandmother beamed as the dogs fussed over me.

"I guess so," I smiled as Hansel and Gretel yelped and turned in circles. "Quite a welcome!" The two slinky brown hounds followed us down a brick walkway along the side of the house that led to a screened porch off the kitchen. My grandmother went through the paces of preparing breakfast, and in a short time three plates of scrambled eggs, crisp bacon strips, and grilled tomatoes were set on the simple pine kitchen table. With her small hands snug inside potholder mitts, Nan popped a hot buttermilk biscuit on each plate.

My grandfather checked to see that the lawn sprinklers were functioning properly, and, satisfied the grounds were being attended, he wiped his shoes on the hemp mat by the screen door and took his place at the kitchen table.

"Do you have the list ready?" he asked as Nan hovered around the table, pouring coffee.

"Let me warm that, Tim?" she said, pouring coffee into my mug, ignoring her husband.

"That's fine," I replied while slipping crumbs of buttered biscuits to Hansel and Gretel, begging at my feet under the table.

"I need to get to the market early," my grandfather pressed, clearing his throat, "before everything is picked over."

"You know I'll have it ready, Daddy," Nan said sweetly, placing the coffee pot back on the burner.

"Your grandmother and I are working today, but Mrs. Pembroke said we can have Saturday afternoon and all Sunday off to show you around. We told her this was your first trip to Florida."

"Maybe we could take Tim to the dog races or to jai alai," Nan suggested, as she jotted notes on the grocery list.

"He's underage, but I know a few of the guards at the track, so maybe we can get him through."

"Don't worry, Pop," I smiled. "I don't gamble."

"It would be nice for you to see the greyhounds. They are so graceful and fast."

"Your grandmother always seems to pick the winners. She doesn't know a darn thing about the sport, but she wins all the time."

"Oh, Daddy," she dismissed. "It's just the luck of the Irish. But I do look at the eyes of those beautiful dogs. I can tell if they're focused and if they're going to run well."

"Mrs. Pembroke left a guest pass for you at the Colony," my grandfather changed the subject. "She thought you might like to use the pool and the health club. Just give this to the attendant," Pop said handing me an envelope.

"You can have lunch there too," my grandmother chimed in. "I hear the outdoor café is very nice…of course, I've never been."

"Sounds great, " I said getting up from the table. "I think I'll put on shorts and take a walk first."

"You can't miss the Colony, son. It's just two blocks over, past Worth Avenue, right on the beach."

I walked down the freshly hosed brick driveway and slipped out the gate onto Chilean Avenue, heading toward the beach. The residential street was quiet except for a few squawking tropical birds and the swishing of palm fronds, flapping high above in the gentle ocean breeze. The elegant homes were set back, hidden behind imposing gates and twenty-foot hedges of trimmed ficus trees, offering only a hint of the opulence beyond.

I crossed Hibiscus Avenue, and in the next block the mansions grew larger and more imposing, until I reached South Ocean Boulevard, Highway A1A, which hugged the long stretch of Atlantic coast. Waves unfolded gently, creating bubbles of white foam on miles of pristine beaches where seagulls and sandpipers skipped and fluttered in the retreating surf. A young man in khakis rolled up to his knees, a sweatshirt tied around his waist, waded barefoot on the wet sand. He was tossing a plastic Frisbee into the air to a panting golden retriever who obediently plunged into the surf to retrieve it. The dog dropped the yellow disc in front of him, shaking vigorously to release a shower of salt water from his soaked coat, eager for a repeat run. Aside from the scurrying birds, the young man and his dog were the only signs of life on the beach.

A long stretch of sidewalk with a low retaining wall separated the highway from the sand. Lonely, unoccupied cement benches dotted the promenade every hundred yards. A workman with a broom swept sand blown onto the sidewalk back toward the beach and deposited papers and trash into a green plastic can on wheels that he pushed in front of him.

I walked south, passing Peruvian Avenue, another residential street of villas hidden behind lush hedges and imposing gates. The snipping sounds of gardeners pruning prickly bougainvillea branches growing over trellised fences, the whirring hum of gas-powered mowers hugging green velvet lawns, and the scraping of rakes across paved walkways completed the symphony of morning maintenance. It was just past nine, but there were no visible signs of the people who actually inhabited these lavish homes.

The next intersection was Worth Avenue, the commercial hub of Palm Beach. It was a four-block palm-lined esplanade of elegant stores, boutiques, art galleries and restaurants. Moss baskets of fresh-faced pansies hung from the arches of colonial Spanish-style buildings. Small brick vias crept off the main sidewalk, inviting passersby to explore shops tucked away in small cottages.

I walked down the famous street, peering into display windows of Saks Fifth Avenue with haughty, faceless mannequins draped in elegant evening gowns. Classic watches rested on gray velvet pedestals behind bulletproof glass at Tiffany's. I paused to study the menu posted in a brass display stand at the entrance of Ta-boo, where a busboy was folding napkins and wiping bamboo bistro chairs on the patio, preparing for the lunch crowd. The young man smiled at me, and I nodded back before continuing down the avenue. Reaching the end of the commercial district at Cocoanut Row, I crossed the wide street, turning to retrace my steps toward the beach.

The Colony was set back from Worth Avenue, shielded from the retail stores by acres of tropical green foliage and a row of tall, well-manicured palm trees. I walked up the circular drive to the coral-colored, sprawling main building and stopped under the porte cochère to ask directions from a doorman dressed in a white Moroccan uniform.

"Through the lobby and out the glass doors to the gardens," he pointed. "Follow the walkway past the bungalows and you'll come to the pool and tennis courts. The attendant there will assist you."

I crossed the formal lobby, its walls covered in tropical green and white banana leaf wallpaper. Cushy sofas and wingback chairs upholstered in pastel floral prints sat on aged Oriental carpets; a gas-burning fireplace flickered in the far corner. Small iron swan-shaped signs pointed to the pool, interspaced in the bright red and white petunia beds along the concrete walkway around the bungalows, eventually leading me to a gate with an imposing sign, "Pool and Cabana Club. Guests and Members Only." A handsome, blond man in tennis shorts and a white polo shirt monogramed with the Colony crest logo was folding towels and spreading cushions on lounge chairs by the pool.

"Am I in the right place?" I asked.

"You must be Halladay." He pressed a buzzer to open the gate to the pool and cabana area.

"How did you know?" I asked, caught off guard to be called by name.

"You're the only outside visitor today," he smiled, picking up a clipboard to make a notation with a pencil dangling on a string. "You're Mrs. Pembroke's guest."

"Yes."

"My name is Sven."

"I'm Tim. Tim Halladay."

"This is for a locker," Sven said, handing me a curled elastic wristband with a small key attached. "Number thirty-seven...through there in the men's locker room. You can change into your swim trunks if you want to use the pool. Your things will be safe in there."

"I would like to use the pool," I said taking the key.

"It's heated," Sven warned. "Kind of like a bathtub, but our guests like it that way."

I was the only one in the sterile, tiled changing room. A long wooden bench ran down the center aisle in front of two rows of steel gray lockers secured with combination locks and nameplates on each door. Number thirty-seven, the one I'd been assigned, was open and empty. The aroma of disinfectant and chlorine permeated the air, creating an antiseptic environment. I stripped naked and stood on the cold cement floor in front of the locker, lingering before putting my clothes and gym bag inside. Aware I was becoming aroused, I slipped into my orange bathing trunks with mesh nylon lining, adjusted myself, and slammed the metal locker door shut.

Sven was skimming the surface of the pool with a net on the end of a long pole, scraping up leaves and bougainvillea flowers that had blown into the gently lapping blue water. He'd set up a chaise lounge with towels in front of a cabana and had tied back the cream-colored canvas curtains.

"You can use Number One. There's nobody here today. Most of the hotel guests are attending an ornithology conference in the ballroom…watching slides about migrating birds and endangered puffins," he laughed. "Well, almost no one," Sven nodded toward a woman in a black bathing suit, large sunglasses covering her eyes, reclining on a lounge at the far end of the pool by the diving board. She appeared to be dozing in the warm sunlight; a copy of *Town and Country* was open across her lap. "She's famous," the pool attendant whispered. "Very famous… These people come here for privacy and do not want to be disturbed."

"Think she'd mind if I took a swim?"

"She'd probably like that," Sven winked.

I slipped into the bath-like water, and began doing laps in the Olympic-size pool. I turned to do a series of backstrokes, alternating my legs, kicking and unfolding my arms behind, creating geysers of rippling water. I swam for a long time, pushing back each lap from the tiles in the deep end under the diving board, thrusting my body toward the opposite shallow end, finally resting and floating in the pool squinting at the overhead sun.

Sven was waiting when I climbed the metal ladder, emerging with my bright orange swim trunks clinging like a deflated balloon.

"That was quite a workout," Sven said patting my shoulders with an oversized white towel. "Hope you didn't overdo it."

"I'm fine," I said, wrapping myself in the soft terry.

"You can relax over there," Sven pointed to a chaise lounge at the end of the pool in front of Cabana One. "Let me know if you need anything."

I stretched facedown on the canvas cushion. The gentle lapping of water from the pool filter system and the swishing of palm fronds overhead lulled me into a contented, light sleep in the warm Florida sunshine.

"You've been out over an hour," a soft voice woke me. "And you're getting burned."

I rolled over to face Sven sitting beside me on the chaise lounge.

"I guess I dozed off," I said sitting up.

"Let me put some of this on your back."

"What is it?"

"Coconut oil. It'll help prevent peeling and you'll smell delicious," Sven grinned as he rubbed a generous amount of the oil in his palms and started massaging my shoulders.

"You have to be careful in this sun, especially with fair skin like yours."

"Yeah," I said, feeling the gentle rotating movements of Sven's hands on my back.

"How old are you, Tim?" he asked unexpectedly.

"Sixteen."

"Okay," Sven said, slapping me lightly on the back with coconut oil. "Do you want some lunch?" he got up, wiping his hands on a towel. "The food is very good here, and you better get out of the sun."

"Sure. I guess so."

"What would you like? Mrs. Pembroke's guests can have anything they want."

"I don't know. Maybe a tuna fish sandwich and some ice tea."

"You are so white bread," he laughed. "I'll put the order in, but you stay out of the sun."

I looked over the cobalt rippling water of the pool, gentle waves slurping into the filtration ducts. The mysterious woman in the black bathing suit and sunglasses was gone, leaving Sven and me alone in the pool area. I pulled the plush terry towel across my shoulders and felt the sting of sunburn. I stretched out on the chaise lounge in the shade of the cabana, closing my eyes, luxuriating in the lush surroundings.

"Your lunch is here," Sven announced as the waiter placed a tray on a glass-top table in the cabana. "He doesn't have to sign," Sven said, picking up the leather folder containing the check. "He's Mrs. Pembroke's guest."

I sat up, trying to drape the towel over the erection in my orange bathing trunks.

"I ordered you some vanilla ice cream," Sven smiled as I sat in a plastic chair in front of the small table in the cabana. "They make it here in the kitchen…like nothing you've ever tasted."

Sven brought me a terry cloth robe with the Colony logo on the lapel pocket. "Put this on. You don't have to sit in that wet towel."

I slipped my arms into the cushy robe, as Sven folded the cloth belt in front of me. "Isn't that more comfortable?" he said backing away. "I have to set up some more places around the pool. The bird people will be finishing lunch in half an hour, and they will flock down here in droves. They heard there was a sighting of a white swan in the pool," he laughed. "You can stay as long as you like. I've blocked out Cabana One for the rest of the day. Just stay out of the sun. You're getting burned."

Sven went about his duties, spreading towels on chaise lounges and opening several cabanas, tying back the canvas drapes. He placed slim leather-bound cocktail menus on plastic tables between the chairs and turned the volume up a few decibels as salsa music floated over the area.

"How's lunch?" Sven asked returning to the table.

"You were right about the ice cream."

"Thought you'd like it."

"This has been really nice, but I think I'm going to go," I said placing the starched white napkin on the table.

"You're welcome to stay as long as you like."

"Looks like it's going to get busy, and I'm not big on crowds. I think I'll take a walk on the beach. I can't come to Florida without putting my toes in the Atlantic."

"You can walk for miles and not run into anyone."

"Sounds perfect."

"Wish I could walk with you."

"That would be nice," I smiled getting up.

Sven patted me on the shoulder. "Make sure you put some coco-nut oil on that burn."

"I'll do that," I said moving toward the locker room.

"See you again, kid," Sven winked. "By the way, when did you say you turn eighteen?"

CHAPTER SEVEN
(July 14, 1967)

● ● ●

The blast from the recorded reveille bugle rang across Fort Jackson, the sun peeking up above dew crying on the surrounding hillsides. I had drifted back to sleep after my late-night trip to the outhouse chicken coop and my encounter with Dildo. I rolled over in the bunk, the memory of Sven drying me off at the pool fixed in my head, my white boxers sticky with pre-cum. I slid from the top bunk, draping a towel in front of me and walked to the shower stalls. I stood under a stream of hot water, closed my eyes and rubbed soap over my shaved head.

"Gotta let the hot water run," Dildo smiled, adjusting spigots on the adjacent shower. He unfolded the towel around his neck and twisted it into a knot, slapping me on the ass. "Want some of this?" he said diverting his eyes downward to his full nine-inch erection.

"Not my thing," I said, shutting off the water, wrapping a towel around my dripping body.

"Maybe not now, college boy, but after a while you gonna be begging for it," Dildo laughed, lathering up. "When all that saltpeter shit they're feeding us in the mess hall wears off, you'll be wanting it bad, just like all the other white faggots."

Charlie Company fell into formation outside the barracks. Sergeant Washington snapped the riding crop into his palm and shouted orders for the "pussy platoon" to start jogging around the athletic field, ordering two more runs up and down drag-ass hill. The rest of the morning was filled with routine calisthenics: monkey-bar hang, belly crawl under barbed wire, and the rope climb which left my arms with burns and scrapes from falling off the twisted lines above sand traps.

"Pathetic," Washington said as I slid down a raw rope suspended from a magnolia tree limb, dropping to the ground. The DI kicked clay grit into my face shouting, "Give me twenty, you pussy college boy."

After lunch we fell in outside the mess hall. Washington called attention as Lieutenant Crawley, dressed in fatigues, came to address the assembly.

"Listen up, men," the DI instructed. "Lieutenant Crawley is here to take you through the next exercise."

"Thank you, Sergeant," the officer said, stepping in front of our formation. "At ease, gentlemen," he motioned. "This afternoon we're going to have some fun…at least fun for those of you who like fireworks. All jokes aside…this is serious stuff. What I'm holding in my palm is a grenade," he said, raising his right arm over his head. "Think of this little gray pineapple as your third ball. It may save your life some day when you're in the jungle facing Charlie."

We were fascinated as the lieutenant walked up and down displaying the small weapon with a circular wire pin attached. "We're going out to the firing range where each of you will have a chance to see how this little baby works. Okay, Sergeant, let's move out."

The DI led Charlie Company in a cadenced jog to a remote area of the base depleted of trees and vegetation. A Quonset hut stood in front of a five-foot wall of sandbags, beyond which was a barren stretch of red clay mounds with wooden markers indicating 100-, 200- and 300-yard distances. A chain-link fence with coiled, razor barbed wire on top surrounded the area, the size of several football fields.

Upon arrival, we were issued protective helmets and goggles. Lieutenant Crawley demonstrated the proper stance, the sequence for pulling the pin out of the grenade, and then the final throw-through to launch the weapon toward its designated target. Each man was given three inactive shells to practice the maneuver.

I gripped the cold pineapple-shaped weapon in my palm, stood gracefully in position as if in Miss Van der Meer's dance studio, and hurled the gray metal object across the sandbag barrier. The metal decoy landed with a thud in the dirt just a few feet away.

"Oh, Christ, college boy," Washington shouted down my back. "Is that what they teach you to do in those fancy schools? You threw that thing like a fucking wet potato chip. You wanna fuckin' get us all killed?"

Lieutenant Crawley stepped in, backing the DI off. "Give it another shot, Halladay," he encouraged. "You'll get the hang of it."

But I knew then that no matter what I did, I would never get the hang of it. Just like at Assumption School when kids were selected for the softball or basketball team. We lined up waiting to be picked, the Skins verses the Shirts, and I was always last. No one wanted me to play on their team. One day Mr. O'Leary, the gym teacher, found me curled up in the changing room after practice, my knuckles bloodied from beating on the door of my locker. My parents were called to school for a meeting with Mother Superior and Mr. O'Leary. The consensus was that I might benefit from outside coaching. I guess they thought it might help build my self-confidence.

The next morning my dad placed a call to Joe Duffy, our next-door neighbor. He asked Mr. Duffy if his son, Mike, would be willing to coach me in some basic baseball and basketball exercises. He explained that I was having problems in the physical education class and maybe Mike, who was two years older, and an accomplished athlete at Staples High School, could give me some pointers. They made a deal that Mike would be paid fifty cents an hour to coach me.

From the start Mike and I were uncomfortable with the arrangement, which was forced on us by our parents, but the next Saturday morning we rode our bikes to the playground behind Bedford Elementary School a few blocks away. Mike had brought a basketball, and we started some basic dribbling maneuvers, passing the ball back and forth. After a while I caught on to the rhythm, running and passing the ball. But when it came to hoops, I was a disaster. The more times Mike passed me the ball and demonstrated how to jump and project it, the worse I got.

"Maybe we should hang it up for today," Mike said sensing my frustration. A light drizzle had started to fall, and the cement pavement on the playground was slippery. "Let's try it again next week," he said as we got on our bikes to ride the few blocks home.

The following Saturday Mike brought two gloves, a bat and three baseballs. We started with basics, but I was totally inept at throwing or catching the ball. I was embarrassed and didn't want to admit that it was the first time I'd ever thrown a baseball or held a glove.

The next Saturday we headed for the playground, but by this time we both knew the situation was hopeless. We tossed the basketball around a few times, passing it back and forth until it came to me and I just held it in my hands. I dropped the ball and kicked it toward Mike. "You know this is never going to work."

"Yeah, but your dad is paying me."

"I know," I said, dejected. "But we can still hang out."

"You mean like babysitting?"

"I guess you could call it that, even if I'm a little old."

"You wanna come over and watch TV at my house?" Mike asked, picking up the basketball.

"Sure," I said relieved to quit the playground.

For the next few weeks we rode our bikes on Saturday morning to Bedford Elementary, circled the basketball court, dribbled a couple of balls, throwing them back and forth toward each other, and then headed back to Mike's room to watch cartoons on television until it was time for me to go home for lunch.

Although Mike was a star player on the Staples High School baseball team, he had a tough time making grades. He had been held back twice at Assumption School for failing to pass basic reading exams, but was finally put through to the public high school because, I guess, the frustrated nuns could do nothing more to improve his test scores. By pushing Mike on, he was no longer their responsibility.

Mike Duffy, at sixteen years old, was six feet tall with a bushy head of red curly hair, which he slicked down with Vaseline petroleum jelly. His chalk-white complexion was splattered with orange freckles, and while he may have appeared to be a clumsy, awkward clown in the hallways of Staples High, he was a star in his flannel-striped uniform on the baseball field, where he looked like a young Mickey Mantle. Mike told me one day that his dream was to become a professional baseball player, but his inability to focus on classroom studies forced him to drop out of high school his sophomore year, ending any chance of his getting an athletic scholarship and squashing his ambitions for a career in sports.

●●●

"You get two more shots with the dummy," Lieutenant Crawley instructed. "Then you get the real thing. Think you can handle that?"

"I'll try, sir," I answered.

"Good, soldier. You'll get the hang of it."

I stepped back into position, bending my right knee and lifting upward, throwing my arm forward, thrusting the metal pineapple shaped dud into the air. The object flew out of my hand and landed halfway before the 100-yard marker.

"Better, Halladay," the officer encouraged. "But not quite there. Let's try it again. See if you can give it more push."

I repeated the exercise, and this time the dummy grenade landed a bit farther out.

"Getting there, but this one's for real," the officer cautioned, handing me a live grenade. "Just pull the pin and throw it as hard and far as you can."

I took the metal pineapple in my hand, looked squarely at Lieutenant Crawley, and got into position.

"Whenever you're ready, Halladay."

I faced the markers in the field, dug my boots into the sand, and stretched into position. I fantasized I was in Miss Van der Meer's class about to take off in leaps to the *Carousel Waltz*. I pulled the metal ring on the weapon—it felt heavier than the three previous practice duds—stretched my arm back and hurled the metal pineapple into the air. It skimmed over the top of the sandbag barrier and fell with a thud a few yards beyond.

"Oh, Christ!" the lieutenant yelled, hurling himself against me, pinning me to the ground. "Don't move," he ordered as he pressed his body on top of me. Our metal helmets clashed and scraped and I could feel the officer's breath on the back of my neck. In seconds the ground shook like an earthquake, and a shower of clay pellets and stones rained over our bodies. The officer's grip tightened when the small bomb exploded, and I felt the lieutenant's belt buckle pressing hard into the top of my butt. As the dust settled, Crawley pushed back and asked, "You okay, Halladay?"

"Yes, sir," I responded turning slightly to see the officer stand up to brush himself off.

"There's one in every group," Crawley said under his breath.

"Sorry, sir," I said, getting up to salute the officer.

"Don't be sorry, soldier. Just get on with it."

CHAPTER EIGHT

(July 20, 1967)

● ● ●

For the next week basic training continued much the same—reveille at 5:30, jogging around the track and up drag-ass hill, awful food at breakfast, and a day of relentless, strenuous exercises. I had devised a plan to visit the chicken coop outhouse at three in the morning, occasionally running into Dildo who shared the same hang-up about communal crapping.

This morning was another muggy oppressive South Carolina summer day, but for me it was different: it was my twenty-second birthday. Growing up, my birthday was a special occasion. When I turned eight, Aunt Blade came up from Georgetown to celebrate. She had ordered a gourmet basket from Gristedes, and that morning we set off in the family Lincoln for a picnic. We drove up Route 7, turning off into a public rest area just south of Danbury. We got there early enough to secure one of the few wooden picnic tables. As Blade spread a red-checkered tablecloth and Mom put out paper plates, napkins and plastic cups, Kathy and I blew up colored balloons. Mom poured cups of lemonade and Blade unloaded wrapped birthday presents from the car.

"Here, Tim," she said, handing me a large box with a blue ribbon from the Bonwit Teller department store in New York. "Open it before we have lunch," she beamed. Inside was a red silk cowboy jacket trimmed with white leather collar and cuffs. My eyes bulged in amazement as I slipped into the elegant jacket and skipped around the picnic table to the delight of my aunt, while Mom looked on, chagrined at the extravagant gift.

A loud clap of thunder rumbled overhead and fat drops of rain started pummeling the area. Mom and Blade quickly ushered Kathy and me into the back seat of the Lincoln as the two women rolled up the red-checkered tablecloth. They gathered paper plates, plastic utensils, napkins and cups, stuffing everything into the trunk of the car. The basket of salads, sandwiches, my birthday cake and unopened gifts, were quickly gathered up as Mom and Blade scrambled into the front seat and slammed the car doors shut. The four of us sat inside watching the sky grow dark as loud blasts of thunder and flashes of lightning struck while hail and rain pelted the car.

The storm passed in twenty minutes—soft beams of sunlight created shafts of pale color through the dense maple trees hovering over the picnic table where the balloons now lay flattened and lifeless.

"I guess we'll have to finish this party at home," Mom said as she turned the key in the ignition and wiped the condensation dripping on the inside of the windshield.

"Well, that was a fast picnic," Blade laughed. And for years to come whenever we drove by the recreation area on Route 7, I would smile and fondly remember the "fast picnic."

Two years later when I turned ten, I spent that birthday at my grandparents' farm in Wilmington, a small town in southern Vermont, nestled between the larger cities of Bennington and Brattleboro, just across the Massachusetts border. The main house, built in 1885, was perched high on a rolling hill that sloped down to Route 9. A railroad track ran parallel to the busy highway and followed the North Branch Deerfield River into the center of town. Haystack Mountain, shrouded by clouds and fog in the morning, loomed in the background. The large wooden farmhouse had eight bedrooms with a dormitory in the attic. Nan ran the summer home like a hotel—aware of every guest, and how many heads she had to feed at each meal. There were three indoor bathrooms, one on each floor, but no heating except for the wood burning stove in the kitchen and two fireplaces, one in the large front parlor and the other in the dining room. Bed sheets were warmed by hot water bottles snuggled under the covers at night. Even though it was summer when days were warm, temperatures at night could drop into the forties and occasionally hover near freezing. It was what locals referred to as "good sleeping weather."

The farmhouse was filled with visiting relatives and friends that July when Kathy, cousin Will and I arrived for our designated stay. The three of us were the oldest of the nine Halladay grandchildren: I would turn ten in another week, my sister was eleven, and Will was twelve. We were assigned space in the attic, a large stuffy expanse under the eaves of the old farmhouse where sleeping bags had been laid out. A wooden ladder led up to the attic dormitory with a bathroom at the foot of the landing on the third floor opposite a stained glass window that in the afternoon let in pools of colored light.

My grandfather's two spinster sisters, Harriet and Hattie, who ran a dress shop on Church Lane in Westport down the street from the firehouse, occupied one of the large bedrooms on the second floor. Uncle Earl, Harold's younger brother, and his wife, Aunt Eve, stayed down the hall in the other bedroom. Aunt Flo, Nan's sister, was in the front room on the third floor. The other guests, Mamie Dunnigan and Margaret Soderstrom, were assigned two of the small rooms on the third floor. My grandparents slept in a large room on the first floor, off the kitchen. The other rooms were left vacant for last-minute guests, and when no other company was expected, Pop would post a "Room to Let" sign at the foot of the winding driveway on Route 9.

Kathy and Will and I went hiking through the rolling fields. We built small dams with stones in the running brook gurgling down the hillside by the farmhouse, catching tadpoles and hoping to snare a small trout, which never happened. Nan gave each of us a cardboard pint container to gather berries for pies and pancakes. The three of us set out on our quest, crossing Route 9, pushing into the heavy brush along the railroad tracks and the North Branch Deerfield River where wild blueberry bushes thrived among tangles of poison sumac. We picked through the prickly brush, scratching our arms and exposed legs below the knees of our shorts, until we had each filled a container with fresh berries.

Marching proudly into the kitchen where Nan was sprinkling flour across a wooden carving board, preparing to roll a mound of dough for her biscuits, I announced, "Here, Nanny," offering her a pint of freshly picked blueberries. Kathy and Will followed with similar offerings.

"Oh, my," Nan gushed, wiping flour-covered hands on her apron. "What have you done? I mean so many..." Then, looking at our scratched arms and clothes spiked with bristles, she exclaimed, "You must have been in the sumac to get all these berries. Don't you know it's poisonous?"

Flustered and concerned, Nan undid her apron and ordered, "You go upstairs and take a bath immediately to get that poison off your skin. Wash with Ivory soap before you break out," she said shooing us out of the kitchen.

"Yes, Nanny," I said obediently as the three of us marched up to the attic.

"You first," Will said to Kathy. "Tim and I will wait."

"It seems so stupid, taking a bath in the afternoon," she said, slipping down the ladder and running hot water in the tub.

Will and I were alone in the hot farmhouse attic, the sound of Kathy's gushing bath water coming from below.

"I guess Nan is worried about us getting poison sumac. She thinks a bath will make it all go away," he laughed, stripping off his T-shirt and dropping his khaki shorts onto the floor.

My eyes gazed at Will's smooth, hairless body, staring at the bulge in the front of his undershorts and the suggestion of curly hair peeking out of the elastic waistband.

"Yeah, a hot bath takes care of everything," I laughed, undoing the top button of my cut-offs, letting them fall around my ankles. "Sure is hot up here," I said as we stood in the stuffy attic in our underwear.

"Think we got any poison?" Will asked, inspecting his arms and legs.

"Guess we'll have to wait and see." I looked for any blemishes on my arms and legs.

"It's all yours," Kathy called up the ladder, fluffing her hair with a towel. "I'm going out on the back porch to dry off."

The sounds of gurgling water draining from the bathtub echoed up into the attic dormitory.

"You first," Will said.

"No, I'll go last. In case we run out of hot water."

"Whatever," Will said slipping down the wooden ladder and turning on the spigots as water streamed slowly into the claw foot tub. Will slipped out of his undershorts and climbed into the bath. "I'll be out in a minute," he said, submerging under the water, kicking his feet to create a circle of bubbles.

I turned toward the window on the landing, pressing my cheek against the cool surface of the crafted green clover, tracing lead filings between the pieces of cut colored glass with my finger.

The next morning Nan prepared a stack of blueberry pancakes for the guests at the farmhouse. She placed a platter of bacon and sausage patties, a basket of biscuits, toast and homemade jams, on the large wooden table in the kitchen. A pot of coffee percolated on the wood burning stove.

"Everybody help yourself," she invited, "this is homestyle," directing her comments to a young couple who'd responded to the "Room to Let" sign Pop posted the night before.

"Tomorrow is Timmy's birthday. We're going to have a party on the lawn, and everyone's invited," Nan said wiping hands on her apron.

"How old will you be, son?" Uncle Earl asked, twisting a cigar before striking a match to light it.

"Ten," I responded.

"Ah, the big ten," Earl coughed as he blew out a huge puff of smoke across the breakfast table. "I remember when I was your age," he said, stretching back in the wicker chair he was sitting in, causing it to creak.

Uncle Earl was Pop's younger brother, a short, barrel-chested hairy man with a booming coarse voice. He was hard of hearing, a shortcoming he never acknowledged, but compensated by talking loudly and definitively. He ran a lawn mower repair shop in Westport, and bored everyone with his dissertations about the latest gas-powered engines. His wife, Aunt Eve, was the relative no one talked about. At six feet tall and close to two hundred pounds, she towered over her husband. Eve was a dark woman with a bulbous nose and thick lips who appeared more beastly at every family gathering.

One rainy afternoon while thumbing through old issues of *National Geographic*, getting excited by pictures of natives wearing loincloths, I came across a photo of a woman who looked remarkably like Aunt Eve. The caption indicated the woman was suffering from elephantiasis, a rare disease contracted mostly by people living in the jungles of the Amazon and in remote parts of Africa. Then I did the unthinkable, and clipped the page with my Swiss Army knife, returning the magazine to the glass-case lawyer's cabinet in the attic of the Wilmington farmhouse.

Aunt Eve was kind and caring, offering to rub calamine lotion over the itchy poison sumac bumps on my arms and legs. I felt guilty when I showed Kathy and Will the picture from *National Geographic* of the gorilla woman. Will joked that it was an early photo of Aunt Eve, who from then on he called "Aunt Steve."

Mamie Dunnigan was another relative who spent time at the farm in Wilmington. She was supposedly a distant cousin, but her direct family tie was vague. Mamie was a plump, jolly woman in her fifties who'd never married. She had a head of tight red curls that looked like geranium blooms cut off and stuck into her scalp. She laughed constantly, even at Earl's stories about repairing lawn mowers. Her pie-shaped face and girly disposition endeared her to everyone.

"Mamie has offered to take you to the movies tonight," Nan announced. "There's a special showing at the Town Hall auditorium. It starts at six o'clock, so we'll have an early dinner before you go."

The local movie house in Wilmington was only open on weekends, and the offerings were predictable science fiction, horror movies or Dean Martin and Jerry Lewis comedies. Members of the local book club at the library, frustrated by the lack of culture in town, banded together to find a way to bring more artistic and dramatic films to Wilmington. They made an agreement with a movie theatre in Brattleboro to rent one film a month for a screening at the Town Hall. This month's selection was *Come Back, Little Sheba*, based on the prize-winning play by William Inge, staring Burt Lancaster and Shirley Booth.

Folding chairs were set up in the auditorium and a white screen mounted on a metal tripod was propped up in front of the room. The projector was perched on a ladder behind rows of folding chairs, and even though the sound was turned up loud, we could hear the rotating clicking of the reels, as a bright beam of light streamed out over our heads.

I saw tears rolling down Mamie's round pink cheeks when she reached for a handkerchief in her purse. Shirley Booth was longing for her lost dog, Sheba, as her drunken husband, Burt Lancaster, stormed around the kitchen. He was outraged that a young woman renting a room in their house had brought home a handsome track star; he was posing as a model for a poster she was painting. I was fixated on the muscled athlete sitting on a stool dressed only in gym shorts.

"That was a beautiful movie," Mamie offered as the four of us walked back to the farmhouse on the hill.

"Sad," Will commented.

"Downright depressing," Kathy added.

"I wish we had seen the dog. I kept waiting for Sheba to return," I said.

"That's the whole point of the movie, stupid," Kathy shrugged.

The next day was my birthday. Pop and Uncle Earl had moved four white Adirondack chairs and the wicker furniture off the front porch onto the mowed lawn area above the sloping hill and carried two picnic tables from the back of the house.

Nan and Flo had made potato and macaroni salads, and a heaping pot of baked beans. My birthday cake—a Duncan Hines Devil's Food chocolate mix—sat in the icebox overnight under a glass cover. Having finished preparations for the picnic, Nan and Flo shed their aprons and sat out on the back porch to have a cigarette, puffing contentedly, looking up at Haystack Mountain in the distance.

Mamie had bought a bag of plastic balloons at the dime store in Wilmington, and she coerced Harriet and Hattie into helping her blow them up and tie them into a huge, colorful bouquet they secured to one of the picnic tables. Pop made it clear that no presents were to be part of the birthday celebration; his grandchildren did not want for anything and already had more than most boys and girls their age. The picnic party was enough for any ten-year-old boy.

My parents were not coming up to for my birthday, since it fell during the week and they both had to work. Mom had given Pop a card when he was in Westport checking in on Mrs. Pembroke, and asked if he would see that I got it on my birthday.

Laughter and sounds of conversation echoed up to the attic where I was getting dressed. I had packed my red satin cowboy jacket, the present I'd received from Aunt Blade two years ago. It was getting a little tight, but if I left it open and unzipped it still fit. I slid down the ladder to the landing and peered out the stained glass window. I could see blurred images of my relatives on the lawn, the balloons billowing in the breeze, even more colorful through the window.

I walked across the silky green lawn, resplendent in my cowboy jacket. It was a glorious Vermont summer afternoon, and I was enveloped in the swarm of balloons, surrounded by hugging relatives. I freed myself from the tangle of attention, backing up toward the table where I noticed an envelope with my name printed in Mom's distinctive hand. I opened the fanciful card of lions, tigers, monkeys and giraffes to reveal the "Happy Birthday" greeting inside. It was signed "Love, Mom and Dad." I slipped the card back into the envelope and pushed it under a paper plate on the picnic table.

Aunt Flo filled cups of lemonade, and Nan sang out for everyone to take a plate as she unfolded wax paper from the platters of sandwiches on the table.

"Everyone, help yourself," she instructed. "And don't miss Flo's baked beans...they're her special recipe."

The adults swarmed around the table while Kathy, Will and I stood aside.

"You get the best parties...born in July and being up here on the farm," Kathy sulked.

"What do you mean?"

"A picnic on the lawn with all the relatives. My birthday's in March, and if I'm lucky I get to invite some classmates over for cake and pin the tail on the donkey."

"Yeah, but everybody brings presents," I retorted.

"Big deal."

"Here, Timmy," Nan said, bringing a paper plate of food. "For the birthday boy. Will and Kathy, go help yourselves before everything's gone."

"See what I mean," Kathy smirked.

When the last of the sandwiches and baked beans had been scooped up, the crowd gathered around to sing the traditional birthday song as I blew out ten wax candles on the chocolate cake. Although Pop did not approve of presents, he did allow a display of small fireworks and sparklers for the occasion.

Uncle Earl and Aunt Eve were passing around hissing sparklers to everyone to wave circles in the air, when Mamie shrieked, "Timmy, don't move."

I froze in the white Adirondack chair I was sitting in, my plastic fork stuck in the piece of chocolate birthday cake.

"Be still," Mamie said moving slowly toward me, tossing the hissing sparkler in her hand onto the lawn.

"On the chair," Mamie pointed. "Look, but don't move."

Just off my shoulder, perched on a white plank of the chair, was a regal praying mantis. The exotic insect looked at the gawking humans surrounding him, folded his front spindly legs, and sat erect.

"He's beautiful," I whispered, slouching into the chair and making eye contact with the beautiful green bug. No one spoke as sparklers expired on the lawn. The graceful creature slipped from the white board of the Adirondack chair and gingerly climbed across my red satin cowboy jacket and perched on my face, placing its front claw on my eyebrow.

A lone car passing on Route 9 below and the soft rippling of the North Branch Deerfield River were the only sounds that broke the silence as everyone stared in awe—until the beautiful green creature sprang off into the grass, disappearing into the security of his kingdom.

"Did you know when they mate, the female bites the head off her partner," Kathy said.

"Oh, that's just an old wives' tale," Pop dismissed.

"And it's illegal to kill them," Kathy stated definitively.

● ● ●

After the morning jog, I was called out of formation.

"Halladay," Sergeant Washington shouted. "Report to Colonel Knight's office at nine hundred hours."

What the fuck is this all about? I thought as I fell out and returned to the barracks to change into a clean set of fatigues. I jogged to the main administrative building and walked down the long hallway on the first floor.

"You Halladay?" the corporal at a desk in the antechamber asked.

"Yes."

"Take a seat, and I'll let Colonel Knight know you're here."

I sat on a wooden bench waiting for instructions as the corporal leaned back from his typewriter and pressed the intercom button.

"You can go in," he nodded, pointing to the large mahogany door behind him.

I entered the impressive office lined with bookcases of leather-bound volumes. A large bronze sculpture of an eagle stood on a pedestal behind the officer's desk, flanked by the U.S. flag to the left and the South Carolina flag on the right.

"Halladay here," I stood at attention saluting the officer.

"At ease, soldier," the officer said, returning the salute. "Have a seat." He pointed to two leather armchairs facing his massive desk.

"Yes, sir," I said, sitting down not at all at ease.

The officer put down the pen in his right hand and closed the file he was reviewing. "So, how are things going?"

"Fine, sir…uh, just fine."

"Good. Glad to hear that." And after an uncomfortable silence the officer asked, "You know why you are here?"

"No, sir. Not really."

"I understand you had a chat with Lieutenant Crawley about OCS," the colonel paused, "but you didn't think it was right for you."

"He said the only openings were in Infantry, and...well I didn't think that was..." I floundered.

"Crawley reported to me that you would be an excellent candidate for OCS."

"Yes, but..."

"Don't interrupt me," the colonel ordered. "I didn't ask you a question." He glared intensely at me. "You know you are the only college graduate going through training in Charlie Company?"

"Yes, sir."

We sat opposite each other, an uncomfortable silence filling the office.

"Halladay." The colonel leaned forward, his steel gray eyes directed at me like lasers. "The Army needs men like you. Smart men who can make a contribution...make a difference...not just some street thug, junkie or punk who might as well be doing time in prison. For them, the Army is a good deal—free food, free clothes, free training...and as an added bonus they get paid. Sure, they might get their ass shot off in combat. That's a risk we all take. But the odds are a lot better than working the streets in Bridgeport or Harlem."

The colonel let his words register. "Halladay, you're not like that. You come from a good upbringing. You went to the right schools and graduated from William & Mary, where great men like Thomas Jefferson and James Monroe were educated." I was astounded at the colonel's knowledge of my background and education.

"So don't let that go to waste," Colonel Knight said standing up. "Lieutenant Crawley will be expecting you to fill out the proper paperwork."

"Yes, sir," I saluted, turning crisply and walking past the corporal seated in the outer office pecking at the typewriter.

As I jogged back to the barracks I tried to replay the scene that had just unfolded in the commanding officer's chambers. I felt I'd been railroaded into signing up for Officer Candidate School. I knew it was a suicide mission to be a Second Lieutenant in the Infantry, assuredly deployed to Vietnam, and I knew in my heart I was not equipped to lead a platoon of young men to their deaths in the jungles of Southeast Asia. It wasn't that I was trying to get out of combat duty; I would have willingly followed orders and crawled through the jungles with the other guys, even if it meant getting my ass shot off. If I had wanted to get out of serving in the military, I would have checked the goddamn box and none of this shit would be happening. But I knew I couldn't be the one ordering guys to their deaths. I just couldn't do it.

I rejoined Charlie Company outside the mess hall after lunch, assuming my usual position in the front row. Sergeant Washington did roll call and at the conclusion shouted, "Halladay…are you supposed to report to Lieutenant Crawley?"

"No, sergeant," I shouted back. "Not to my knowledge."

"Fall in and do laps around the course with Charlie Company," Washington instructed, eyeing me suspiciously.

The afternoon training session was a repeat of hand-to-hand combat, only this time more intense than the introductory round. I was again pulled out to demonstrate the maneuver, exchanging blows with the corporal. After a five-minute duel, we were both sweating, eyes locked, bobbing back and forth on our feet. Washington slapped the riding crop in his palm and shouted, "That was pathetic. You're supposed to kill the enemy, college boy, not prance around like a fairy at a high school prom. Halladay, drop and give me fifty."

I sprawled out on the ground, arched my back and pressed up and down, as I started the count.

"You're cheating, college boy," Washington snarled after ten push-ups, kicking my outstretched right arm, sending me facedown into the gritty sand.

"Fuck this," came a muffled curse from one of the recruits watching the demonstration.

Sergeant Raymond Washington beamed with a broad smile, knowing immediately where the comment had come from. "You got a problem, Rodriguez?" he glared at Razor.

"Give the kid a break?" Razor spoke up shifting back and forth. "You been pickin' on Halladay since we got here."

"You think the Army is for sissies…for little faggots who don't want to be picked on?" Washington bellowed, dragging Razor out of formation. "You don't think, you fucking spic," Washington roared slapping Razor across the face with the leather riding crop. "Now you and your sweetheart, college boy here, report to the commissary where you will be on KP until further notice. You're both suspended from training."

• • •

"**T**his is not how I expected to spend my birthday," I joked as Razor and I sat on milk crates on the loading dock.

"Cigarette?" Razor offered an open pack of Camels he had rolled up in his sleeve.

"I don't smoke," I said, "but I think I might try anything tonight."

Razor flipped his lighter and lit the cigarette I held clumsily between my fingers. He watched as I inhaled and then spat out a gasping cough.

"You really don't smoke," Razor laughed, slapping me on the back.

"No shit, Sherlock," I choked, pounding my chest with a fist. "This is supposed to be fun?"

"You'll get used to it, and then you'll see."

"I'm sticking to beer," I said squashing the unfinished cigarette onto the tar pavement of the loading dock.

"So why is Washington riding your ass every day?"

"Is he?"

"Yeah. It's college boy, do this—college boy do that—and then give me twenty or fifty. What the fuck's that all about?"

"They want me to sign up for OCS."

"And?" Razor probed.

"The only opening is Infantry. And I'm not doing that."

Razor puffed on his cigarette, pushing smoke rings into the air, leaning back to look up into the night sky. He took another drag, cupping a fist to tap me on the arm saying, "So I guess that's why we're here cleaning the grease trap."

"Yeah," I shrugged. "And I didn't get any mail today. I thought I might get a card from my mom, or my aunt who always remembers my birthday, or my girlfriend—but nothing."

"You got a girlfriend?" Razor pushed back, squinting.

"Sort of," I tried to avoid the question.

"I thought you were…you know…" Razor said, lighting another cigarette and puffing smoke circles into the humid night air. We sat in silence on the milk crates watching the filthy water from the hosed-down kitchen floor stream down into the grease trap.

"Mind if I try another cigarette?"

"Help yourself," Razor said, smiling as he passed me the pack. "Hey man, it's your fucking birthday!"

"Yeah, it's my fucking birthday," I said, awkwardly cupping a cigarette in my palm as Razor flipped open his lighter.

CHAPTER NINE
(July 21–August 5, 1967)

● ● ●

The next morning Razor and I fell into formation with the other members of Charlie Company, our suspension from training forgotten. I had become so used to the routine that I actually looked forward to the long morning jog around the track and up drag-ass hill. Those years of dance training had developed my leg muscles to the point I could outrun anyone in the company. While chanting the Jody, I fantasized I was rehearsing for a part in a Broadway musical, with songs of Rodgers and Hammerstein humming in my ears.

One morning after breakfast, we were marched to the administration building and herded into a classroom for eye examinations. A contraption with metal plates and a chin rest was attached to a bench encased by black curtains. It looked strangely like a voting booth. One by one we were ushered into the chamber, dark drapes drawn, as the doctor flipped lenses back and forth while we held up a fan-like patch covering one eye, answering questions, "Better? Brighter? Clearer?"

I sat on the bench and went through the process of reading rows of letters, calling them out until coming to the bottom line I could not decipher. I was then given a series of charts to view, asking which letters were brighter, the green or the red. I froze, not knowing how to respond.

"Halladay, which is it?" the doctor snapped impatiently. "The red or the green?"

"I don't know, sir. They look the same."

The doctor pushed his glasses up over his forehead and grabbed the clipboard from the nurse standing beside him, removing the top page and handing the clipboard back to her. "Continue here with the others," the doctor instructed. "Halladay, follow me."

The doctor led me to an empty classroom across the hall, pointing to a chair at a desk in the front of the room. "Have a seat. I want you to look at some charts."

The doctor pulled out a folder from the briefcase he was carrying and spread out a series of cards splattered with inkblot images.

"Now, I want you to tell me what you see as you look at each card. Tell me your first impression."

I studied the cards, looking at the gothic illustrations.

"What do you see?"

"Zorro," I responded immediately.

"Anything else?"

"Captain Enrique is there on the left," I said, starting to enjoy the game.

The doctor spread out three more cards and asked the same question, "What do you see now?"

I picked up the cards, studying them, trying to focus on the black, abstract images.

"It's the Lone Ranger," I said definitively. "And there's Tonto hiding in the bushes."

"And there?" the doctor asked, flipping another card on the table.

I looked at the splotchy image, trying to determine what I was supposed to see.

"And?" the doctor tapped his pen on the clipboard impatiently.

"A praying mantis."

"All right, Halladay," the doctor said scooping the cards off the desk. "You've had your fun. Now I want you to look at something else."

The doctor produced a different series of cards with dotted color circles that looked like cheap linoleum tile samples, placing them one at a time in front of me.

"Tell me what you see."

"I don't understand," I said, turning toward the doctor. "What am I supposed to see?"

The doctor stepped back, looking suspicious, handing me two more cards. "What numbers do you see?"

I looked closely, squinting, but all I could see was a bunch of dots.

"Sorry, sir. There's no number. Just dots."

"You mean you can't see the green number six?"

"No, sir. It's just a blur."

"Look again, carefully, soldier. Concentrate, and tell me again what you see."

I stared at the card intently, and slowly, as if emerging through a heavy mist, the number nine emerged.

"Do you see anything now?" the doctor probed.

"It looks like the number nine," I replied, "but I'm not sure."

The report went up to Lieutenant Crawley that I was color blind. The handicap was possibly an advantage since, although unproven, it was suspected color blind soldiers had the ability to see through camouflage in the jungle. Ironically, my inability to see green propelled me to an even more desirable status as a candidate for OCS.

Training exercises continued, and every day I gained strength from the relentless push-ups. Never had I been in such good physical shape. I became adept at the monkey-bar crawl, a hand-over-hand exercise across a rack of suspended ladders. Even though I completed the laps back and forth, Washington ordered me to demonstrate the maneuver again and again until I dropped from exhaustion into the sand and was then ordered to do fifty push-ups for giving up.

"Is that what they teach you in those fancy schools?" Washington sneered, as I pumped up and down in front of the company.

It was four weeks into basic training, a Friday evening after chow. Charlie Company was lined up in formation outside the barracks waiting for roll call. Ray Washington walked up and down in front of us, slapping the riding crop in his palm as the corporal called out names.

"At ease, men," the sergeant directed, looking out over us. "Some of you have caught on, got with the program and maybe, I say maybe, you might one day be qualified to be soldiers in the U.S. Army."

Washington flipped the cigar he was sucking, squashing it with his boot into the sand and spat out a wad of spit. "I said some of you," the DI emphasized, "but there's always a few pussy faggots who don't get it...or maybe this time only one." Washington glared at me.

"You men are going to be issued a twenty-four hour pass, effective tomorrow at zero seven hundred hours. There's a bus that leaves the base every hour. You are free to go into Columbia and enjoy the local sights. You'll find the people in the community welcoming, some of them very welcoming." Washington winked. "Just know you are soldiers in the U.S. Army and you're expected to act accordingly. Always remember to respect your country and your flag and be back here for roll call Sunday morning or you will be reported AWOL."

The men cheered as the corporal handed out vouchers for permission to leave base, the first time in four weeks. As I pressed forward in line to get my pass, the corporal brushed me aside, saying, "Sorry, Halladay. You're not on the list."

"What do you mean…I'm not on the list?"

"Someone has to stay here and help out in the kitchen. And you've been elected," the corporal laughed. "But don't worry. You don't have to do the grease trap. We found another sorry bastard to do it this time."

"Fuck!" I cursed in disbelief.

Razor and Dildo stood behind me, advancing and taking their passes from the corporal.

"That really sucks!" Razor looked at me.

"And Halladay…here's your mail," the corporal said tossing me a packet of envelopes bound by an elastic band. "Must have been redirected."

Back at the barracks, I crossed my legs and sat on the coarse wool blanket atop my bunk, breaking the rubber band around the letters that had already been opened. The first piece of mail I looked at was a large oversized card, a Hallmark greeting from my parents with a sappy Joyce Kilmer poem about trees and a wonderful son growing up in the forest of life. It was signed in ballpoint in Mom's distinctive neat script, "Love, Mom and Dad."

I recognized Aunt Blade's card with a Washington D.C. postmark and a broken wax seal on the back of the envelope. Inside was an oval-window card with a flourish written, "Don't spend it all in one place! Hope you're doing fine. I know you are…you must look so handsome in uniform. Happy Birthday! Love, Blade."

There was no money inside; it too must have been "redirected."

I thumbed through the envelopes—cards from my sister and grandparents, two letters from Karen, and an envelope from Yale Drama School. I placed the stack of mail under my pillow and stretched out on the bunk. I closed my eyes, trying to understand what I had done so fucking wrong to be singled out as the only one in the company not getting a weekend pass.

The next morning, I was awakened by the sound of running showers. The heavy scent of after-shave lotion permeated the barracks as guys laughed and joked, getting ready for their day of freedom. I turned over on my side pretending to be asleep. When everyone had left, it was eerily quiet, the only sound coming from the dripping showerheads at the end of the hall.

I reported to the commissary as instructed. The women who served grits and scrambled eggs every morning were behind the counter preparing steaming trays of food, placing them into warming bins.

"You here for kitchen detail?" asked a heavyset black woman whose hair was wrapped in a tight mesh net—the same woman who encouraged me to eat every day.

"Yes."

"What you do to get this gig?" she asked.

"Luck of the draw," I shrugged.

"Well you come in here, honey." She opened the hinged half-doors at the end of the counter. "We could use some help today from a strong thing like you."

I started with the crates of milk and orange juice delivered to the loading dock overnight. I stacked the dolly and rolled it to a large metal refrigerator in the kitchen. I could tell the woman was watching me when she asked, "How come you was the only one in Charlie Company not gettin' a pass?"

"Got me," I said avoiding the question.

"Must be somethin', honey…because they let all those other monkeys off the base."

"Somebody's got to help you ladies out," I smiled. "Besides, what's there to do in Columbia?"

"It's not such a bad place—sure would be more fun than unloading milk crates and slopping a mop around this kitchen floor." She stood up and returned to the steaming bins of food as a line of soldiers from Alpha and Echo Companies lined up. Kitchen detail was light since two of the four basic training units, Bravo and Charlie, had been issued passes. I spent the rest of the morning cleaning the gas burner stovetops, wiping off built-up grease using steel wool pads and Ajax until my hands were rubbed raw from the harsh white cleanser.

"You should be protectin' yourself when you use that stuff," the woman said, tossing me a pair of yellow rubber gloves. "That ammonia in there will eat the skin right off your fingers. I know, honey."

I walked back to the barracks after a full day of kitchen detail and stretched out on my bunk, drifting into a light sleep. Loud laughter and stumbling boots woke me up. I looked at my watch; it was just after three in the morning. Razor and Dildo staggered in, arms draped across each other, calling out, "Hey, college boy!"

I sat up, my legs dangling over the thin top mattress. "You guys are drunk." I squinted as Razor and Dildo shuffled back and forth in front of me.

"Pissed…fucking pissed," Razor slurred.

"Fucking pissed," Dildo echoed, producing a pint of Jack Daniels from his hip pocket and taking a swig.

"You better get rid of that," I said. "You can't have booze in here."

"Fuck…then we'll just have to destroy the evidence," Dildo said, taking another gulp. "What about you, college boy?" he slurred, shoving the pint toward me.

"I don't drink that shit."

"Hey, you must be thirsty after washing dishes all day," Dildo laughed as he placed his broad dark palm on my thigh, inching a middle finger up under my boxers.

"I don't want it."

"Well, maybe you'd rather have some of this juice." He swaggered back, unzipping his fly and pulling out his huge cock. "This what you want, college boy?"

"Fuck off." I recoiled on the bunk. "You guys are drunk."

"Fuckin' A," Dildo said, stroking his huge cock. "I'm fuckin' wasted…but you want it…I know you want it, you pretty white faggot."

"Knock it off," Razor said, pushing him back. "Go jerk off somewhere else, you fuckin' gorilla."

Dildo stumbled backward, his dark eyes dilated. He took a swallow of whiskey, slobbering and crashing into the metal bunk bed. He regained his balance momentarily, then shuffled toward the entrance of the barracks. He slammed into the doorframe, brushing against the switch, turning off the overhead lights.

"I'm going to the chicken coop to take a shit and jerk off," he slurred, his pants still opened as he staggered out of the darkened barracks.

"He's really fucked up," I said, facing Razor who had straddled his arms on either side of me on the bunk, trying to steady himself.

"That Jack Daniels shit makes him crazy," Razor grinned.

"Guess so," I laughed, aware that Razor was now slouching closer, his head bowed. "So where are all the other guys?" I asked looking around the empty barracks.

"Went to Sambo's for breakfast," Razor slurred. "They're coming back on the last bus. Wanted to stretch out leave to the last minute."

"Don't blame them," I said, aware that Razor was now only inches away, his breath heavy with liquor.

"You shoulda been out partying with us," Razor looked up with glazed eyes. "Coulda been fun. But you had to pull that kitchen detail shit."

"Somebody has to do it."

"Yeah, but kid…they're always picking on you. That fucking Washington is a real sorry ass motherfucker. All that college boy shit. Don't you get pissed off and want to smash his fuckin' head in?"

"Sometimes."

"If I was you, I'd just do it. Kick the stupid motherfucker in the balls and say fuck off." Razor stumbled, trying to stand upright, then fumbling forward pressing his face into my chest.

"Hey, man," I said, pushing up and gently placing my hands on his shoulders to steady him. "I feel like it every day, but you know that's not how it works."

Razor lifted his head, looking me directly in the eyes. "Yeah, man, but it really pisses me off to see you get beaten up every day. It really fuckin' pisses me off."

"Yeah, and look where that got you," I said. "We both got the grease trap on my birthday."

"But we had a party," Razor stumbled back, laughing, then crashed forward with his face falling into my lap. I cradled the young Puerto Rican boy's shaved head in my palms, sensing his heavy liquored breath warming against the fly opening of my boxers.

The barracks was dark and deserted. The other guys were still out wolfing down pancakes at Sambo's; Dildo was throwing up and jerking off in the shit-house chicken coop.

"Hey, man…you better get into bed," I said quietly, lifting Razor's head off my responding crotch. "You've had a long day."

Razor looked up, his eyes half-closed, and then fell like a rag doll to the floor. I slid down from the upper bunk and cupped Razor under his arms and rolled him onto the lower bed. I unlaced his boots, pulling them off with a hard tug. I unfurled a blanket and draped it over Razor who looked like a corpse lying on the thin mattress.

"Aren't you supposed to be my battle buddy?" Razor purred, exhaling deeply, clutching my hand.

"Yeah, guy…I'm your battle buddy," I said softly, peeling my fingers away from his tight grip.

I slipped back to the top bunk, clutching the lumpy pillow like a lost teddy bear. I rolled onto my stomach, letting my right arm dangle down toward my snoring friend below.

"Yeah…I'm your battle buddy," I whispered into the pillow.

CHAPTER TEN
(August 6, 1967)

● ● ●

Sunday morning and no reveille sounded; it was the only day we were allowed to sleep in and not line up in formation. I awakened to a commotion of guys stumbling into the barracks just before seven when their twenty-four hour passes would expire. I rolled over and tried to go back to sleep, but it was hopeless. I sat up and thumbed through the pack of unopened mail I'd stashed under the pillow. There was a plain white envelope, obviously not a birthday card, addressed in Mom's familiar neat handwriting. Inside was a yellow legal-size page written on both sides:

July 23, 1967

Dear Tim,

I hope you are doing well and are coping with Army life. How is the food and are you taking care of yourself?

We've only heard from you that one time when you sent a postcard giving us your mailing address at Fort Jackson. I'm sure you don't have much time to write letters, and I guess they don't want you using the phone unless there's an emergency.

I'm sorry to have to write this letter to you, but we've had some bad news here in Westport. You remember young Ronnie Bankhead—he used to babysit for you and Kathy—and then he went off to West Point.

Of course I remembered Ronnie, the handsome guy who let me stay up late watching television, the babysitter who taught me how to play strip poker. Ronnie was something of a hero in town, with his picture in the newspaper when he'd graduated from West Point. A few months later when he was deployed to Vietnam, his photo in full dress uniform appeared on the front page of *The Town Crier*. The caption read: "Second Lieutenant Ronald Seth Bankhead, III to serve in Vietnam."

> *A week after you left, Kay Bankhead interviewed four lo-cal boys on her radio show. They all had just returned from Vietnam—I think you know one of them—Danny Chalfont, who went to Prep, but was a few years behind you. The same day when Kay got home, there were two marines waiting out-side her front door.*

I dropped the letter on the pillow because I knew what was com-ing. Mom went on to quote from the newspaper article how Lieu-tenant Ronald Seth Bankhead had been killed with four other men in a helicopter crash when their aircraft strayed into Cambodia and had been shot down. I immediately knew it was no accident since it was widely suspected that the U.S. was conducting unauthorized missions in Cambodia.

> *Your father and I attended the service at Assumption, and it looked like the whole town turned out. It was so sad and a shame for such a nice young man to lose his life like that.*

I stared out across the rows of bunk beds in the barracks, the wheezing sounds of snoring, hungover soldiers breaking the silence. I turned over the yellow page of Mom's letter and continued reading.

> *But even worse, a week after the burial in Arlington, Kay was found dead in the garage of their home on Dogwood Lane. As you can imagine it was a terrible shock to Seth, as well as to your father and me.*

I had to stop. Two deaths in one letter was more news from home than I was ready to handle. Mom had clipped both obituaries from *The Town Crier* and enclosed them. Ronnie looked like a prince in his full dress uniform, but the photo of Kay must have been lifted from a press kit twenty years old. The article listed the popular radio interviewer's death at forty-six, an accident. But it was hard to be-lieve an intelligent woman, who just days before had buried her only son in Arlington Cemetery, could have turned on the ignition of her husband's 1955 Thunderbird and forgotten to open the garage door.

> *I'm sorry for all the sad news, but you knew the family*
> *and of course your father does a lot of business with Seth. I*
> *thought you might want to send Mr. Bankhead a card or a*
> *note saying how sorry you are for his loss. Just a thought, but*
> *I know your father would appreciate the gesture. Please take*
> *care of yourself and let us know how you are doing. We love*
> *you.*
>   *Mom and Dad*

I crumpled the yellow page into a ball and stuffed it under my pillow. Sunday morning was time to sleep in, write letters or go to chapel. Despite my religious cynicism, I decided to attend the nine o'clock Sunday Mass conducted in the non-denominational chapel by a visiting priest from St. Peter's Catholic Church in Columbia. The chapel was an unused classroom on the first floor of the administrative building where red, blue and yellow rolls of cellophane had been taped to the windows to create the illusion of stained glass: in reality it only made the room look more like a tacky cocktail lounge in Atlantic City. The Jewish boys had use of the space on Saturdays, and Protestants took over after the Catholics left Sunday morning.

I sat on a creaky bench retired from the mess hall, now used as a makeshift pew in the chapel. I knelt on the cold tile floor as the priest raised a host, breaking off a piece like a potato chip, mumbling the words, "Body of Christ." Although I hadn't been to Confession since graduating from Fairfield Prep, I walked in line with other soldiers to receive Communion, letting the priest place the wafer on my tongue. The tasteless disc dissolved on the roof of my mouth, and I swept my tongue back and forth to make sure the Body of Christ did not cling to my teeth. I tuned out the sounds of "Agnus Dei" droning from the priest and buried my face in my hands, praying silently—if you can call thinking morbid thoughts a form of praying.

I had heard that the remains of a lot of soldiers killed in combat were nothing more than empty uniforms and bags of sand and stones, shipped home in coffins to unsuspecting families. I mean, when you think of it, why would the Army risk getting more guys killed by sending them out into the jungle under hostile fire to the wreckage of a downed helicopter to scoop up bones and teeth to ship back to the U.S. for burial. I clutched my face, begging whatever god was listening, not to let my empty uniform come back in a box—my face framed in a graduation photo from Fairfield Prep the only hint of my existence—sandbags and stones for my pillow.

CHAPTER ELEVEN
(August 7–September 4, 1967)

● ● ●

It was halfway point in basic training—only four more weeks before we would all move on to another base. I was resigned to my role as company demonstrator, and tried to ignore the college boy moniker. I knew I'd never be issued a weekend pass, because no matter how flawlessly I demonstrated an exercise, Sergeant Washington found some fault and ordered me to drop for twenty, thirty or fifty push-ups. As the DI paced back and forth, slapping the riding crop and kicking sand into my face, I clearly understood I was being punished for refusing to register for OCS.

Every weekend I was assigned kitchen detail, helping ladies in the commissary, while Razor, Dildo and the guys in Charlie Company went into Columbia to play pool, get drunk and shove what little money they had into the blouses and panties of hookers on Jefferson Street. If lucky, the guys might get a hand job—fucking was out of their price range.

"Why don't you come with us?" Razor egged me on. "Who the fuck will know?"

"I could get my ass thrown in the brig."

"Couldn't be any worse than mopping the kitchen and picking up cigarette butts and trash."

"Yeah, it could. I just want to get through this shit and move on."

I had made it to the last week of basic training and was alone in the barracks on Saturday night. The guys had gone into Columbia, but after a long day of cleaning stovetops and scrubbing down steam trays in the commissary, I was happy to be by myself. No mail had arrived that week—either it was being redirected or my friends and family had gotten tired of writing and getting no response.

The final days dragged on. My demonstrations as college boy were flawless by now, and I didn't wait to be ordered; I just dropped automatically to do push-ups, cursing Washington under my breath as he slapped the riding crop.

"You men can be proud," the DI started. "You came in here like a sorry-ass bunch of pussies, and now look. Somebody might even mistake you for soldiers," he smirked. "I know you probably think you've been through a lot of shit these past eight weeks." Washington fixed his glare on me. "But this is nothing compared to what you'll face out there in the jungle with Charlie."

The corporal stepped up behind Washington, holding a stack of yellow envelopes. The DI studied us, and after a long pause ordered, "At ease, gentlemen. Corporal Donovan will be passing out your orders. Read them carefully. Everyone will be moving out tonight, so make sure you pack up your gear and be ready to leave. Details of your next assignment are in your orders."

The corporal started calling out names—Gonzalez, Murphy, Shapiro, Rodriguez, Brown, Halladay—until all the envelopes were distributed.

Charlie Company stood waiting as Washington turned his back on us and looked out over the jogging track and up drag-ass hill. He snapped the riding crop several times, then shouted across the field. "For your information, gentlemen. Charlie Company came in first with the most commendations and awards…again! We beat the shit out of those sorry fuckers in Alpha, Bravo and Echo."

Razor looked at me and grinned. "Must a been 'cause of you, college boy."

"Yeah, right," I shrugged.

Washington stood erect as a marble statue, then pivoted around on his boots and yelled over our heads, "Gentlemen…dismissed!"

Back in the barracks we ripped open our orders. I sat on the upper bunk and flipped through the pages to discover I was being deployed to Fort Eustis in Virginia, a short distance from Williamsburg. Eustis was transportation headquarters, T-School, where soldiers were taught helicopter maintenance and other support skills.

Razor and Dildo sat on the lower bunk, sorting through pages they'd pulled out of the yellow envelopes.

"Where you guys going?" I leaned down from my bunk.

"Leavenworth," Razor said throwing the papers on the floor. "Fucking Leavenworth, in the fucking cornfields. We're going to fucking Kansas."

I sat up stunned, knowing that a transfer to Fort Leavenworth, the main training center for artillery, was a sure ticket to deployment in Vietnam.

"Yeah, they're gonna teach Dildo and me how to stuff ourselves into a big metal tank and roll around in the jungle till we get our dicks blown off by a fucking land mine or some other booby trap Charlie has planted out there, just waiting to see our balls blown sky high."

I slipped down from the upper bunk and stood in front of Razor. "I was hoping we'd all be going to Eustis together."

"No fucking way, college boy," Razor cursed bitterly. "You privileged white guys get all the pussy assignments. Spics and niggers like us get what's left over. I'm going to take my last crap in the chicken coop," he said, stomping out of the barracks.

Dildo looked at me blankly. "He's pissed off about Leavenworth. Nothing to do with you, kid."

"Yeah, right," I said, hauling my duffel bag out from the storage locker.

"Hey, man," Dildo said running his hand up and down his pants. "Want some chocolate banana before you get on that long bus ride?"

"Stow it, King Kong. Haven't you got it by now? It's not my thing?"

"Coulda fooled me, college boy."

Razor returned from the chicken coop, picked up his gear and left, slamming the screen door behind him. I sat in the deserted barracks, the only member of Charlie Company not going to Kansas. The bus to Fort Eustis would not leave for another two hours.

It was just past midnight when we pulled up to the Fort Jackson exit gate. The MP on duty looked at the manifest of the twelve of us onboard, then waved us through. As the wooden cross arm folded down behind the departing bus, a cheer rose up from the guys onboard as we left basic training and drag-ass hill.

I had taken a window seat in the back. I didn't know any of the other guys on the bus, although I recognized most of them from the mess hall. I swiped my palm across the condensation on the window, steamed up from the air conditioning. Blurry images of the rural South Carolina countryside slipped by: telephone poles strangled by creeping kudzu vines, shanties tucked in the scrub bush, a mangy dog alongside the dusty roadway scratching his ear with a back paw. The bus picked up speed as it lunged and turned onto Interstate 77 North. I pressed my cheek against the damp window, drawing circles with my forefinger on the dripping dirty glass, knowing that my battle buddy, Razor, and crazy Dildo, were at the same time on a bus speeding away in the opposite direction. I knew I would never see them again.

I dozed off as the darkened bus—straining to reach the 55-mile-per-hour speed limit—hummed along the highway. Passenger cars and eight-wheelers pulled into the passing lane to get around, and occasionally a supportive truck driver would blast an air horn and give a thumbs-up out the window.

The sound of downshifting gears when the driver applied the hissing brakes woke me out of a light sleep. I rubbed my fist across the window, and looking down, saw a ribbon of red taillights. In the distance, flashing patrol cars blocked the road. State troopers in Smokey Bear hats strode between rows of stopped vehicles. They pointed flashlights into windows and ordered people to open the trunks of their cars; truck drivers climbed out of big rigs and opened rear doors of their trailers for inspection.

"Some problem, here?" our bus driver asked as he pulled back the lever to open the front door. The state trooper outside did not respond; he stepped onto the bus waving a large silver flashlight.

"Where you headed?" he asked.

"Fort Eustis. These men just completed basic and are being deployed for further training."

"Pick up anybody on the way?" The trooper glared at the driver.

"No. This is a military vehicle."

"Got a manifesto of who's onboard?

The driver retrieved a clipboard from behind his seat and handed it to the officer who counted the men onboard. He nodded apparently satisfied. "You can move on when traffic opens up."

"Mind if I ask what this is all about?"

"Yeah, I mind," the trooper said, pointing the flashlight into the driver's face. "Just get these men to where they have to be."

The bus door flapped shut after Smokey Bear disembarked and continued his inspection of vehicles lined up behind. I looked out the window, and as the bus inched toward the flashing lights ahead, I saw the highway sign, "Florence. Next Three Exits."

I slumped into my seat as the bus slowly regained speed, crawling past the roadblock, continuing on the journey north. I curled up and rested on my duffel bag, listening to the humming tires of the bus rolling rhythmically underneath. We were passing through the junction onto Interstate 95 North, crossing the state border into North Carolina.

It was daybreak when I opened my eyes, squinting to make out signs for Rocky Mount. When the bus approached the outskirts of Richmond, the sun was burning cruelly in the Sunday morning sky. I looked at my watch: it was just after ten when the bus turned off the Interstate and pulled into a truck stop. The driver opened the door and called back as we were stretching and yawning from the uncomfortable overnight ride.

"Pit stop," he announced. "Suggest you men get out and stretch your legs and do whatever you have to do. We'll be here about thirty minutes while I gas up, before heading down to Eustis, another hour from here. Go eat, shit, piss, fuck—whatever—but be back on the bus at eleven hundred hours. I don't want to send a posse out looking for any stragglers. Got that, men? Don't fuck up, and don't get me fired."

After taking a piss in the long urinal trough in the men's room, I washed my hands and splashed cold water on my face. I reached for paper towels, but the dispenser was empty.

"Class place," came a voice from behind.

I turned around to a pale freckled-faced kid whose red hair was just starting to sprout back onto his head like a newly seeded lawn.

"Yeah," I laughed. "But not as bad as the chicken coop."

"Nothing could be that bad."

"I hope Eustis is better," I said.

We left the restroom, shaking our hands dry in the warm morning sunlight. I slipped a quarter into a vending machine outside the bathroom and pulled out a Coke that landed with a thud in the dispensing bin. The red-haired boy followed, depositing a coin, retrieving a Dr. Pepper.

"You like that shit?" I asked.

"It's okay," he said, popping open the soda can.

"But the taste," I grimaced.

"You were in Charlie Company, weren't you?" he asked, taking a swallow of Dr. Pepper.

"Yeah."

"And weren't you on KP every weekend, in the kitchen cleaning the grease trap. What was that all about?"

"Luck of the Irish."

"Nobody gets it every week. You must have done some bad shit to get that fucked."

I ignored his comment and dropped the empty Coke can on the pavement, crushing it with my foot. "Better get back on board," I said, picking up the crumpled can and tossing it into a garbage container outside the restroom.

The driver checked off our names, all twelve accounted for. The bus pulled away from the gas pump and edged onto the turnoff road away from the Interstate, heading toward Newport News and Fort Eustis. The flashing neon sign on high metal poles above the truck stop behind us beckoned travelers with the promise of "Food—Fuel."

It was just before noon when we pulled up to the entrance of Fort Eustis.

"All accounted for," the MP at the gate said handing the clipboard back to the driver, waving the bus forward as the crossing arm lifted upward.

"Looks like we're here," the red-haired boy sitting in the seat in front of me said, turning around. "By the way, my name is Tom. Tommy Driscoll."

"Tim Halladay," I returned, shaking his hand.

"Okay, gentlemen," the driver announced, opening the door. "We're here. Make sure to collect all your stuff. This is the end of the ride for me. Thanks for not falling out along the way and getting my ass in a sling," he said good-naturedly. "And good luck, gentlemen."

Two soldiers were waiting at the entrance of a brick building with large metal letters mounted over the doorway—"Fort Eustis—Transportation Headquarters." We disembarked, unloading our gear on the grass.

"Welcome to Fort Eustis. I'm Sergeant Haggerty and this is Private Perkins. We're here to see you men get settled. Let me get a roll call first to make sure everyone is here. Then we can move ahead."

The sergeant started reading off names—"Baker, Murphy, Schultz, Driscoll, Abrams, Shapiro, Lopez, Palmer, Kowalski, Halladay, Weinberg, Romero…" as each of us yelled out "Here!"

"All accounted for," Perkins reported to the sergeant as he checked off names on the manifest.

"All right men, now listen up," Sergeant Haggerty said. "I know you're just coming out of basic. We've all been there and we know what a hellhole that is. But you're here now…and this is different."

I jabbed Tommy Driscoll standing next to me and whispered, "Is he the Welcome Wagon?"

We were then led by Sergeant Haggerty down a row of one-story wood buildings and directed to a barracks with bold block letters stenciled on the side, "C-404."

"Gentlemen, this is where you will be housed while you're at Fort Eustis." The sergeant nodded to the building behind us. "You will occupy the right-hand side of the facility—six cubicles, two men to a unit. On the opposite aisle are soldiers who got in last night from Fort Benning. You'll be attending the same classes, so make nice. Each of you has your own footlocker and storage closet. I encourage you to pick up locks at the PX to secure your stuff, but that's up to you. You've been assigned space in alphabetical order. You can draw straws or flip coins to decide who gets the upper or lower bunk."

Haggerty started reading off names: "Abrams and Baker—number one; Driscoll and Halladay—number two," as PFC Perkins checked us off on the clipboard.

"Looks like we're camping out together," Tommy said.

"Guess so," I responded, picking up my duffel bag.

"Should be careful who you pee next to at a truck stop," he joked.

We settled into our new quarters, a luxury suite compared to where we'd been sleeping the past two months at Fort Jackson.

"You got a preference, upper or lower?" Tommy asked.

"I don't mind the top," I said. "Was upstairs all the time at Jackson."

"Okay with me," he said relieved. "I'm afraid of rolling over in my sleep and falling out."

We proceeded to unpack. I folded my socks, boxer shorts and T-shirts and placed them on the top shelf in the upright metal locker, my green dress uniform on a hanger below. Fatigues, one pair of jeans, toilet kit and my small stack of letters took up the rest of the limited space in the footlocker.

Private Perkins returned. "You men can finish putting your gear away when you get back. The area will be secure while you're having lunch." The PFC nodded toward an MP who was standing by the door. We marched the short distance to the mess hall, an extended wing off the central administration building. It looked the same inside as the commissary at Fort Jackson, a cavernous room with rows of tables and a cafeteria-style lane with bins of food trays behind glass partitions.

"Have seats over there." Sergeant Haggerty directed us to tables set with napkins, stainless utensils and plastic cups of iced tea. "These fine ladies will be bringing you a welcome lunch. Be nice to them since they're working overtime on a Sunday, when I'm sure they'd rather be home with their families."

"When did we check into this resort?" Tommy winked at me.

"I don't know, but I like it already. Did you see the latrine in the barracks?" I asked.

"No, what of it?"

"There are actual toilets in cubicles with doors. Not like that shit-hole chicken coop at Jackson."

"You mean we're coming back to civilization?"

"Something like that."

The two ladies who'd prepared the welcome lunch set plates of fried chicken, mashed potatoes with gravy, and string beans in front of us, then passed a basket of buttermilk biscuits. We were digging in when Sergeant Haggerty pushed through the swinging doors of the mess hall and yelled, "Attention!"

We instantly dropped our fried chicken legs and stood up rigid around the table.

"At ease, gentlemen," Captain Oliver ordered as he entered the dining room. "Sit down and continue your meal. It's probably the only decent food you've had in a while."

We sat back in the folding metal chairs, scraping them across the linoleum tiles under the table, and looked up at the officer who had addressed us.

"I'm Captain Oliver, Commanding Officer at Fort Eustis. You men are here because you've demonstrated abilities in basic training that qualify you to acquire specialized skills." He looked across the tables littered with gnawed chicken bones and buttermilk biscuit crumbs. "Our motto at Fort Eustis is, *Nothing Happens Until Something Moves.* Remember that. In the coming weeks you'll come to appreciate its full meaning. You'll understand the importance of what we do here, and what it means to make things move. I hope you'll take full advantage of the opportunities you get here. Very well then, carry on, men," he said, saluting and turning abruptly to exit the mess hall.

"Well, that was something." Tommy Driscoll nudged me as he reached for another fried chicken leg. Before I could comment, paper plates of strawberry shortcake with foaming whipped cream were placed on the table.

"Wow, this is like being at home."

"Don't get used to it, honey," the jovial woman serving the table whispered, pressing her large bosoms against my shoulder. "This is just day one. You'll see."

• • •

"**D**id you know it's Labor Day?" I called down to Tommy on the lower bunk. "How'd we manage that day one in MOS training is a fucking holiday? They didn't even tell us."

"Fuckin' lucky," Tommy said, pulling a pillow over his head and rolling under the covers.

"I mean, how crazy is that? We get here on Sunday, have a great fried chicken meal, a pep talk from the Captain about opportunities we're going to have and all that 'Nothing happens until something moves' bullshit, and now we're here with nothing to do. How screwed up is that?"

"Guess nothing's moving today," Tommy said, smothering the pillow over his head. "Just let me sleep in."

"And on top of it, we can't leave the base. Not here long enough to get a pass."

"Where you gonna go anyway?" Tommy muffled from under his pillow. "We're in the fucking swamps of Virginia."

"Not exactly," realizing Fort Eustis was not far from my college in Williamsburg.

I slipped down from the top bunk and headed to the showers. Most of the guys were sleeping in, taking advantage of the holiday, but a few were sitting in their boxers, smoking and playing cards in the lounge. The black and white TV in the background, sound turned down and the snowy screen flipping at annoying intervals, was broadcasting the Jerry Lewis telethon for muscular dystrophy.

I was alone in the shower, luxuriating in the cascading hot water raining over my face and closed eyes, feeling the torment and bullying at Fort Jackson washing away in the drain. I was determined to get a fresh start at Fort Eustis and leave all the shit from basic training behind me.

Private Perkins had shown us around, pointing out the mess hall, the PX and the gym where we were welcome to work out, play basketball or swim in the pool during off-duty hours. The base was eerily quiet as I walked down the tar roadway lined with single-story, white wooden housing units. I wandered toward the rifle range, the James River in the distance, passing no one on the way. Most of the enlisted men and officers must have taken off for the long weekend. Orientation was scheduled for seven hundred hours the next morning, when we were expected to be in uniform, standing inspection outside building C-404.

It was hot and sticky, a steamy morning in the Virginia Tidewater area, the kind of oppressive climate I'd become used to, having spent the last four years in Williamsburg attending summer-school classes and working as a waiter at the King's Arm's Tavern. I thought about going back to campus when I got a pass, yet I was apprehensive. I was well aware of the anti-war sentiment among students. Shit, only a few months earlier I had been participating in demonstrations against the atrocities being carried out in the jungles of a foreign country halfway around the world. And now here I was with a shaved head, wearing the green uniform. This was the real fucking world—beyond student idealism.

Today I was confined to the dusty fields within the barbed-wire perimeters of Forth Eustis. My paperback copy of *The Catcher in the Rye* stuck to my palm as I passed the posted warning signs indicating "live fire danger" on the rifle range whose guns were silenced in deference to the holiday.

I walked to the edge of the bluff overlooking the James River. In the distance, I could see rusting rows of gray hulls tied together, like toys in a giant bathtub. They were abandoned ships from World War II—the mothball fleet—left there like ghostly reminders of what could happen again.

I sat leaning against the trunk of an old elm tree, following Holden Caulfield through the pages of the dog-eared paperback until the light faded and I could no longer make out the small type.

"What did you do today?" Tommy Driscoll asked when I returned to the barracks.

"Not much. Took a long walk around the base, checking things out. Found a quiet spot out by the river overlooking the mothball fleet. You can't believe how many abandoned war ships are just tied up out there."

"Yeah, I can," Tommy said. "Another good use of taxpayers' money."

"Whatever."

"Did you eat?" Tommy asked.

"Not hungry," I answered as I kicked off my sneakers and dropped my jeans, folding them and laying them flat in the footlocker. "I'm turning in," I said grabbing the metal pole on the side on the bunk bed.

"You're from Connecticut, aren't you?" Tommy asked, stopping me from climbing to the upper bed.

"How'd you know?"

"Just did," Tommy said. "I am too."

"Where?" I asked.

"Westport."

"No shit...so am I."

"How come I don't know you?"

"Went to Assumption, the Catholic school."

"I was at Bedford Elementary and then Staples. It looked like you Catholic kids weren't having much fun—lined up in the playground in your blue uniforms with old women in black robes hovering around like crows."

"They gave us a good education."

Then, changing the subject, Tommy asked, "Did you know the West Point hero from Westport who got blown up in Cambodia?"

I closed the lid on my footlocker without looking at Tommy. "You mean Ronnie Bankhead?"

"Yeah, I think that was his name."

"I heard about it."

"The paper said their helicopter strayed over the border into Cambodia and got shot down. What do you think?"

"It could have happened."

"I've heard a lot of crazy shit about what's going on over there," Tommy commented suspiciously. "So you knew this West Point guy?"

"I knew the family," I said, climbing to the upper bunk.

"Imagine going through the fucking military academy and ending up in a blown-out helicopter in a jungle on the other side of the world."

"Shit happens," I said, hugging my pillow.

"Yeah, shit happens," Tommy agreed.

CHAPTER TWELVE
(September 5 - September 24, 1967)

● ● ●

The recorded reveille bugle blasted across the base at five hundred thirty hours. We showered and were putting on fatigues when Sergeant Haggerty entered the barracks and announced, "Everybody up and lookin' sharp. You need to assemble outside on the grass at six hundred hours." He looked at his watch. "Line up in the same order as your sleeping quarters—the men from Jackson in the first two rows and you guys from Benning behind. After roll call we'll be heading over to the mess hall for breakfast and then on to orientation. Be ready to move out."

"First day of school," Tommy said, drying himself off with a towel, letting it drop to his ankles, revealing a semi-hard erection protruding from a curly patch of ginger pubic hair. I pulled on my socks, pretending not to notice.

We assembled outside C-404, as Sergeant Haggerty took roll call and Perkins checked off names. After breakfast, we were moved to a large classroom on the first floor of the administration building.

Captain Michael Oliver entered and we rose to attention. "At ease," the officer instructed. "Take your seats." Oliver had a medium build, thinning light brown hair starting to reveal a shining spot on the crown of his scalp. He wore tortoiseshell, horn-rimmed glasses in front of sea-green eyes. I suspected he was a career officer who landed this assignment at T-School after doing his time in Vietnam.

"For the next eight weeks," he began, "you will be attending a number of classes." He went on to chalk subjects on the blackboard, explaining that some of us would be studying troop movements and cargo distribution, while others would be trained in the technical aspects of helicopter maintenance. "All vital to the objective of making things move."

"He could have been a priest," Tommy jabbed me as we listened to the orientation.

"Would have made a good one."

I was assigned to troop movement class while Tommy went to more technical helicopter repair. We shared the same sleeping quarters but did not see each other during the day except for meals in the mess hall. I carried heavy manuals of airline schedules, resembling bulky Yellow Pages directories, and studied various ways and routes to move men and equipment around the world. Tommy came back covered with purple grease stains, and he spent long hours in the shower soaping over the stubborn oily smudges on his hands and arms.

The classroom exercises were a fucking snap for me, college boy. I might not have been able to throw a grenade to save my life, but I could sail through a test on how to move containers of grain, weapons and troops from Omaha to distant ports around the world. Because I had near-perfect scores on all written exams, I was taken out of class and assigned duties to process orders for troops moving out: typing forms outside Captain Oliver's office. At times it felt like I was functioning as a glorified travel agent, only instead of sending honeymoon couples to Bermuda, I was writing one-way tickets for young men to Vietnam.

"You're doing good, Halladay," Sergeant Haggerty commented one day as he placed a pile of orders on my desk. "And Oliver likes you."

"I try," I said, diffusing the compliment.

"Captain Oliver authorized a weekend pass for you, even though you've only been here two weeks. Thought you might like to take in some of the local color."

I was astounded. It was the first acknowledgement I'd done anything right since being inducted into the Army, and the first time I'd been given an authorized pass to leave base.

"Lots of hot pussy in Norfolk and Virginia Beach, but look out for your wallet," the sergeant cautioned.

"I'll be careful," I smiled. "You can be sure of that."

My pass was valid from zero six hundred hours on Saturday until twenty-four hundred hours on Sunday. I had the whole weekend.

The next morning I crept down the aisle to the showers. The TV was flickering in the lounge, unwatched and the channel unchanged for the last few days. Jerry Lewis had long since signed off and left the building.

The sun broke through the early morning clouds, casting long fingers of light across Fort Eustis. It was September: hot, humid and sensuous, as though summer would never retreat. Few people were stirring on the base as I walked on the tar road toward the entrance gate. I showed my ID and weekend pass to a disinterested MP who motioned me through. It was several hundred yards down the paved entryway of the base before I came to the old highway. I knew if I turned left I would eventually reach Williamsburg. I passed Lee Hall Farm where the gently sloping pastures hugged the railroad tracks. Meandering cows with droopy brown eyes looked at me suspiciously as I trekked down the two-lane road. The Interstate had long ago siphoned off through traffic heading north to Richmond and Washington, bypassing Williamsburg.

An occasional car sped by, kicking up sand and pebbles. I wiped sweat off my forehead as the sun burned through the morning clouds. A battered Ford pickup sailed past, then skidded to a stop with its brake lights blinking. I jogged forward to the stopped truck and peered into the open passenger-side window.

"Wanna ride?" the woman asked. Before I could answer she said, "I know you guys aren't supposed to hitch-hike, but I can offer you a ride, can't I?"

"Thanks," I said. "It's sure hot walking out here."

"Get in, kid," the woman offered. "How far you going?"

"Just up to Williamsburg," I answered, climbing into the cab.

"Me too," she said, jerking the truck into gear, peeling off down the road. "On my way to work."

I looked at the woman—dyed reddish-blond hair, curls brushed along her plump white cheeks—clacking a wad of chewing gum. She was wearing a tight Beatles T-shirt over melon-shaped breasts, her nipples pointing out George and Ringo. Her chubby legs pinched a pair of ragged cut-off denim shorts, and her bare feet stretched to reach the clutch and gas pedal.

"I'm Orleane," she said, rolling the wad of gum, taking it from her mouth with her fingers and squashing it into the ashtray.

"I'm Tim."

"On my way to the Lord Paget Motel," the woman offered. "I do front desk during the day and bookkeeping when it's not too busy, which is most of the time now summer's over."

"Thanks for stopping."

"You new at Eustis?"

"Two weeks."

"Why you going to Williamsburg, and not Norfolk or the beach?"

"I went to school there."

"Oh, one of them college boys!" Orleane arched her eyebrows. "Now you're in the Army! How the fuck did that happen?"

"Drafted."

"Ain't that a bitch!" she laughed.

"Yeah," I shrugged as we drove along the back road for the next few miles without speaking.

"So where you from, kiddo?" Orleane asked breaking the silence.

"What?"

"I mean where'd you grow up?"

"Connecticut."

"A fuckin' Yankee! I shoulda known. But you're still cute, honey."

Orleane downshifted the truck and pulled into the Texaco filling station on the outskirts of Williamsburg. She got out of the cab and swabbed the windshield with a handheld rubber squeegee, scraping off bugs and dirt, wiping dripping water around the windows with a paper towel. She disengaged the nozzle of the fuel hose, and held back the lever with her fingers as she filled the truck with gas. She pushed the nozzle back into the holding arm of the gas pump and slammed the cab door shut before edging the pickup into a shaded area, turning off the ignition.

"I'm gonna take a piss," Orleane said as she withdrew the keys and slipped them into her cut-off shorts. "Wanna come in?" she said nodding to the rest room. "I'll give you a blowjob."

"What?" I backed off.

"You know, like I'll suck your pretty dick."

"Thanks for the ride," I said sliding down from the cab of the truck. "I can walk the rest of the way."

"Just as I figured. Queer as a two-dollar bill. You pretty guys are too fucking cute…all the same," she said, raising her middle finger and slamming the door to the women's bathroom.

It was less than a mile to the historic district of Williamsburg. I jogged the distance, pebbles crunching under my sneakers as I pushed open the wooden gate behind the King's Arms Tavern on Duke of Gloucester Street and walked past the outbuilding where I had dressed in my "Tom Jones" costume. Every night after getting dressed for the evening shift, I'd tie three-foot-square white starched napkins around the necks of tourists who giggled over being served peanut soup and Sally Lunn bread—dinner presented with a flourish by waiters in ruffled blouses and Weejun loafers with strap-on brass buckles.

I heard the locker-room chatter of guys getting dressed for the lunch seating, making disparaging jokes about tourists lined up outside the tavern, who on a good day would maybe leave a fifty-cent tip on a twenty-dollar check. I wanted to push open the door to the locker room and say, "Remember me? I used to work here a few months ago." But I rubbed the stubble of fuzz on my head, knowing that I was now no longer one of them. I pushed open the white slatted gate with the heavy metal ball suspended on a chain that pulled it closed behind me with a thud.

"Hey, Halladay? Is that you?" I heard a booming voice. "Halladay!"

I turned to face Nate Burwell, the wine steward I'd worked with at King's Arms the last four years.

"Guilty," I smiled, embarrassed.

"What the fuck!" Burwell shouted. "What the fuck!"

"I know."

"Man...look at you. What the fuck happened? Your hair..."

"Don't rub it in. It's bad enough."

"You're supposed to be at Yale."

"It didn't quite work out that way."

The burly wine steward wrapped his arm around me, giving a warm hug. "What are you doing here?"

I proceeded to tell Nate how I'd gotten drafted after graduation and that I was just transferred to Fort Eustis.

"That's fucking incredible. You're stationed just down the road at Eustis?"

"Funny how shit happens."

We moved to a picnic table in the garden behind the tavern. "Wait here," Nate said, disappearing briefly to return with two cold Heinekens. "I don't usually drink before lunch," he popped caps off the beer bottles, "but this is a special occasion. Cheers, buddy!"

Sunlight filtered through the grape leaves and morning glory vines winding across the wooden trellis overhead as we sat and shared memories of times working at the historic tavern.

"So why didn't you just tell them?" Nate asked unexpectedly.

"You mean check the box?"

"A lot of guys do."

"Guess I'm not a lot of guys," I said, putting the half-empty beer bottle on the table.

"You coming in to say hello? It's still a half hour before we open."

"I think I'll pass," I said standing up, brushing my shaved head.

"Sure, kid," Nate smiled, punching me lightly on the shoulder. "I understand. You take care of yourself."

My sneakers squished on moss-covered bricks as I walked up Duke of Gloucester Street, approaching the Wren Building at the entrance of the college campus. I paused to look into the windows of Stair & Company, the corner antique store with hand carved model ships, shiny brass telescopes, Hepplewhite chairs and gate leg tables on Oriental carpets. I continued past the movie theatre with a poster of the Beatles' *Hard Day's Night* in the display frame. Next door, Earl Levitt men's shop offered herringbone sport coats and Shetland crewneck sweaters folded in neat pastel colors in the window. Every well-dressed young man at William & Mary had a house account at Earl Levitt's. Credit was no problem because Earl knew that come graduation the parents would pay any charges their sons had run up.

Greek's restaurant was on the corner, not the real name of the establishment, but dubbed that because the Greek immigrant family who owned the place served daily specials for two dollars to students rejecting the garbage served in the campus cafeteria.

I crossed the intersection where Richmond and Jamestown Roads came to a circle in front of the Wren Building. I paused outside the Student Center. The kiosk in front was plastered with notes from students looking for rides to D.C., fliers offering modern dance classes, and notices announcing demonstrations against the Vietnam War.

The door to the campus bookstore was propped open with a rubber wedge. A new girl was sitting behind the checkout counter, leaning on her elbows, thumbing through an issue of *The New Yorker*, sipping on a straw from a plastic Dairy Queen container.

"Where's Amanda?" I asked.

She looked up, annoyed at the distraction from the cartoons in the magazine. "Who?" She pushed up her brown horn-rimmed glasses.

"Amanda...the girl who works here?"

"I don't know. I just started yesterday," she said, sucking up the last bubbles from her drink.

"Thought you might know her."

"Sorry," she said, disinterested, and turned back to the magazine, tossing the empty Dairy Queen container into a wastebasket under the counter.

I strolled through the deserted bookstore, stopping in front of the fiction section to pick out a copy of Faulkner's *Light in August*, a book I'd only thumbed through senior year and had always wanted to read. I was fascinated by the professor's challenge to delve into the seeming misuse of the word "further" in the opening paragraph of the novel where Lena is describing her journey from Alabama to Mississippi in a horse drawn wagon—when the word "farther" was seemingly correct.

"That it?" the girl asked.

"Yes," I said, handing her a five-dollar bill.

She rang up the purchase and handed me change, then settled back on the stool, licking her thumb to turn the next page of *The New Yorker*.

The bus schedule posted on the bulletin board outside the bookstore indicated the next local to Norfolk, stopping at Fort Eustis, wouldn't leave until four o'clock, almost two more hours. I decided to walk and headed down Duke of Gloucester Street past Bruton Parish Church, Chownings Tavern and the Kings Arms, exiting the historic district onto the two-lane highway leading back to the base. I needed to use a bathroom and paused in front of the Texaco filling station where only a few hours earlier Orleane had offered me a blowjob. but decided to pass, and walked another mile before cutting off the road at the entrance to Carter's Grove Plantation. I unbuttoned my fly and let a long stream of piss wash over the kudzu vine and poison ivy crawling along the embankment.

It was hot and muggy as I trudged along the back road. The afternoon sun burned like an iron against the nape of my shaved neck. An occasional car sped by, whipping dry dust off the road. The traffic coming south from Richmond was on the Interstate; only locals working at the base, or people who lived in the trailer camp adjacent to the installation, took this road.

I'd been walking more than an hour and was now far beyond the Williamsburg city limits, when a red Mustang convertible screeched to a stop fifty yards ahead. The immaculately polished car looked out of place on the back road.

I jogged up to the stopped car and was standing next to the passenger door, sweating and out of breath when the driver asked, "Need a ride?"

"Thanks," I said.

"Get in," he offered. "How far you going?"

"Just to Eustis."

"On the way," he smiled, peeling back onto the highway. He shifted the Mustang from second to third gear in a deliberate motion, his hand gripping the stick shift ball as he brushed against my left knee. The driver reached to turn up the volume on the radio, blaring out "Don't Come Home A' Drinkin'" by Loretta Lynn.

Glancing to my left, I got a good look at the driver as a warm blast of air washed over the windshield. His hair was bleached white by the sun, evidence of long days at the beach, yet his brows were dark brown, arched over sea-blue eyes. The fine hair on his forearms looked like milky feathers against his honey-colored skin. His chest was subtly defined, a smooth stomach in a rippled V that disappeared into the open top button of his cut-off jeans.

"How long you been stationed at Eustis?"

"Two weeks," I answered.

"You don't look like the typical GI Joe," he smiled. "I mean not many guys on base read Faulkner," he commented, referring to the paperback on my lap.

"I like to read." I smiled, thinking it was only a few hours ago that I was riding on the same backcountry road in a Ford pickup truck with Orleane who wanted to give me a blowjob.

"Something funny?"

"It's just this was my first pass since I've been in the Army."

"And you went to Williamsburg?"

"Yeah."

"You should go down to Virginia Beach. I go there all the time."

"I can tell," I said.

The car drove on, passing the cows at Lee Hall Farm, country music mixing with the warm breeze flowing over the windshield.

"What company you in?"

"C," I responded.

We drove another mile before I saw the white dome of the water tower poking up through the trees in the distance. A chain-link fence with circular razor barbed wire coiled on top defined the perimeter of the military installation.

The Mustang slowed and pulled onto the sandy shoulder of the road.

"Here is fine," I said as the car came to a stop. "I can walk to the main gate."

"You wanna stop some place for a beer or something?" he asked unexpectedly.

"I have to get back to pull CQ," I lied. I was keeping true to my self-imposed pledge not to fool around with anyone while in the military.

"Maybe some other time."

"Yeah, some other time," I repeated getting out of the car.

"By the way, what's your name?

"Tim," I said, closing the car door. "Tim Halladay."

"Nice to meet you," he said leaning across the front seat and extending his right hand. "I'm Eddie Arkansas." He smiled, aware of the strange name. "No shit. Real name."

"It's different," I admitted. "Good to meet you, Eddie Arkansas… and thanks for the ride." Just then I noticed a clear plastic dry cleaner's bag on the backseat with the familiar khaki uniform inside—corporal striping on the sleeve.

Eddie Arkansas shifted the Mustang into gear. "So long, Tim," he said as the car pulled away. "See you around."

Pebbles and sand spat out from the rear tires as the bright red Mustang driven by blond, tan Eddie Arkansas—Corporal Eddie Arkansas—disappeared off into the fading afternoon sun down the old Virginia highway.

Back in C-404 barracks, I climbed onto my bunk. It was Saturday night, so everyone who wasn't pulling duty had taken off. It was after midnight when I woke up to the sound of dance music drifting across the base from the officers' club. A few drunk enlisted men were singing off-key near the bowling lanes. I walked down the hall and got a Coke from the vending machine, taking a long swallow and letting the fizzing bubbles stream out of the corners of my mouth down onto my chest.

I grabbed a towel folded at the foot of the bed and headed toward the showers. My body was sticky and sweaty from the long afternoon walk, and I welcomed the hot water pouring over my head, pretending I was anywhere in the world but the Army. After twenty minutes, I turned off the spigot and emerged onto the tiled floor of the shower to dry off. I looked at my reflection in the clouded mirror above the sink, trying to recognize Tim Halladay.

I slipped into a clean pair of white boxers and stretched out on the upper bunk. Music from the officers' club continued to drift across the compound, and the enlisted men who'd been singing earlier were now engaged in a drunken brawl. The only light in the deserted barracks came from the television set at the end of the hall, the sound tuned down, but the picture flickering relentlessly.

The image of Eddie Arkansas stuck in my mind: his soft white-blond hair, honey-colored skin and swimmer's body—the sight of him driving the red Mustang convertible, barefoot in cut-off Levis—the tightly drawn muscles on his chest, the trace of white fuzz against his flat stomach, and the faint form of a barely detectable V disappearing beneath the open top metal button of his jeans with no trace of a tan line.

My boxers were damp with small circles of sticky fluid uncontrollably emitted by the fantasy. I slipped the shorts below my knees and kicked them to the floor. Naked atop the brown wool blanket, I spat into my palm, and slowly and repeatedly stroked to the music from the officers' club, surrendering and paying homage to the image of Eddie Arkansas—Corporal Eddie Arkansas.

CHAPTER THIRTEEN
(September 25–October 16, 1967)

● ● ●

My weekend pass was still valid, but I stayed on base. After my venture to Williamsburg, I didn't feel like going anywhere. I spent Sunday afternoon reading Faulkner under the elm overlooking the James River. I leaned back against the old tree and gazed out over the mothball fleet anchored in the river, *Light in August* opened across my lap. I studied a column of tiny red ants climbing across the toe of my sneaker, a microscopic army in their world with their own Bravo and Charlie Companies.

On Monday morning I was stationed at my desk outside Captain Oliver's office. My main responsibility was to type orders and process paperwork for soldiers shipping out.

"Halladay," Sergeant Haggerty announced, dropping off a stack of files on my desk. "Oliver wants to see you. Like now. Hope your boots are polished."

"What did I do?"

"Guess you'll find out."

I pulled back from the desk, leaving an incomplete form in the typewriter. I knocked on the captain's door.

"Come in, Halladay," the officer gestured, getting up from his desk. "Have a seat. This isn't the Inquisition."

"Yes, sir."

"I've been watching you, Halladay," he said. "I've been watching you since you got here," he paused. "I understand you had some problems at Jackson."

"I got through it, sir."

"They gave you shit because you didn't sign up for OCS," the captain said, not expecting an answer. "The fact is, Halladay, the Army needs men like you. Smart guys with a head on their shoulders."

"I didn't think I was cut out for Infantry," I started.

Oliver leaned forward. "I'm not trying to talk you into something you've already made up your mind about. I may think you could be a hell of an officer, but that's a decision only you can make." Oliver sat back, folding his arms. "I've seen the way you conduct yourself," he continued, not giving me an opportunity to speak, "and I've put in a request to have you appointed my permanent aide."

I sat silent, not knowing what to say.

"You'll be excused from further classes and assigned a full-time desk job with the rank of Private First Class. You will report to me and be responsible for administrative duties. That should be no problem for you," the officer said.

"Yes, sir."

"You will be required to participate in some training exercises, which I'll get into later, but I'm sure you can handle it. That will be all, Halladay. Now get back to your desk. There's probably a shitload of paperwork piled up out there."

"I'm sure, sir," I said standing up. "Thank you for the vote of confidence."

"Yes, soldier," Oliver said, slipping his hand into the pocket of his pressed khakis and tossing me a set of keys. "And when you break for lunch, take my Camaro down to the motor pool to get it washed… and tell them…no water spots."

"Yes, sir," I said clutching the keys. "No water spots."

I returned to the desk, where another stack of manila envelopes had been dropped off during the short time I was in Captain Oliver's office—orders that needed to be processed for the graduating class from helicopter maintenance school, twenty-four young men being shipped off to Vietnam.

"Guess you lucked out for this assignment," Haggerty sneered, looking at my overflowing in-box. "Whose ass you been kissing?"

"Somebody has to do it," I said, deflecting the sergeant's sarcasm.

"Must be pretty good at it, college boy."

"I just follow orders."

"Sure, pretty boy…and make sure there's no water spots on the captain's shiny Camaro."

I returned to my typewriter and finished entering information on the form, sending another eighteen-year-old to Vietnam.

The next few weeks were uneventful. I stood in formation every morning, and after roll call reported to my desk where I typed stacks of orders for the guys completing training at T-School—all being deployed to Vietnam. Fridays, at noon, I drove the captain's Camaro down to the motor pool to get it washed.

"How you like being Oliver's lackey?" the private teased as I dropped off the car.

"I follow orders, just like you," I retorted. "Just make sure there's no water spots."

"Yes, sir," the GI mocked, tossing a wet chamois in the air. "Whatever you need for the captain."

I was plowing through a stack of orders, typing transmittal forms, when Captain Oliver came out of his office, stood behind and placed a hand on my shoulder. "Sorry to interrupt your work, Halladay," he said, "but I need you to come into my office."

"Yes, sir." I stood to attention.

"Relax, Tim," the officer said, calling me by my first name. "Nothing to worry about."

I followed the officer who closed the door and motioned me to sit down.

"You've been doing a good job," he started, "and I know the transition from civilian life to the Army hasn't been easy for you."

"I'm trying."

"I see that," Oliver acknowledged. "You've been doing a fine job, but now I need you to step up to the plate for a special assignment."

"Yes, sir," I responded.

Oliver gazed out the window, his back to me. "You'll be going to Fort Story in Virginia Beach for the next few weeks."

"Fort Story?"

"You will still be based at Eustis and maintain your quarters here, but you'll be on special detail for the next few weeks."

"What kind of special detail, sir?"

"You'll be given instructions when you get there. Be packed with fatigues—you won't need civilian clothes—and be ready for departure at zero seven hundred hours tomorrow. And, Halladay," he emphasized, "you are not to discuss this with anyone."

"Yes, sir." I stood up and saluted.

"Halladay, I wouldn't have picked you for this assignment if I didn't think you were the best man for the job."

"Thank you, sir. I appreciate your confidence."

I was packing my duffel bag when Tommy Driscoll came into the barracks, his hands and arms covered with grease stains from maintenance class.

"You going on vacation without me?" he joked as he pulled off his T-shirt and kicked out of his fatigues.

"Not exactly," I said, folding socks and underwear into the pockets of my duffel bag.

"So what the fuck you doing?" Tommy asked.

"I'm being reassigned to Fort Story."

"You're shitting me!" Tommy said in disbelief.

"Why? What's wrong with that?"

"You know what goes on down there? The kind of shit they do?"

"No, what? And how do you know so much about it?"

"Because everybody with a pea brain knows what goes on at Story."

"I don't know what you're talking about."

"Well, you sure as hell will find out, you sorry fuck," Tommy said, stripping naked and heading for the showers at the end of the hall.

I finished packing, disturbed that my bunkmate knew about this place I was being reassigned while I didn't have a fucking clue what to expect.

● ● ●

An MP pushed open the door to the barracks a few minutes before seven hundred hours. "Halladay," he called out, "you ready to move out?"

"Ready," I said picking up my gear. I climbed into the jeep, and we drove off into the morning mist, passing through the entrance gates of Fort Eustis without being stopped, and headed south toward Virginia Beach.

"So how'd you get picked for this assignment?" the MP asked as he lit a cigarette and shifted the jeep into high gear.

"Got me." I shrugged. "I don't even know what I'm supposed to be doing."

"They didn't brief you?" the MP asked, taking a long draw on his cigarette.

"Captain Oliver said I was being reassigned to Fort Story for a few weeks…to be ready to move out this morning."

"Guess they know what they're doing," the MP said as the jeep turned onto the Interstate. A half hour later we exited onto Route 60, the old road to Virginia Beach, then drove through miles of scrub pines and sand dunes. As we got closer to Chesapeake Bay and the Atlantic Ocean, the driver turned onto a two-lane road with a sign marker pointing to Cape Henry Lighthouse.

"Where is this place?" I leaned out the open door and breathed in the warm salt air.

"You'll see," the MP said, lighting another cigarette. The jeep bounced over the bumpy road for a few miles, passing a series of white wooden signposts in the sand dunes: "Restricted Area," "Authorized Military Personnel Only," "Caution: Live Ammunition."

We came to a stop in front of a guardhouse flanked by a high chain-link fence topped with coiled, razor barbed wire disappearing into the bushes on either side of the entrance—a white wooden sign arched overhead announcing "Fort Story." Two soldiers in camouflage fatigues stood guard with M-14 rifles drawn. Another MP emerged from the gatehouse and approached the jeep.

"This the new guy?" he asked as the driver handed him a sealed manila envelope.

"Private Halladay." The driver nodded toward me.

The guard opened the file, looked at it, staring at me. "Welcome to Fort Story, Halladay." He handed the envelope back to the driver and waved to the guards. They lifted the heavy steel bar securing the gates and pushed the barrier open as we passed through. The driver shifted into four-wheel drive to proceed along the sandy, unpaved road through muddy gulches. Overgrown holly bushes and ferns scraped the sides of the vehicle as we navigated to a clearing half-a-mile away.

"They call it the *moat*," the driver said as we came out of the muck and stopped on a paved section of road in front of a two-story wooden building. White paint peeled off the clapboards weathered from years of sun and harsh salt winds. Cape Henry Lighthouse rose in the distance, Chesapeake Bay and the Atlantic Ocean beyond. It was a beautiful Indian summer October morning with waves licking the shores of the endless sandy beaches along the coast.

"This used to be a hospital for veterans returning from World War II, but now it's HQ for Fort Story."

"Could use a coat of paint," I commented, climbing down from the jeep.

"More than that, kid," the MP said. "Report in there at the desk." He pointed, handing me the manila envelope. "They know you're coming. People don't just drop in here," he said. The MP shifted and sped off down the stretch of tar-paved roadway heading back to Fort Eustis.

I walked up the creaky steps of the administration building and reported to the PFC at the desk.

"Sign in here," the soldier said, handing me a clipboard without looking up. "Let me see your orders."

I handed him the manila envelope and signed in on the board with a ballpoint pen attached with a string.

"Okay, Halladay. Major Bengert will see you shortly. Have a seat."

I sat on the bench, my duffel bag cradled between my feet. I waited as the indifferent soldier pecked away at the typewriter on his desk. I looked around the dingy quarters—everything looked old and used, as though abandoned years ago.

"Halladay?" I heard my name called from the inner office.

"Yes, sir." I shot up, saluting the major standing in the doorway.

"At ease, soldier." The officer waved his hand, directing me to enter. "Sit down," he said closing the door.

Major Frank Bengert walked with a slight limp and had a beer-belly bulge sagging over the polished brass belt buckle on his khakis. He settled into a creaky chair behind a gray metal desk and stared at me.

"We do things a little different here at Story," he started. "A lot different than Eustis," he emphasized. "The first piece of business is you have to read this and sign it."

I looked at the form, a complicated legal document in small type and in language impossible to comprehend, with an X marked in blue ink indicating where I was to sign.

"You don't have to read all the fine points," the major said, anticipating my questions. "It only means you will not discuss any of the programs or activities you participate in while you're here at Fort Story. Not with anyone—military or civilian." The major paused, leaning back in his chair.

"Sure," I said, jotting my signature on the line.

"You see, Halladay," he started to explain, "we have programs at Fort Story that are highly confidential—top secret and classified. We need to be sure our men understand the sensitivity and the seriousness of what they may be exposed to here."

"Yes, sir," I responded automatically.

"Very well, Halladay. Captain Oliver recommended you for this assignment."

"I'm just not sure what I'm supposed to be doing."

"You wouldn't be here if your commanding officer didn't think you were up to it." Bengert stood and folded his arms across his chest. "You may have heard of an elite squad of infantrymen called tunnel rats."

"Yes, sir, I've heard of them."

"It takes a special type of soldier to qualify for that assignment, and not many make the cut. It's our mission here to flush out those individuals who measure up and make sure they get the training they need to carry out their mission."

Major Bengert unrolled an elaborate chart curled up in a long cylinder mounted on the wall of his office. It was an intricate drawing of a jungle with a maze of tunnels and underground compartments. It looked like an advertisement for an ant farm I'd once seen in *Boy's Life* magazine.

The major extended a metal pointer that he traced over various images on the chart. "Charlie has been very clever," he started. "They've built these elaborate underground complexes beneath the jungle floor." He pointed out lush palm trees and dense foliage across the top of the illustration. "They're like fucking underground cities," he continued, scrawling across diagrams of subterranean rooms, hallways and storage areas. "They've built dormitories, training areas, even hospitals—all underground. They can live in these complexes for weeks, even months, as long as they get supplies. It's fucking incredible. We have to get in there and blow these suckers to bits because they're coming up out of the fucking ground and attacking our men, coming out of the jungle floor like ants." The major's face was flushed and drops of sweat formed over his eyebrows.

"So, Halladay." The major folded the metal pointer into his palm and placed it back on the desk blotter. "I suppose you're wondering how you fit into this picture."

"Yes, sir."

"We have a selection process to weed out men equipped for this difficult detail. We need to train men to infiltrate this underground system, to get down into the tunnels and blow the fuckers up."

The major sensed my anxiety, and laughed.

"No, Halladay." He returned to the leather chair. "You don't come close to the cut. How tall are you?"

"Five-ten."

"And what, about a hundred forty pounds?"

"Yes, sir. About that."

"You're too tall and too heavy. The maximum requirement is five-four and maybe a hundred twenty pounds. Smaller and lighter is better. We're looking for the spics and wetbacks, the scrawny kids who didn't do anything right in basic, the ones who couldn't throw a grenade to save their life. You know, the real losers."

I sat in silence, wincing that I actually did fit the profile, aside from my height and weight.

"So Halladay…since you are obviously not tunnel rat material, why are you here?"

"Yes, sir. I'd like to know."

"Fair enough," Bengert said sitting back. "We have a specific process to determine just who are the right men for this mission. A lot of guys volunteer for the wrong reasons, maybe thinking they're going to become some kind of hero or whatever the fuck is in their twisted minds. But the truth is, only a handful of men are actually cut out—mentally and physically—to take on this mission." Bengert stared at me, searching for a reaction. "That's where you come in."

"I do?"

"We have a program here called Escape and Evasion. It's actually phase one of Operation Tunnel Rat. It's a weeding-out exercise where we determine who goes on to the next stage of intensive training. And you've been assigned to be a member of that team."

"I'm not sure I understand, sir."

"You'll be reporting to Sergeant LaVern. Three tours in Nam and a Purple Heart."

"Sounds impressive."

"You'll be a member of his squad in training exercises," the major said. "LaVern's one of our finest men. He may come off a little out there, but that's what we need for this kind of detail."

"I see."

"Do what LaVern says, and you'll be fine." The major ended the conversation. He stood up and opened the door. "Get one of the MP's to show Halladay to his quarters," the major instructed the soldier outside his office. "Drop your gear off and report to LaVern at his camp. He knows you're coming."

Within minutes an MP appeared in the hallway. "You Halladay?"

"Guilty," I said trying to make connection with someone at this strange place.

"I'll drop you off at the barracks where you can stow your stuff. Get in and I'll take you there. It's just the next building over that sand dune. But don't get too attached to the place because you aren't going to be spending much time there."

"What do you mean?"

"They haven't told you shit, have they?" the MP smirked, turning on the jeep's ignition and heading up the hill where we stopped in front of a one-story wooden building.

"Welcome to the Fort Story Hilton," the driver joked. "Your name is posted on a room inside the door. Secure your stuff in a locker. I'll wait for you out here."

I found "Halladay" printed in Magic Marker on a page of yellow legal paper taped to the door of the first room in the dingy barracks. I pushed the door open to find a cot with a bare mattress and an open footlocker at the base of the bed—no other furniture in the dank room. A horizontal hinged window just below the ceiling let in light through a screen with a hole in it that looked like someone had punctured it with a fist. I placed my duffel bag in the locker and secured it with a combination lock I'd bought at the PX.

I shut the door and walked to the latrine at the far end of the barracks to take a piss in the metal trough where a slow trickle of running water crept down the wall of the urinal. There was a communal shower area with four spigots, a pair of water-stained sinks in front of a cracked mirror, and two toilets in cubicles with no doors—not exactly the cushy quarters I'd had at Eustis, but I did have my own room.

I bent over the dirty sink and splashed water on my face, then walked down the deserted hall past six identical rooms, yellow pages with scrawled names tacked on each closed door. There was no one else in the musty barracks.

"You ready, Halladay?" the MP called from outside. "Sergeant La-Vern is expecting you at the camp. I'll drive you over."

"The camp?"

"They didn't tell you shit, did they?" The MP leaned over the steering wheel of the jeep.

"What's this camp?"

"You'll find out soon enough," the MP said, lighting a cigarette. "Man. Will you fucking find out!"

CHAPTER FOURTEEN

(October 16, 1967)

● ● ●

The jeep's bulky traction wheels dug in when the MP diverted the vehicle off the paved roadway into thick brush. Muddy sand spat up over the windshield as we navigated the swampy terrain. Bamboo fronds and scratchy scrub pine branches scraped the sides of the vehicle maneuvering deeper into the swamp.

"Where the hell is this place?" I asked, spitting out bits of mud and leaves that flew into my mouth.

"Nowhere," the MP said. "Nowhere anybody wants to be."

"How would anyone ever find this place?"

"They can't," the driver said. "That's the point."

The jeep continued pushing into the swamp, the waterholes becoming increasingly difficult to navigate and the overhead growth of vegetation creating a natural canopy, filtering in only slim fingers of sunshine.

"Hold on," the MP cautioned. "We've got to get through this next marsh. It can be tricky."

Water came across the floorboards and washed over my boots as the jeep plunged into the rushing current. The MP worked the four-wheel-drive vehicle, artfully pushing back and forth, shifting gears, until the jeep emerged grunting like an elephant from the muddy current, coming to a stop on a sandy embankment.

"We're here." The driver turned off the ignition and pulled out a towel from under his seat. He wiped his face and arms and threw out branches that had snapped into the vehicle. "Here, kid," he said, tossing me the towel.

I grabbed the cloth, wiping mud and grit off my face and hands. The MP hopped out of the jeep and walked a few paces toward a tent behind a fire smoldering within a circle of stones.

"He's here," the MP called out.

Sergeant LaVern emerged, bare-chested, his fatigue pants sliding down below his rippled tight stomach. He was smoking a hand-rolled cigarette and had a growth of stubble on his deeply tanned face. His eyes looked like huge brown walnuts. Both arms were painted in tattoos: a snake curled around his left limb and a Valentine heart on his right bicep with the words "love/hate" burned into his skin.

"You're Halladay," the sergeant said, looking at me, taking a long drag on his cigarette, before squashing it with the heel of his boot.

"Yes, sir."

"I'm taking off," the MP announced, getting back into the jeep. "I'm done here." He spun the wheels in the sand and drove back into the swampy marsh.

"So, Halladay." The sergeant pulled a joint from his hip pocket and sat on one of two sawed-off tree stumps facing the smoldering fire pit. "Sit down and take a load off." LaVern leaned forward and touched the cigarette to a smoking coal. He took a long puff and inhaled deeply, looking toward the leafy canopy overhead. Exhaling in a deep breath, he passed the joint to me. "Here, kid...have a toke."

"Thanks," I backed away. "I don't smoke."

"Well, you better fucking start if you want to survive here."

I leaned forward to accept the crude cigarette, looking at it suspiciously before pressing it between my lips and sucking in. My mouth and lungs filled with sweet-tasting smoke and I coughed in short bursts.

"You'll get the hang of it, kid," LaVern laughed, taking the joint back. He sat on the tree stump, his eyes closed, blowing smoke rings into the air.

"So, Halladay," he said exhaling. "You come recommended by Oliver over at Eustis."

"I report to Captain Oliver," I said, starting to feel mellow from the marijuana.

"We do things different over here."

"I still don't know what I'm supposed to be doing."

Sergeant LaVern looked at me, sucking the last juice out of the joint before flipping the stub into smoldering coals. He flicked a few specks of green off his lower lip. "Let me give it to you straight, kid," the sergeant said, resting his left tattooed arm across my shoulder. "Welcome to hell...the fucking asshole of the world."

I sat on the tree stump next to the sergeant, facing the glowing coals in the fire pit.

"You heard of tunnel rats?" LaVern asked, standing up, not waiting for an answer. "Well, this is where we weed them out. There's only a few sorry fucks who ever qualify for the assignment, and it's our mission to determine who gets to move on."

LaVern knew I did not understand, so he continued. "This is a training exercise. They call it Escape and Evasion, kind of a fancy military term for torture," he laughed. "We get away with all kinds of shit no other base could handle."

LaVern weaved back and forth and lit another joint. "This is base camp." He gestured toward the pup tents in the surrounding bushes. "I have ten men who patrol the swamps, looking for the enemy."

"What enemy?" I asked.

"The pussies who were released to navigate this course. An hour after you left Eustis this morning, a bus carrying twelve men pulled up to the same gate you came through. Only, they didn't get waved through like you. They weren't special like you, college boy. Their mission is to get through the swamp and bivouac on the beach. It's just over two miles from the gate through the swamp to the sand dunes and ocean. The men are armed with an M-14, a knife, and they carry a backpack of gear weighing a hundred pounds."

LaVern paced around the fire pit and came up behind me, squatting down and breathing stale breath close to my face. "But not many of the fuckers make it to the beach." He grinned broadly, revealing a ridge of yellow-stained, crooked teeth. "You know why, Halladay? Because they get lost and disoriented in the swamp. And they get caught," LaVern boasted as he stood up.

"Caught?"

"Captured by my men, all ten of them who've been here over a year. They know every inch of that swamp, every snake and bug and critter crawling in the slime and muck. They know that swamp better than their bitch's pussy."

"Impressive," I commented at the sergeant's graphic description.

"The men going through this course are supposed to be trained in survival techniques, but they don't know shit. They get into that swamp with water and snakes up to their balls and they act like scared little faggots."

I winced at the slur, but sat on the tree stump looking out into the dense foliage surrounding the camp.

"One or two might make it through to the beach, usually the scrawny spics. Must be from crawling through fucking rain forests in Puerto Rico. I don't know, but they ain't enough to fill the program. So we have to weed out some more fuckheads who might make it through as tunnel rats."

LaVern extended the joint to me.

"I'm good," I said passing on the sergeant's offer.

"Suit yourself…" LaVern smirked, taking a long draw. "Let me show you some of the toys we have around our little country club. We'll be using them when my boys bring in the first sorry fucks they capture."

I followed LaVern down a path past pup tents to a clearing in the brush, about a hundred yards away. A large tent sat on the perimeter, its canvas flaps propped open. In the center of the clearing was a low oval of stones surrounding a mound of gray ash emitting thin spirals of smoke. Two Y-shaped poles, joined by a rope, straddled a grave-like opening covered with a coarse rope cargo net.

"Take a look," LaVern motioned as he pulled back a corner of the net. I stepped to the edge and peered down into the dark pit, stumbling backward as I recoiled from the sight of dozens of slithering snakes in the bottom of the muddy hole.

"Don't worry, Halladay," he laughed. "They're not poisonous. They're my babies."

The sergeant picked up a long pole with a metal fork hook attached to the end and thrust it into the pit. He scraped across the bottom of the pit and with a hard jerk, he lifted up a three-foot black snake squirming and wrapping itself around the bottom of the pole.

"Come to Daddy," LaVern cooed affectionately, staring at the darting reptile hissing its razor tongue in and out like a lightning bolt. "This is Hanna," he grinned, pointing the snake at me. "She's my favorite."

"She's great." I backed up slowly.

"A good bitch," LaVern said, kissing the reptile on the head, sliding his fingers down the back of her squirming tube-like body. He pulled the pole back and gave it a hard jerk, sending Hanna back to the bottom of the pit. "This is only one of the attractions we have here at Fort Story Disneyland."

I looked at the sergeant, not sure whether he was insane or stoned—or both.

LaVern strode off into the brush to take a piss as I checked out the encampment. Two oil drums, overturned in the sand, with cut-out holes in the lids, were stacked next to the large open tent. Fifty yards back, along the edge of the swamp vegetation, were three crude wooden crosses, looking like ghosts from a Ku Klux Klan rally.

LaVern kicked sand into the air with his boots as he stomped back to the snake pit. His fatigues were unbuttoned and he flapped his dripping cock in the air. He stared at me, and getting no reaction, he folded his dick into his fatigues and buttoned up.

"So, Halladay," he started. "Your job is to help me process the prisoners."

"Prisoners?"

"The sorry fucks who don't make it to the beach…and that might be all of them, if my men do their job."

"Tell me what to do."

"When we get the prisoners here," the sergeant became serious, grabbing my shirt and pulling my face close, "it's our job to break them."

A shrill whistle shrieked from the swamp beyond the camp, and the sound of footsteps breaking through dense brush crackled through the steamy air.

"Sergeant LaVern, we got two here," a voice called out of the jungle. Then shots rang into the air as four men emerged. Two soldiers in camouflage, brandishing rifles with bayonets drawn, black paint smeared under their eyes and across their cheeks, prodded two infantrymen whose hands were tied behind their backs.

"Well, well," Sergeant LaVern gloated. "Our first visitors to Story Disneyland."

The soldiers with painted faces pushed the prisoners onto their knees alongside the stone rim of the campfire. One of the camouflaged soldiers rested his rifle against a Y-shaped pole by the snake pit and grabbed an armful of bamboo and driftwood stacked next to the large tent. He heaved the dry kindle onto the smoldering coals while his buddy stood by, pointing a rifle at the two captured soldiers kneeling by the fire, now starting to crackle into short flames. The captured men looked at the sergeant, and then at me. I was standing silently in the background.

LaVern paced back and forth in front of the two men on their knees. He halted, digging his boots into the sand while taking a long drag on the joint between his fingers, then nodded to the soldier pointing a rifle at the captives.

"On your feet," the soldier barked, swiping the sharp tip of his bayonet inches from their faces. The two men stood up clumsily, hindered by hands tied behind their back.

Sergeant LaVern approached and pressed close to the first captive, exhaling heavy marijuana breath. "Identify yourself," he demanded.

"Fuck you," the kid spat back defiantly.

"No, fuck you, scumbag," LaVern shouted, thrusting a full fist into the soldier's groin, sending him into a doubled-over convulsion.

"Maybe your buddy will be more cooperative," the sergeant smirked, moving to confront the other captive. "Now you want to get with the program," LaVern sneered, sizing up the young Latino soldier. "Let me see…you a spic or wetback? Let me guess."

"What's it to you, you doped-up asshole," the boy fought back, kneeing LaVern in the shins and sending the sergeant stumbling back toward the fire pit.

The camouflaged soldier flew forward and smashed the defiant kid in the face with the butt of his weapon, sending the boy, nose bleeding, into the sand.

I stood by horrified, not believing what I was witnessing.

"Looks like we've got a couple of fucking live wires here," LaVern laughed. "Just what the doctor ordered." The sergeant approached the two captured soldiers, both on the ground, and kicked sand into their faces.

The soldier with the drawn bayonet prodded the men to get up as his comrade piled another heap of bamboo and brush on the fire, turning it into a crackling blaze.

"Halladay," the sergeant yelled. "Bring me those cocksuckers' uniforms. I'll find out who the fuck they are."

I approached the captives—two men I might have passed in the PX at Fort Eustis yesterday—two men who were now here in this surreal nightmare in the swamps of Virginia.

"He wants your fatigues," I said.

The soldiers untied the captives' hands and stripped off their uniforms, dumping them in a pile. I picked up the discarded fatigues and deposited them in front of LaVern, who was standing before the roaring fire pit—a bottle of Jack Daniels dangling from his left hand.

"Save the boots and gear, everything else comes here," the sergeant directed, taking a swig of bourbon.

The prisoners stood naked by the blazing fire, cupping their hands in front of themselves, looking at me with contempt.

"Lopez?" the sergeant hollered, holding up a shirt, reading the black letters on the uniform. "You from San Juan?"

"My family's from Cuba."

"Oh!" LaVern laughed. "I thought we cut off all you sugar canes. What did you do, float over on a '55 Chevy?"

The Cuban boy lunged forward but was restrained by his buddy. "Let it go. It's just training."

"Some fucking training," the boy cursed under his breath. "What's this psycho supposed to be teaching us?"

"Well, Lopez," the sergeant said wiping the green fatigue shirt between his legs. "I was hoping you were one of those hot Puerto Rican pretty boys...the ones who like to take it up the ass."

I stood frozen as the crazed sergeant hurled the boy's shirt onto the fire.

"And you, Tucci," the sergeant said, stretching the other soldier's shirt across his face, reading his name. "You one of those fucking Itralian wops?"

The boy stood rigid, eyes locked with LaVern who was swaying back and forth, the bottle of Jack Daniels in his hand.

"Name, rank and serial number," LaVern shouted into the boy's face.

"Fuck you," Tucci shot back, "you sorry, drugged-up, fucked-up son of a bitch."

LaVern's eyes bulged and bubbles of spit oozed out of the slits of his mouth, as he screamed, "We got one!" The sergeant stumbled around in circles, as if in a tribal dance, then, coming face-to-face with the captured soldier, he smashed the bottle of Jack Daniels across the Italian boy's skull, sending him bleeding into the sand.

I rushed over to the dazed soldier, wiping blood off his face with a sweaty T-shirt I pulled from the pile of clothes dumped in front of the fire.

"Halladay," the sergeant yelled. "Get that sorry fuck up and over to the pit. We got work to do here."

I helped the stunned boy to his feet, wiping the cut on his forehead.

LaVern staggered unsteadily before the captive and grabbed the boy's jaw in his hand. "Your company and position," he snarled.

The boy had been drilled never to reveal that information, and even though this was supposed to be a training exercise, all sense of reality was lost.

"Your company and position," LaVern repeated tightening his grip on the boy.

"Fuck you, asshole," Tucci spat into the sergeant's face.

"Whoa," the sergeant laughed, reeling back and releasing his grip. "I think we got a real one here."

The sergeant nodded to the two soldiers, who leaned their drawn rifles against a tree stump by the fire and moved toward the pit, rolling back the coarse rope cargo net.

"Ah, my babies." LaVern exhaled a cloud of marijuana smoke, then moved to the edge of the pit to take a prolonged piss onto the swarm of slithering snakes below. He shook his dripping dick, then ordered, "Halladay! Bring that sorry spaghetti-bender over here."

I nudged Tucci toward the sergeant, then backed away. The naked boy, hands tied behind his back and blood clotting on the side of his head, stood in front of the sergeant.

"So let me ask you one more time," LaVern started, his pupils dilated and popping. "Your company and position?"

The soldier stood tight-lipped, refusing to answer.

"Cat got your tongue...? Well, maybe my ladies can loosen you up."

The two soldiers standing by approached Tucci, one grabbing his arms and the other his feet, lifting him up and suspending him facedown over the open pit. LaVern gloated as he took a swig from the Jack Daniels bottle.

Tucci twisted and turned, trying to free himself from the soldiers holding him, but he was no match. He stared down at the swarm of slithering snakes below and screamed.

"Maybe you can remember now." LaVern hovered over the naked soldier, drooling bourbon saliva from his mouth. "Company and position?" he demanded.

The boy gritted his teeth, still refusing to talk, fighting to free himself from the tight grip of his captors.

"Still can't remember?" LaVern sneered into Tucci's face. "Well, it looks like Hanna's gonna have an early dinner," he roared as the two soldiers holding the captive lowered him to the rim of the snake pit.

"Okay, babies," LaVern leaned into the pit, "you gonna have a nice ripe Itralian sausage to chew on."

The soldiers' grip loosened on Tucci's arms and legs as he stared down into the muddy pit of slithering snakes. He heard the soldiers counting "one-two-three" as they rocked him back and forth, and then he let out a terrifying scream. "No! God, no!" He twisted and fought, sobbing and begging not to be dropped into the pit.

Crows in the overhead swamp trees screeched and flapped their wings, flying into the clear October sky, frightened, as if warned that a terrible predator was approaching.

Tucci screamed, "Bravo Company, 129th Battalion, Fort Eustis, Virginia." He sobbed, wringing in terror as the two soldiers lifted him away from the pit and dropped him in the sand, letting him squirm in the muck as the boy wept uncontrollably and wrapped his hands around his head.

LaVern walked away from the scene. "I thought we had one here," he said to himself, disappearing into the dense swamp foliage.

The trembling boy was sobbing, curled in a fetal position in the mud as I approached him with a towel that I used to wipe slime and crusted blood off his face.

"Get him out of here," one of the soldiers ordered. "Hose him off," he instructed, pointing his drawn bayonet toward a makeshift shower next to the large tent on the perimeter, "and get him a uniform out of the pile inside. He's going back to Eustis…back to greasing helicopters."

I draped my arm across the boy's shoulder and guided him toward the shower, whispering into his ear, "I think you're done here."

Shrill whistles pierced the steamy air as members of LaVern's squadron pushed four more captured men into the campsite. The prisoners were quickly stripped and tied to the wooden crosses propped up at the edge of the clearing.

LaVern emerged from the brush, surveying the new arrivals with a menacing sneer, then yelled out, "Halladay? Where's that pretty little Cuban fuck?"

"Private Lopez?" I asked hesitantly.

"No, Ricky fucking Ricardo," LaVern shouted.

"He's over here, sergeant," I said nodding to the slight Latino boy kneeling by the fire pit, his hands still tied behind. He looked like a marble faun sculpture in a Rome museum, his solid uncut penis dangling between his taut thighs.

"Come here, sugar cane," LaVern motioned. "I already know your name and rank 'cause I got your uniform and dog tags, so we don't have to go through that bullshit," the sergeant laughed. "But I need more information that only you can provide."

The Cuban boy fixed his large brown eyes on the sergeant and stood defiantly.

"Company and location?" LaVern pressed up to the boy's face. "Now you can tell me what I need to know, and we'll get along just fine. Or you can make it difficult. It's up to you, sweetheart."

Lopez stood rigid, refusing to respond.

LaVern staggered back, looking intently at the young man, then turned to the soldiers standing around the fire pit. "Looks like we got a lot of cats out here today. Lots of fucking cats with their tongues tied."

Sergeant LaVern hurled himself against Lopez, the two men standing, pressed against each other, eyes locked.

"I'm going to ask you one more time," the sergeant hissed. "Company and position."

"Never."

LaVern pushed back from the Cuban, amazed at his audacity. "Never is a long time. Sure you mean that?"

"Never in your fucking life."

The sergeant glared at the naked boy standing defiant, hands tied behind his back. "You're a pretty piece of sugar," LaVern slurred, staggering forward, taking a long swig of Jack Daniels. "Maybe I can convince you another way."

The two camouflaged soldiers moved forward, pointing their bayonets at the captured boy, creating a barrier between the sergeant and the prisoner.

"Fuck it…" LaVern backed off. "I'll ask you one more time…Company and position."

The soldier was silent, his bull-brown eyes fixed on the crazed interrogator.

Egged on by the boy's determination, LaVern laughed, "Guess my ladies will have to settle for a Cuban sandwich today."

The soldiers dropped their weapons and picked up the captured boy, suspending him over the open pit.

"You want to reconsider your answer?" LaVern challenged, still getting no reply. "Turn him over," the sergeant shouted. The boy stared into the muddy cavern of slithering reptiles below, closed his eyes and gritted his teeth.

"Last chance," LaVern bellowed. "Company and position."

The only sounds from the prisoner's lips were the whispers of "Hail Mary, full of grace."

The soldiers released their grip on the boy, no longer struggling or trying to get away, dropping him into the muddy, reptile-infested pit, no scream or shouts of terror coming forth, only the hushed mumble of "blessed art thou among women."

I sank to my knees at the side of the smoldering fire pit, pounding my fists into the sand, feebly trying to trace the sign of the cross on my chest.

CHAPTER FIFTEEN

(October 17, 1967)

● ● ●

The jeep pushed through the marsh, headlights bobbing like a hand-held flashlight through dense brush. I'd fallen asleep on a cot in one of the pup tents, after Sergeant LaVern and the men from his squad disappeared into the jungle, heading toward the sand dunes and the beach, laughing and celebrating.

"Get in." The MP driving the muddy jeep motioned to me. "This is the last bus out of here."

I looked around, aware I was the only one left at the campsite. The fire in the pit had pissed out hours ago, and everyone, prisoners and captors, was gone.

"Captain Oliver sent a directive to make sure we bring you back to the barracks," the driver confided. "He must think a lot of you."

"The captain's been very decent to me since I arrived from Jackson."

"Guess so," the MP winked. "Not every GI gets this kind of treatment."

The jeep sloshed through the swamp, bouncing and jerking back and forth as I held onto the roll bar. We came to a stop in front of the clapboard building where I had stowed my duffel bag earlier that day.

"Thanks for the lift."

"Don't get too comfortable, Halladay, because we're going to be moving out of here in a few hours."

"What do you mean? I just got here."

"There's a hurricane off the coast of Florida and she's gaining strength. Her name is Edith and the bitch is moving north, predicted to come up the coast, maybe hitting the Outer Banks by tomorrow night. If that happens and it moves onto Virginia Beach, Fort Story is right in her path. Couldn't happen to a nicer place, if you ask me. Wipe this fucking shit hole off the face of the earth."

The wind was brushing through the trees at a steady pace, and the crickets and frogs had ceased their nocturnal chorus.

"Stay tuned, Halladay. But you better be ready to move out. Maybe no more time for the war games you guys were playing today."

"Thanks for the heads-up."

"I'm sure Captain Oliver wants you high and dry on safe ground," the MP said as he thrust the jeep into gear and sped off.

Lights were on inside the barracks as I pushed open the screen door and approached the room with my name still taped to the door on a flapping piece of yellow paper. Four men were playing cards in the lounge at the end of the hall outside the latrine. Although they had washed off the black charcoal smudges from their faces, and were now sitting in Army-issued white floppy boxer shorts, I recognized the men as Sergeant LaVern's squad who had rounded up the prisoners.

"Well, look who's here," one of the soldiers called out as he saw me. "College boy."

I winced at the thought that my nickname followed me everywhere, even in this remote, desolate outpost.

"Come join the party. We got beer...not too cold, but what the fuck," he laughed popping open a hissing can. "Best we can offer in this fucking flea-bag motel. I'm O'Malley," he stood up unsteadily, "and these fine men," he burped, introducing the others, "are Tedesco, Feeney and Goldberg, our token Jew boy."

"Cheers," I said, accepting a can of beer and pulling up a folding beach chair to join the guys around a milk crate functioning as a coffee table where the men had thrown their cards in a jumbled pile.

"We're just dealing our next round," O'Malley said.

"Didn't mean to interrupt," I said, taking a swig of beer.

"So what did you think of your first day at Fort Story Disneyland?" O'Malley leaned forward staring at me.

"Not exactly what I expected."

"They just dumped you into this hell hole to find out for yourself," Tedesco commented. "Like there's no fucking rules...like anything goes."

"Same as over there—with Charlie," O'Malley cut in. "Only here it's pretend."

"Could have fooled me," I said.

"Wait till you're in the jungle sitting on a bamboo stick rubbing against your balls with a land mine attached to the end of it in a hole three feet underground, waiting for you to cut a fart that'll blow you into a million pieces, sending you up to the fucking satellites. That'll get your attention pretty fucking quick."

"But why all the torture and harassment shit?" I asked.

"Here's the drill," O'Malley started. "The mission is to screen out a few guys who go on and be trained as tunnel rats. They're the scum of the earth—the losers—the guys who can't get anything right. The guys who can't do shit. That Cuban kid today—Lopez. He's perfect."

"The one who prayed when you dumped him into the snake pit," I asked.

"Yeah, that scrawny sugar cane."

"Had to step in," Tedesco said, "before LaVern got carried away and went crazy. We had shit like that happen before, and we all got called out on it because some kid claimed he was raped during training."

"Maybe 'cause he wasn't moved on to tunnel rat, but instead sent back to helicopter repair," Feeney spoke up.

"Fuckin' doesn't matter," O'Malley cut him off. "We all got busted with no passes for ninety days just 'cause crazy LaVern got his rocks off with some twerp. That ain't gonna happen again."

The wind was picking up outside and tree branches whipped against the weathered clapboard siding of the barracks.

"Looks like that storm's getting nasty," O'Malley said, collecting cards strewn over the top of the crate, stacking them in his hands, then shuffling. "You gonna join us for a hand?" O'Malley asked, tapping the neat deck on the crate.

"Poker?" I asked.

"That's the game. No cover to join, but you got to catch up with the rest of us."

"What do you mean?"

"Well, you're sitting there in full combat gear and the rest of us are in our skivvies. Doesn't seem fair, does it guys?"

"Have another beer, Halladay," Feeney grinned, tossing me a new can. "We're ahead of you."

"What the fuck," I said popping open the metal tab on the beer and unbuttoning my fatigue shirt. A few swigs of warm beer and I was sitting in my underwear with the guys, cupping the cards dealt me, trying to remember the rules of poker—the game Ronnie Bankhead had taught me while babysitting.

"If we get moved out of here because of this fucking hurricane, you won't get to see the rest of this horror movie," O'Malley said tapping the remaining cards in the deck, placing them in front of him on the crate.

"What do you mean?"

"We only interrogated two prisoners today," Tedesco said, taking a swig of beer, "that pathetic Italian pussy, Tucci, and the praying Cuban kid who passed with flying colors. The other four we rounded up are in the cage. LaVern was too stoned and out of it, so we had to suspend exercises until morning."

"The cage?"

"It's a holding area behind the big tent at the campsite. We usually only keep prisoners there until they're brought up for questioning, but sometimes, like today, when LaVern goes over the top, we have to hold them overnight," Tedesco continued.

"There are guys are out there with this storm coming in?"

"Yeah, along with four of our men who are tracking the other fuckers who are still slithering through the swamp trying to get to the beach."

"You mean we just left all those guys out there?" I said, clutching my cards toward my chest.

"They got blankets, C-rations and a hose for running water," Feeney explained. "You think they're gonna get a fucking Motel-6 in Cu Chi?"

"What about the other guys out in the swamp?"

"Don't worry about them, Halladay. That's the way it is…just the way it is."

"Yeah, but…" I started.

"There are no buts," O'Malley said gripping my arm and pulling me forward. "The guys all volunteered for this assignment, and they knew it was no piece of cake. They are the losers, the nobodies. This is their last chance, and the ones who make it will do anything to survive. Do you have any fucking idea what that feels like…you coming from fancy prep schools and college?"

"No," I withdrew.

"So have you had to suck Oliver's cock yet?" O'Malley said, offhand.

"What?" I laughed nervously.

"Well, you are the flavor of the month." O'Malley peered over the fan of his cards.

"What's that supposed to mean?"

The other players sat around the circle, holding cards close, watching the exchange, grinning.

"Oliver's a good guy," O'Malley continued. "Don't get me wrong. He does his job at Eustis…and most of the men respect him, and like him…well, some like him a little more," he snickered. "But at the end of the day, he's an okay guy and looks out for his men…as much as he can since most of them are shipped off to Nam every eight weeks."

"He's been pretty decent to me," I said.

"Decent, your ass," Tedesco butt in. "He saved you from being shipped out and getting your balls blown off with all the other poor suckers heading off to the fucking jungles."

"Has he given you the keys to the Camaro yet?" Feeney interjected.

"I take the car to the motor pool to get it washed."

"That's how it starts," Feeney said studying his cards.

"It's not like I took it off base and went for a joy ride to Virginia Beach or something."

"Goldberg, you need a card?" O'Malley asked. "You been fucking quiet as a church mouse, all night. Sorry, I meant a synagogue mouse."

"I'll hold," he said, ignoring the comment.

"Hit me," Tedesco said tapping his fingers on the table, studying his cards. "Again," he instructed.

"What about you, college boy?" O'Malley challenged.

"You know, I wish you wouldn't call me that," I shot back. "I'm just one of you guys."

"Oh, no…no…no, you're not," O'Malley stared. "You're one of the chosen few. Ain't that right, Goldberg? Just like in the fucking Bible?"

"I don't know what you're talking about, you sorry ass. I thought we were playing poker."

"Okay." O'Malley backed off. "Anybody else need a card?"

The men studied their hands, trying to calculate what the others were holding.

"Bets are closed, gentlemen," O'Malley announced, spreading his cards across the crate. "Full house," he beamed, showing three tens and a pair of Jacks. "Anybody beat that?"

"I got two pair," Tedesco said, showing matching fives and sevens."

"Two kings," Feeney revealed.

"And you, Goldberg? What you got?" O'Malley challenged.

"Nothing. A bunch of crap. You guys got all the good shit," he said, throwing his cards onto the crate.

"And you, college boy. You got a surprise up your sleeve, like a fucking flush or something you been hiding?"

"No such luck," I admitted spreading my cards. "I got nothing."

"Well, it looks like you and Goldberg are the losers this round," O'Malley laughed, "and seeing as we don't take money here at this casino, you'll just have to surrender your shorts."

I looked at Goldberg, who was used to the routine as he stood up and slid out of his boxers, tossing them onto the makeshift table where the cards were strewn.

"Your turn." O'Malley popped open another beer, grinning at me. "Time to settle your losses with the house."

"Yeah, sure," I said, wondering how I'd ever gotten into this fucking situation, but knowing I had to play along. I lowered my shorts, rolled them into a ball, and hurled them onto the milk crate. "If that's what the house needs," I laughed, trying to control a semi-erection.

"Oliver's going to love you, baby," O'Malley snickered. "A feisty little flavor of the month."

The lights flickered in the barracks as a tree branch pounded the outside of the building and the storm picked up intensity.

"Well, gentlemen," O'Malley slurred, standing up, swaying back and forth as if being driven by the winds. "We can't leave our buddies, college boy and Jew boy standing here with their dicks wagging out with a fucking hurricane banging at the door. Come on, you guys," he said, pointing to Tedesco and Feeney. "On your feet and get with the program."

The other soldiers stood up and stripped off their shorts, hurling them onto the milk crate. "You know the drill," O'Malley continued. "That deck has to be retired." He referred to the cards on the crate under the pile of underwear. O'Malley moved forward, familiar with his role in the ritual, gathering up the white shorts and tossing them in a heap behind him. The five of us stood naked in a circle, arms across each other's shoulders, locked in an embrace like members of a primitive tribe.

"You know this deck has to go," O'Malley hummed as we swayed back and forth in a circle, jerking off. "Everybody has to drop a load onto the deck so it can be retired forever."

"This ain't no queer thing," O'Malley mumbled as he stroked himself. "I love pussy as much as anybody. We all love pussy. I can't wait to get my tongue up in some juicy cunt and suck that fuzz into my nose when I'm eating down there. But being here in this hell hole for months on end, and all the shit that goes on with crazies like LaVern, fucks you up…like you don't know where the fuck you are or where the fuck you're going."

I tried to fit in, standing naked with the four other men, closing my eyes and stroking myself.

"These cards will never be used again," O'Malley said, squeezing me, locking his arm around my neck. "Once they're cum stained, they're not playable…at least not in this house," O'Malley said as he pulled back, looking at me directly as he shot his wad across the cards.

"You know, you're pretty, Halladay, but I'm not that way."

"Me neither," I said, backing away and walking naked down the hall to my room where the yellow page with my name on it had been whipped off by the howling winds of hurricane Edith bearing down on Fort Story.

CHAPTER SIXTEEN

(October 18, 1967)

● ● ●

Rain pelted the barracks, spitting in through the fist-hole opening in the screen above my bunk, slapping the sides of the wooden building and roof like sticks against a drum. Torrents of water came in through the window as I pulled the coarse wool blanket over my head. The screen door of the barracks thumped repeatedly, slamming like a warning signal.

"Attention, men," a bullhorn blared, cutting through the howling wind. "We're moving out at zero seven hundred hours. Get your gear together and be prepared to leave. Everyone is moving to higher ground. This is a serious storm, and we have orders to evacuate Fort Story."

I rolled off the cot, wiping my eyes, still wondering if the poker game was a bad, beer-induced dream or a reality. None of it mattered as I zipped my duffel bag and pulled on fatigues, looking around to make sure I'd left nothing behind in the dank cubicle.

A bus pulled up in front of the barracks, and we filed out into the gusty rain. We scrambled aboard, throwing gear across empty seats. I settled in the rear of the bus as the driver turned on the ignition and pumped the gas pedal to get the old vehicle running. Four men wrapped in brown wool blankets clambered on board. One of the guys took a seat in the row behind me, hugging himself in the soaking crude blanket, his bare feet pushing against the back of my seat.

"We're moving out," the spec-4 called from the front of the bus as the driver folded the door shut. "And with any luck, we won't be coming back. If Edith has any mercy, she'll wipe this fucking shit hole off the face of the earth...forever."

A cheer went up from inside as the bus lunged forward, swaying back and forth as it ground out of the sand dunes and gained traction on the road leading away from Fort Story. The chugging bus inched onto Interstate 64, heading north toward Newport News, leaving Cape Henry Lighthouse and the sand dunes of Virginia Beach behind. Cars sped by, whipping up sheets of rain that splashed the bus's steam-covered windows. The restless guys fingered images of breasts and penises on the dripping interior windows, hoping someone in a passing car would notice and honk.

I peered over the seat at the young man curled up in a wool blanket behind me. I opened my duffel bag, fumbled around inside until I found a pair of navy blue jogging shorts and a William & Mary T-shirt.

"Here," I said, passing the clothes to the boy.

"What?" he sat up startled.

"Put these on."

"Why?"

"Because it's fucking cold and wet and you're naked."

He took the clothes, looking at me suspiciously. The bus swayed back and forth on the highway, buffeted by winds and pounding rain from the encroaching hurricane.

"You're one of those guys at the campsite," the boy muttered, slipping into the gym shorts.

"It was my first day. Not what I expected."

"Me neither," he said, pulling the college T-shirt over his head. "I saw what you guys did to that Cuban kid. We were tied up naked to those fucking crosses just watching you sorry fuckheads play sick war games."

"Not my idea," I defended myself.

The bus chugged along, its windshield wipers sweeping back and forth in cadenced rhythm. The sky grew more ominous, and the driver switched the headlights on. I looked over my shoulder at the boy, sitting cross-legged, wearing the clothes I'd given him. "Not exactly Army-issue, but it's better than running around naked under a wool blanket."

"Yeah, after you guys threw our uniforms into the fire."

"My name's Halladay," I said, changing the subject.

"Rodriguez," the boy returned, not extending his hand.

"Where you from?" I asked.

"Bridgeport."

"Connecticut?"

"Is there another one?"

"I don't know. There may be somewhere."

"The only one I know is in fucking Connecticut."

"You enlisted?" I probed.

"Fuck, no. My brother and me both got drafted."

"Your brother?" I leaned over the seat.

"Yeah, Ricky and me both got drafted the same time. I didn't think they were supposed to do that, but what the fuck, it happens. You know, we're fuckin' Puerto Ricans, so it doesn't matter."

"Your brother is Ricky Rodriguez from Bridgeport, Connecticut?" I asked amazed.

"My older brother. You know him?"

"Maybe. Did he do basic at Fort Jackson?"

"Yeah, and they shipped me off to Benning. Guess the Army couldn't handle two Rodriguez boys at the same place," the kid laughed.

"Do you know where he is?"

"Somewhere in Kansas, I think, driving tanks and other heavy shit. I don't know. Haven't talked to him…he may be shipped out by now for all I know. Guess I'll hear from him sometime," the boy said as if talking to himself. "He don't know I signed up for this tunnel rat shit…probably whip my ass good if he found out."

I slid back into my seat, stunned that the boy I'd just handed gym shorts and a T-shirt to was my battle buddy's kid brother.

The forty-mile trip back to Eustis took more than five hours. The old military bus got snarled in traffic on Interstate 64, locked in by cars and vans evacuating Virginia Beach and the surrounding coastal areas. The crackled news reports, fading in and out of transistor radios a few of the men had turned on, were predicting a Category 4 storm would make landfall near Virginia Beach sometime that evening. People were being advised that the Coast Guard would not be able to respond to emergencies if the expected tidal surge came onshore. Power was already out in Hampton Roads and Newport News. The Chesapeake Bay Bridge was closed.

"Looks like we'll get to Eustis just before the storm hits," the spec-4 who'd worked his way down the aisle of the bus said. "Mind if I join you?" he asked, picking up my duffel bag and dropping it on the empty seat across the aisle.

"Help yourself," I said.

"Captain Oliver wants to see you as soon as we get to base. Got a message just before we left Story. Said it was urgent. Can't even wait for the fucking hurricane to pass."

"Whatever," I shrugged.

The crossbar was in the upright position and yellow caution lights were flashing at the entrance to Fort Eustis when the bus crossed unchallenged onto the base past the guardhouse. Wind was howling and hard rain relentlessly hammered the roof of the bus.

I retrieved my duffel bag from the seat across the aisle and turned back to the boy who had draped the wool blanket around his body to cover the borrowed gym shorts and T-shirt.

"What's your name?" I stopped the boy from exiting down the aisle. "I know it's Rodriguez. I mean your first name."

The boy looked at me suspiciously. "Why? What's it to you?"

"Because your brother, Ricky, was my battle buddy in basic...that's why."

"Jimmy," he said. "Jimmy Rodriguez," he repeated before pushing off the bus.

"You Halladay?" the MP shouted as I disembarked.

"Yes." I peered from under my right arm, trying to shield myself from the pounding rain.

"You're to report to Captain Oliver," the MP yelled through the wind. "You know where that is?"

"I know." I crouched, heading toward the administration building. Electric power was out, and plywood sheets had been nailed across windows, creating an eerie feeling of an enclosed tomb inside the building.

"Halladay?" The soldier sitting outside the captain's office looked up. A small vigil light with a flickering candle cast moving shadows along the wall in the anteroom.

"Reporting."

"Have a seat."

From behind the closed door I could hear muffled voices as the winds howled outside. I sat, hands folded in my lap, wondering why I wasn't out on detail with the other men, packing sandbags and shoring up the facility against the approaching storm. The soldier pecked away at the keyboard, sneaking a glance at me through the flickering candlelight, as he unrolled a form out of the typewriter. He was sitting at the desk I had occupied just a few days ago.

The door opened and Captain Oliver stood in the entrance. "In here, Private Halladay."

"Yes, sir," I sprang to attention, saluting the officer.

"At ease, soldier," the officer said, patting me on the back and ushering me into the office, closing the door.

"This is Lieutenant Hadley." Oliver motioned to an Air Force officer standing in front of the desk in the small, stuffy office. "He's from Langley."

"Sir." I saluted politely.

"Have a seat, young man." The Air Force officer gestured, starring intently at me. Oliver settled into the sagging leather chair behind his desk and the three of us eyed each other as Edith clawed her mean fingers outside the building.

"You know, Halladay," Oliver started quietly, leaning forward across the desk. "You've been exposed to some highly sensitive information. Things that not a lot of soldiers will ever see."

"You mean the stuff at Fort Story?"

"Stuff?" Oliver smirked.

"Well, you know what I mean."

The Air Force lieutenant looked impatient, saying, "Aren't we getting off subject here, gentlemen? Like why the three of us are here in this fucking room with no lights and no air conditioning with a hurricane barreling down on our ass?"

"Right," Oliver said. "Let's get on with it."

Hadley pulled out a manila folder from his briefcase and opened it, thumbing through the first few pages, stopping and making a notation with a yellow Magic Marker.

"Private Halladay...do you know a John Nistico?" Hadley zeroed in on me, cupping the folder to his chest.

I was puzzled, caught off-guard by the unexpected question. "You mean Johnny Nistico...from Westport, Connecticut?"

"Yes, that John Nistico," Hadley said, peering over the folder.

"I went to school with him. We were in Assumption together."

"Were you in the same class?"

"We were in first to eighth grades."

"And you were friends?"

"What's this all about?" I asked.

"Private Halladay. You're not here to ask questions," the Air Force officer snapped peevishly.

"Hold on a minute here," Oliver stepped in. "Let's try to keep this discussion civilized."

I looked at Captain Oliver, fearing for the first time that a larger storm was brewing than the one pounding on the shingles of the building.

"His family has an Italian restaurant in Westport," the Air Force lieutenant continued.

"Yes, by the railroad station."

"Did you ever go there?"

I was confused by the unusual line of questioning and looked at Captain Oliver for direction, but the officer raised his finger, motioning me to continue.

"Lots of times. We used to go there on Friday nights for pizza and sausage grinders. Everybody knew it was the best Italian food in Westport."

"And John Nistico worked there?"

"The whole family worked there, even the grandmother who had some secret recipe for spaghetti sauce she brought over from the Old Country."

"What was John Nistico's job?" the lieutenant asked.

I shot another puzzled look at Captain Oliver. "I don't know...I think he worked in the kitchen until he was old enough to wait tables."

"Did he ever wait on you and your family?"

"He might have," I answered, confused. "It was a family business... his dad and brothers and sisters all worked there. They all waited on us. Mr. Nistico liked my dad."

"You know John Nistico is in the Air Force?" the lieutenant probed.

"I heard he'd enlisted."

"Stationed at Fairchild Air Base in Spokane."

"Sounds like he's doing better than me."

"Maybe not," Hadley said unfolding the file.

I looked back and forth at the two officers, wondering what the fuck this was all about. "What does this have to do with me?" I asked.

"Nistico identified you as a partner." Hadley stood up, fingering the edges of the manila folder.

"A partner?"

"He claims you two had sex together," the Air Force officer said.

"What the fuck are you talking about?" I shouted in disbelief.

"Nistico named you as a sex partner," the Air Force lieutenant glared.

"You've got to be kidding." I rebounded, stunned at the accusation. "We went to Catholic grammar school with nuns."

"According to Nistico it was more than rosary beads," Hadley challenged.

I lunged out of the chair toward the Air Force lieutenant when Oliver stepped in, saying, "Gentlemen...let's keep this civilized."

"Here's a copy of the report," Hadley said, sliding the manila file across Oliver's desk. "The inquiry is still open."

Oliver cringed at the uncomfortable scene. He pressed his hands on my shoulders and coaxed me back into the chair.

"I'm going back to Langley," the Air Force officer said, moving toward the door.

"Nobody's going anywhere," Oliver announced. "Eustis is on lockdown until further notice. I-64 is closed. So, Lieutenant, it looks like you will be hunkering down with us for a while."

"I'd rather be going back," Hadley said, "but I have to respect the seriousness of the situation."

"Good," Oliver said, opening the bottom drawer of his desk, pulling out a fifth of Jack Daniels. "I guess you'll have to accept some Army hospitality."

The Air Force officer was clearly uncomfortable, and he avoided looking at me.

"Halladay, you can be excused," Oliver said awkwardly. "We can take up this matter in the morning once the storm has passed."

"Take up what?" I stood facing the captain. "There's nothing to take up because this is all a bunch of bullshit." I glared at the manila folder on the desk.

"We'll discuss this further in the morning."

"There's nothing to discuss because nothing happened," I said defensively.

"Halladay, you're dismissed," Oliver said sternly. "Return to your barracks and wait for orders."

"Yes, sir." I saluted, turning my back on the two officers drinking shots of Jack Daniels, and flew out of the administration building. "Fuck this shit. Fuck the whole fucking Army."

The rain stung my face as I sprinted past rows of housing units whose windows were boarded up with sheets of plywood. I ran faster and faster, heading toward the rifle range where waves exploded over the banks of the James River. The hulls of the mothball fleet were tethered in the heaving waters, slamming against each other like lonely bodies, trying to press close for protection.

I found my elm tree, swaying defiantly in the raging wind, and wrapped my arms around the coarse bark, caressing the trunk like a lost lover. I opened the belt buckle of my fatigues, sliding them below my knees, letting the rain beat on my bare ass. I threw myself facedown in the mud and tightened the leather belt around my thigh, securing myself to a gnarled root of the old tree. The relentless rain streamed down my face as I sank pounding my fists into the muck, sobbing, "Why me?…why me?"

CHAPTER SEVENTEEN
(October 19–October 22, 1967)

● ● ●

Headlights of the jeep cut through thrashing branches in the howling storm as the MP yanked the handbrake and hopped out of the vehicle, sloshing his way toward the river bank.

"What the fuck you doing out here?" he yelled, spotting me hugging the tree trunk. "You out of your fucking mind?" he called out, waving a flashlight beam across my half-naked body. Not waiting for a response, a second soldier jumped out of the idling jeep, shining another flashlight back and forth.

"He's one of those crazies from Fort Story," the MP dismissed. "Still playing war games."

"They're all fucked up when they come back."

"Get up, soldier," the MP said prodding me with the tip of his boot. "We're going in before this monster storm takes us all out."

I looked up, squinting into the flashlight pointed toward my face, rubbing my sleeve across my face as I squirmed in the mud trying to stand up.

The MPs yanked me up, my drenched fatigues falling into a clump around my boots as I was forced to stand up.

"The infirmary?" the first MP nodded.

"Definitely?" the soldier returned as they slipped me, unresisting, into the back of the jeep. The winds lashed mean swipes across the vehicle.

● ● ●

"Want some breakfast?" the orderly asked, pushing a metal cart on wheels into the ward. "We got eggs and cereal," the chubby girl said shifting back and forth on her heels; her name badge read Cindy. "Let me know what you want, hon, and I'll put it on your tray."

I blinked, shaking my head back and forth, trying to get my bearings. I tried to sit up but fell back into the bed, feeling the restraints pinching my arms and ankles. A needle held in place by a Band-Aid covering a patch of gauze was pricked into my right arm. The needle was attached to a thin tube running up to a clear plastic bag of fluid suspended on a metal tripod next to the bed.

"They got you tied down here good," Cindy smiled. "You must have done some bad shit."

"I don't think so," I squirmed in the bed.

"Anyway, honey," she shrugged, "eggs or cereal?"

"I'm not hungry," I said, turning away.

"You let me know if you change your mind," she said, rattling the cart down the aisle toward other patients. "It's all the same to me."

I tossed in the bed, trying to wrest my arms out of the restraints holding me on the metal rails.

"Looks like you had a rough night."

I turned to see a handsome blond doctor pressing against the side of the bed; a nurse with a clipboard was standing next to him. "How you feeling?" he asked, taking my wrist to read my pulse.

"What am I doing here?" I asked.

"Well, for starters," the doctor pressed his fingers on my veins, "you were picked up clinging to a tree by the James River in the middle of a hurricane."

"Oh, that," I said, turning away.

"That would give a lot of people concern," the doctor said. "Pulse normal." He turned to the nurse holding the clipboard.

"You think I could be untied?" I asked.

"I don't think this man is a threat," the doctor smiled, instructing the nurse to cut the tapes away from my arms on the metal rails of the bed.

"Thanks," I said, sitting up, rubbing the residue from the sticky adhesives into little balls and flicking them across the bed. "I feel like I'm in prison."

"Just a precaution," the doctor said, sitting on the bed, nodding to the nurse to go on with her duties.

"A precaution against what?"

"You were pretty messed up when they brought you in, according to the report," the doctor said, placing his hand on my knee.

"Messed up?"

"Relax," the doctor smiled. "I've seen a lot of you guys come back from Story with nightmares."

"I was only there one day."

"Sometimes that's all it takes. I've never been down there, but I've heard about some of the shit that goes on."

I leaned forward, looking at the I-V still taped to my arm. "You think we could lose this?"

"Let's leave it for a while," the doctor said. "You're dehydrated, and from the looks of it," he glanced at the empty tray table, "you're not eating. The I-V will replenish your fluids."

"Whatever."

"We're going to keep you here overnight." The doctor patted me on the leg. "You've got some nasty bruises on your arms," he pointed to black-and-blue blemishes where I had clung onto the tree root, "and some superficial cuts from the pounding you took out there in the storm. Nothing life-threatening," he smiled.

"The chaplain will be in to talk to you," the doctor advised offhand-edly, then, sensing my anxiety, he added, "Just a formality in cases like this. But I have to advise you that you are on medical leave until further notice."

"Medical leave?" I sat up. "What does that mean?"

"You're temporarily relieved of duties. When released from the in-firmary, which will probably be sometime tomorrow, you'll go back to your barracks and wait for orders. Good luck, kid. And eat some-thing." The doctor turned to check on other patients in the ward.

I sat on the hospital bed, my bare feet dangling over the edge. The nurse had lowered the metal safety bars when she cut away the re-straints, so I was able to slide out of bed and stand up, although I couldn't walk far since I was still connected to the I-V contraption. I was dressed in a regulation hospital gown tied loosely and open in the back. I looked around the area but saw no sign of my clothes. The hospital bed abutted a boarded-up window. I could hear the wail-ing wind battering trees outside and blasts of hard rain striking the plywood like relentless rounds of bullets. The lights in the infirmary ward flickered on and off, powered by an emergency generator.

"Private Halladay?" I heard a calm voice from behind. "I'm Father Donovan. May I come in?"

I turned, instinctively grabbing the flowing hospital gown, folding it behind me.

"Sure," I said.

"I'm in hospitals all the time," the priest smiled. "Those smocks, or whatever they call them, are a joke."

"Pretty useless," I agreed.

Without asking, the priest closed the white plastic curtain separating the cubicle from the rest of the ward. "A little privacy," he said, sitting in the one metal chair as I leaned against the side of the bed. "So how are you feeling?"

"I'm okay."

"Good," Father Donovan said, studying me. "Glad to hear that. Probably a blessing you're here, seeing the infirmary is one of the few places on Eustis with power."

"A blessing? I guess that's one way of putting it."

"I understand you were at Fort Story," the priest probed.

"For one day before we had to evacuate."

"This is one of the worst storms we've had in years. Certainly the most destructive one I've ever seen. I understand Fort Story is getting hit hard."

I was starting to become agitated, knowing that the chaplain was not here to talk about the weather. Sensing my impatience the priest asked, "Is there anything you'd like to discuss? Anything you'd like to get off your chest? You know whatever you tell me is in strict confidence."

"I didn't do anything," I said defiantly, offended by the priest's vague insinuation.

Startled by my directness, the priest backed off. "No one said you did anything wrong, son."

"Then why am I here in the infirmary, and why am I being placed on medical leave when I'm not sick?"

"Well, I'm not your doctor, so I can't address that. But there have been some serious issues raised."

"I didn't do anything wrong."

Sensing that the discussion was not going as he'd hoped, Father Donovan rose from the chair and looked at me benignly. "Well, if you ever need to talk—about anything," he paused, "my door is always open."

"Sure, Father," I said. "I'll keep that in mind."

"And just remember," the chaplain pulled the curtain open, "that we are all God's children, and He made us all in His image. God doesn't make mistakes," the priest hesitated before leaving, "but we do...we all do."

• • •

Cindy rattled the metal meal cart into the ward, stopping at my cubicle. "You gonna eat something this morning, baby?" she called out. "You look skinny as a rail, but kinda cute."

"Maybe some eggs." I sat up.

"Got no eggs today." Cindy looked at the cart, lifting a plastic cover off one of the plates. "Pancakes is what we got here. That's about it. We got no deliveries the last two days."

"Fine," I said, not caring what the girl put down in front of me. I hadn't eaten for the last twenty-four hours and was now hungry.

"Here's some maple syrup," she tossed me two packets, "and a can of apple juice. Sorry it ain't cold. That mean old Edith hurricane cut off our deliveries and we got no power except the generator and the gas stove down there, so we doing the best we can."

"We'll survive," I grinned, sitting cross-legged, biting open a packet of maple syrup and pouring it over the limp pancakes.

"You know, honey, you don't look very sick to me," Cindy observed. "I mean compared to the other guys," she said, rolling her eyes in the direction of the patients in the ward who had limbs in slings and heads bandaged, men wounded in combat and shipped back home to recover and start rehabilitation.

"I'm checking out of here today," I said.

"Good for you, honey." Cindy rolled the cart down the aisle. "Hope they cured whatever was wrong with you, but the rest of us still gonna be stuck here."

I picked at the pancakes soaked in fake maple syrup, then pushed back the arm of the tray table and crumpled the paper napkin into a ball, tossing it on top the uneaten breakfast. I sank back into the hospital bed, closing my eyes.

"Wake up, Halladay," the doctor said, gently shaking my knee. "Time to get up. You're checking out of here," he smiled. "We gave you something to sleep," the doctor explained, "and you responded very well. As I expected, you were exhausted."

"What time is it?" I asked.

"A little after five," the doctor said, looking at his watch.

"You mean I slept all day?" I responded, amazed.

"Right through lunch."

"Jesus," I muttered. "Why didn't you wake me up?"

"You needed rest," the doctor offered. "Power to the rest of the base was only restored a little while ago, so you were better off here. But now you can go back to your barracks. Also, we need the bed," the doctor alluded to the space in the cubicle I was occupying.

"Sure," I said sliding off the bed.

"Here are your fatigues." The doctor waved to an orderly standing behind him with a plastic bag labeled "Patient Belongings" and the name "Halladay" written in large black Magic Marker letters. "They've been laundered, but your boots are still muddy," he indicated as the orderly placed the bag on the bed and set my boots on the floor. "This isn't the Hilton. We don't do shoes."

"Understand," grateful to have my clothes back.

"Looks like we're done here, Halladay," the doctor said, making a notation on his clipboard. "When you're dressed, go to the front entrance and an MP will take you back to your barracks."

"I know where it is," I said.

"Army regulation. All discharged patients have to be escorted from the infirmary to their destination. Just procedure. Don't sweat it."

I opened the plastic bag and pulled out my freshly laundered fatigues.

"You'll be getting orders from your CO," the doctor said. "But for tonight, I'd suggest you go to the commissary and get something good to eat. Not the stuff we serve in here. It's Friday night and a lot of guys will be off for the weekend, so it should be quiet."

"I'll do that," I said, slipping out of the flowing hospital gown and tossing it onto the bed. I found my white boxer shorts in the plastic bag and pulled them up around my waist.

"And remember, Halladay," the doctor said, gazing at me, "you're on medical leave. So don't do anything stupid, like try to leave the base."

"I won't."

"Good luck, kid," the doctor said, proceeding down the ward to other patients as I pulled on my clean fatigues. I crumpled the plastic bag and stashed it into a wastebasket in the hall, then walked to the entrance of the infirmary. An MP was smoking a cigarette and leaning against a jeep parked outside.

"You Halladay?" he asked as I emerged into the soft evening light.

"Yes."

"Get in, and I'll take you to your barracks."

"I can walk."

"Just get in and shut up," the soldier ordered, squashing his cigarette out with his boot. "Soon as I get rid of you, I can take off on my weekend pass."

I got into the open jeep as the MP started the ignition and shifted the vehicle into gear. Tree branches and broken pieces of wood littered the tarred roadway as we navigated over the debris field left by the storm. The jeep's huge rubber tires dug into water-filled potholes, spinning sand and dirty water into spiraling cascades.

"Must have been some storm," I commented, looking at the trash strewn across the base.

"She was a fucking Category 4," the MP muttered as he navigated the littered roadway. "We got a lot of water and wind damage...broken windows and roofs torn off, but nothing like Fort Story."

"What happened there?"

"They got hit with the tidal surge. Wiped the fucking place off the face of the earth."

"We were just evacuated," I said.

"You were down there with those crazies?" the MP turned looking at me.

"I was only there one day. It was pretty intense."

"Fucking insane from what I hear," the soldier said stopping the jeep in front of the barracks. "Here's where you get out and I get off."

I slid out of the jeep, then turning I asked, "There were a couple of guys still in the swamp heading toward the beach," I said referring to the tunnel rat trainees who had not been caught and were not on the bus. "Did they get out?"

"Fuck if I know," the MP shifted the jeep into gear and sped away.

The barracks was practically deserted, only a few guys playing cards in the lounge at the end of the hallway. My room was just as I'd left it, but someone had placed my duffel bag on top of the bunk. I unzipped it and dumped everything onto the cot. Music from the officers' club drifted across the compound as I stretched out on top of the clothes strewn across the thin mattress. The sounds of Johnny Mathis singing "Chances Are" drifted into the barracks from the officers' club as I curled up and fell asleep.

● ● ●

"Halladay…it's for you." The corporal hurled a manila envelope across the room, waking me up. "Orders, so you'd better check it out. Get fucking dressed," he said. "And clean those boots before you leave here."

"Right," I said, groggy, still feeling the effects of the drugs I'd been given in the infirmary. I grabbed my boots, caked with dry mud, found a toothbrush, razor and shaving cream in my toilet kit and headed toward the shower. It was Saturday morning so the barracks was deserted except for the few guys sleeping in, not on leave. I ran hot water in the sink over my boots, melting the dry hardened clay as the molten mess swirled in the basin like brown blood. I banged the heels on the side of the sink to loosen the crud and took wads of toilet paper to wipe the black leather dry. It wasn't a spit-shine, but the boots were clean. I dressed in fresh fatigues and folded the clothes spread out on the bunk, stowing them in my footlocker.

It was a crisp October morning as I headed toward the commissary. A crew of enlisted men raked leaves and debris, loading mounds of trash into the back of a flatbed truck. The mess hall was quiet as I pushed open the screen door and picked up a plastic tray, sliding it down the metal rungs in front of steaming food bins. I sat at an empty table and peeled back the lip on the carton of concentrated orange juice, sticking a straw into the V-shaped opening. I sucked up a long swig of fake juice, then ripped open the sealed manila envelope containing my orders. I read over the official document with my name, rank, date of birth, religion and blood type clearly entered in the boxes on the form. Under the assignment section, the instructions were to report to Captain Oliver's office at zero eight hundred hours on 23 October 1967—that wasn't until Monday.

"Mind if I sit down?"

I looked up to see Jimmy Rodriguez holding a tray in his hands.

"Sure. Join the party."

The boy set his tray on the table, pulling up across from me. He dug into the plate of eggs and pancakes, washing it down with a gulp from a container of milk.

"Looks like we ain't going back to Fort Story," Jimmy said, wiping his lower lip with his sleeve. "The shit hole got wiped out by the fuckin' hurricane," the boy announced triumphantly. "We're all on temporary assignment waiting for new orders."

"Sounds like a dream," I commented.

"We won't have to deal with that maniac LaVern," Jimmy said, stuffing a forkful of grits into his mouth. "You want your clothes back?" he asked belching.

"Keep them," I said. "But do me a favor. Next time you talk to your brother, tell him college boy is doing okay."

"You and Ricky did basic at Fort Jackson?"

"We were in the same unit."

"I heard the DI was a real asshole."

"He was doing his job."

"Ricky said he kept pickin' on this one guy, fucking with him all the time 'cause he was some rich college kid." Jimmy stopped, looked at me, making the connection. "Was that fucking you?"

"Your brother was real decent to me. Even got his ass in trouble when he mouthed off to the DI one day telling him to back off. We both got KP on my birthday," I laughed. "Your brother's all right."

"Wait till I tell him I met you and that you burned up my uniform and held me over a fucking snake pit."

"I didn't hold you over a snake pit." I tried to downplay the horror of what went on at Fort Story. "Besides, that was just war games."

"You got a pretty fucked-up idea of games." Jimmy glared at me.

"It's all part of the exercise to prepare guys for the shit they're going to face in the Cu Chi tunnels."

"But this is here with our own guys, and that LaVern is a fucking wacko."

"He's been over there three times and seen it all. Anyway, didn't you volunteer for tunnel rat assignment?"

"Yeah, I did." Jimmy looked down, pushing his tray to the middle of the table.

"Why?"

"Because I couldn't do nothin' else," Jimmy shot back. "My MOS scores qualified me for no training. I can't spell English or even write a whole fucking sentence or answer any of those stupid questions about a train leaving Chicago and another one from New York and what time they gonna meet. All that stupid shit."

"I hear you."

"And look at me. I'm five feet two and 110 pounds. A scrawny shit with no brains and no muscle." Jimmy stared down at the table.

"Sounds like you'll make a perfect tunnel rat."

"Because nobody gives a rat's ass what happens to me," Jimmy shot up and bolted out of the mess hall, leaving his tray of dirty dishes on the table.

I sat there, sipping lukewarm coffee. I picked up both trays, scraping off cold eggs and grits stuck to the plates, crushing empty milk and orange juice cartons, dumping everything into the plastic garbage container. I stacked dirty dishes and flatware in a plastic bin at the end of the line, and nodded to the woman standing behind the steaming trays of food behind the counter, her apron pulled tight across her belly.

I walked out of the commissary, the manila envelope with orders tucked under my arm. I couldn't leave base since I was on medical leave, but I needed toothpaste and shaving cream so I headed toward the PX. A few Army wives were thumbing through circular display stands offering summer T-shirts, bathing trunks and shorts on hangers at fifty-percent off.

I was holding a can of Gillette shaving foam and a super-speed razor when I looked up across the aisle to face Eddie Arkansas, the corporal who'd given me a ride in his red Mustang convertible. Eddie was dressed in khakis, starched and pressed, his skin aglow against the tan color of his uniform. He was with two sergeants. Eddie and I locked eyes across the aisle of toothpaste and mouthwash, but there was no verbal exchange, just a nod and a faint smile.

I placed my items on the checkout counter, paid and jogged back to the barracks where I changed into shorts and a T-shirt. I had no assignment until Monday morning when I was to report to Captain Oliver. Almost everyone was gone except for guys on detail cleaning up debris from the hurricane. The television was turned on in the lounge outside the shower room, the black and white screen flipping and zigzagging in snowy burps because no one had adjusted the rabbit ears on top of the set. I pressed the off button, putting the speechless beast to sleep. I pulled out the Faulkner paperback tucked under my pillow and set out toward the river. I found my faithful elm tree, the one I'd strapped myself to during the hurricane, and punched the trunk like a lost friend. I plopped down, resting my back against the rough bark. The mothball fleet flotilla bobbed in the choppy waters of the James River, hulls rubbing together, waiting for action.

I opened the pages of the novel, but couldn't concentrate. My mind drifted back to the afternoon when Johnny Nistico and I were lifting weights in his garage, stripped down to our Jockey shorts. We were two horny thirteen-year-old boys playing around—that's all— just like all the other guys. I thumbed the pages of the paperback, then slammed the book into the dirt around the elm tree, thinking, *Why the fuck is this happening to me?*

CHAPTER EIGHTEEN
(October 23–November 21, 1967)

● ● ●

Monday reveille—the recording blasted across Fort Eustis, sending crows screeching into the morning air as men hungover from a weekend at Virginia Beach clutched pillows over their heads.

"All right, you scumbags." The corporal charged into the barracks, flicking the lights on. "Get moving. In case you didn't know it, there's a fucking war going on. So get your sorry ass out of bed and in formation at six hundred hours."

The shower was busy with guys lathering up, flipping towels back and forth at each other.

"So, Halladay, what's your detail?" Tommy Driscoll asked, wiping off next to me.

"Report to Captain Oliver's office at eight hundred hours."

"Sounds like a pussy assignment," he said, pulling the towel between his legs, stroking his balls. "Who'd you have to suck to get that one?"

"Luck, I guess."

"Let me know whose dick I have to suck to get such a cushy-ass assignment."

I ignored the comment and got dressed. My orders indicated I was not required to stand formation in roll call, so I jogged to the commissary where I poured a cup of coffee from the large metal urn and picked a carton of orange juice from the plastic bucket filled with ice. Men lined up in formation outside the mess hall, waiting to report to class or detail for cleanup after the hurricane. I walked across the base to report to Captain Oliver's office in the main administration building. His door was closed, although I could hear voices from within. I took a seat and looked at the round clock on the wall. It was five minutes to eight. I shot to attention, raising my right arm in salute, when the door abruptly opened and Captain Oliver and the base chaplain, Father Donovan, emerged.

"At ease, Halladay," Oliver returned the salute.

"Good morning, sir," I responded automatically.

"You know Father Donovan," the officer gestured.

"Yes, we've met."

"We'll discuss this further." The captain nodded to the priest.

"You're looking fit." Donovan glanced at me.

"I'm fine."

"Glad to hear that," the priest said, tapping me on the arm, then turned and walked down the hall.

"Come in, Halladay," Oliver instructed, shutting the door. "I know the last few months have been tough," he started. "It's tough for all of us. We're in a fucking war that nobody wants to be in—one that a lot of people don't support. Do you know what it's like to march in a veterans' parade and have people spit on you and want to beat you with a baseball bat because you're wearing a uniform?"

I sat in silence.

"Okay, Halladay." Oliver leaned forward. "I've gone out on a limb for you, because I think you're a decent kid and have gotten a lot of shit thrown your way. But this stuff from the Air Force, having Lieutenant Hadley from Langley come in here and make allegations from that fuck-up airman at Fairchild in Spokane… I mean I can't ignore that and look the other way."

"I didn't do anything wrong."

"Maybe not," the captain said, settling into the leather chair behind his desk. "But I can't ignore it, especially since another branch of the service is involved."

"You mean it would have been better if I'd fucked around with an Army GI instead of some Air Force fly boy," I shot back bitterly.

"I know you don't mean that," Oliver said calmly, turning around and staring out the window at crews of enlisted men raking up debris, loading branches and piles of garbage and splintered wood into flatbed trucks. An awkward pause filled the room before he spoke.

"For the time being you will continue functioning as my aide," Captain Oliver said without looking at me, "processing orders for the men moving out. We'll let you know when to appear for the hearing."

"The hearing?" I asked.

"You'll be advised," the captain said, indicating the discussion was terminated.

"Yes, sir," I stood up, saluting. I settled back at my desk in the antechamber outside Captain Oliver's office and started thumbing through a stack of folders. It was as if nothing had changed.

For the next few weeks I processed paperwork for men moving out of T-School on to their next assignment. I knew as I typed the forms that I was issuing one-way tickets to young guys who would not come home, except maybe as a memory in a box with stones and sand bags and a photograph inside. Every Friday, I drove the Captain's Camaro to the motor pool to get it washed and filled with gas.

"You Oliver's squeeze this weekend?" the GI teased as I pulled the car up to the pump.

"Just fill it up," I said annoyed.

"Oh, we got a live one here," the soldier smirked as he unhitched the nozzle from the stand and started to pump gas. "You going off to Virginia Beach this weekend with Miss Mike?"

"Funny," I shot back, dismissing the comment.

I fell into the routine of my assignment, feeling more like I was working in a clerical position at an insurance agency than a member of the armed services. I reported to my desk Monday through Friday, plowed through heaps of paperwork, and processed orders. I had weekend passes, but did not leave base. I was tempted to check out the bar scene in Norfolk where I heard a lot of gay sailors hung out on weekends, but I was terrified of getting caught in a raid. I had little interaction with other soldiers on base, and had no buddies to hang out with. I ate alone in the mess hall and spent free time on weekends reading under the elm tree overlooking the James River.

It was the week before Thanksgiving when, thumbing through the stack of manila folders on my desk, I opened one and started entering the information on the transfer form. It was for James Rodriguez being shipped to Schofield Barracks outside Honolulu. I froze and withdrew my fingers from the keyboard. I was typing orders to send Razor's brother to advanced training as a tunnel rat. Playing war games at Fort Story was one thing, but this was real, one step away from being deployed to Cu Chi. By typing and processing the order, I was surely issuing a death sentence to the kid brother of my battle buddy from basic training.

"You okay, Halladay?" Captain Oliver asked, looking at me staring at the typewriter.

"Yes, sir," I mumbled.

"Leave that for now," he said, "and come into my office."

"Yes, sir," I slid back on the chair, leaving Jimmy Rodriguez's orders in the typewriter.

"You know Chaplain Donovan and you've met Lieutenant Hadley from Langley," the captain said, shutting the door. The priest and Air Force officer must have arrived while I was at lunch.

"Yes, sir," I answered.

"Take a seat, Halladay," Captain Oliver nodded. "We'll try to make this as easy as possible."

Lieutenant Hadley began, his arms folded across his chest. "You've previously acknowledged that you know John Nistico."

"We went to the same school," I said. "Assumption in Westport."

"And you were friends?" the lieutenant repeated.

"I knew him."

"Well, according to Mr. Nistico it was more than friends." The Air Force officer let the insinuation float in the stuffy office. Lieutenant Hadley went on to read a report that John Nistico had been caught in the bathroom of a Greyhound bus station in Spokane, having solicited sex from an undercover policeman while sitting in a stall with his pants down and his penis exposed. He was arrested and taken into custody. When the local police discovered Nistico was stationed at Fairchild Air Base, they turned him over to the military.

"We have men assigned to flush out this deviant behavior, trained to find perverts and weed them out, make sure they don't infiltrate our ranks," Hadley said proudly. "Imagine what that could do to morale, our men knowing that queers and cocksuckers were out there in combat, in close quarters, dug into foxholes and sleeping in the same tents. The military is no place for that kind of disgusting, anti-Christian debauchery."

I gritted my teeth, glaring at the Air Force officer, trying to reconcile in my mind how a bunch of soldiers playing strip poker and jerking off on a deck of cards was any different.

"We're all aware of the military's position on this issue," Oliver interjected. "Just get on with it."

Hadley went on to report that John Nistico had been cooperating with the investigation and naming other homosexuals who he knew were currently serving in the military.

"Here is a copy of his sworn testimony." The Air Force officer pushed a file across the desk to Captain Oliver. "He identified you as a sex partner."

"That's crazy," I responded. "We went to grammar school together."

"Are you saying that John Nistico lied? That he gave a false statement under oath? That you two were not queer together?" Hadley glared at me.

I was shaking, feeling attacked and threatened, when Father Donovan stepped in. "Tim, it will be better for everyone if you just tell the truth. God is your only judge."

I looked at the three men. "Johnny and I went to Assumption School from first grade on. Other kids made fun of him because he was fat and had bad skin, pimples and acne on his face."

"But you didn't make fun of him?" Hadley pressed.

"He was okay. Our family used to go to their restaurant on Friday nights for pizza."

"So your family knew Nistico's parents?" Hadley asked.

"My dad knows everyone in Westport," I shot back defensively.

"Where is this going?" Captain Oliver broke in. "What has this got to do with the question at hand?"

"Just trying to get a clear picture of the relationship between Private Halladay and John Nistico."

"Well, I think it's obvious that the boys knew each other and were friends," Oliver offered.

"We've established that, but the question is, how close and what kind of friendship was that?" Hadley insinuated. "Now let me ask you again, Private Halladay. Did you and John Nistico have a homosexual relationship?"

I looked up, sensing anything I said would be twisted and held against me. "Johnny and I were friends."

"So are you telling us there was never anything more than that?" the Air Force officer sneered.

I sat on the edge of my chair, feeling the world closing in. "There was one day," I started, looking back and forth at the men hovering around me.

"Yes, this one day?" Hadley leaned forward.

"Johnny and I were working out in his garage, lifting weights. It was hot and we both stripped down to our shorts."

"And?" Hadley probed.

"We were both sweaty after working out and flexing our muscles when Johnny started rubbing himself under his shorts."

"And what did you do?" Hadley pressed.

"I just laughed. I told him he was a perv."

"But it went on, didn't it?"

"He said we should jerk off together…that's what guys did in the shower after gym."

"And you went along?"

"It was kind of crazy, but we were just fooling around."

"I think we're done here," Hadley placed the file on the desk.

"Thank you." Oliver escorted the Air Force officer to the door. "There's a jeep waiting to take you back to Langley."

"Come over and we'll play eighteen. It's a pretty tough course at Langley. What's your handicap?"

"We'll see," Oliver returned. "Things are pretty busy here right now."

"The Army's always welcome to come over and get its ass whipped by us Fly Boys," Hadley smiled as he exited the building.

Oliver returned and signaled to the chaplain. "Let me have a few minutes with Private Halladay."

The chaplain stood and backed out of the room. "Remember, son, my door is always open, any time, if you need to talk."

"Sure, Father," I said, biting my lip.

The door closed and Oliver sat behind his desk. An awkward silence hung over the room before he spoke. "I know this is difficult for you, for all of us."

"I didn't do anything wrong."

"Maybe not," Oliver interrupted, "but the Army is very clear on these matters."

"Clear?"

"We're in a war, and there is no tolerance for homosexual behavior in our ranks. It could undermine the morale and confidence of our men."

"Yeah, right," I muttered flippantly.

"You have a problem with that?" Oliver challenged.

I did not respond, thinking about guys jerking off in the showers, the strip poker games, LaVern raping a naked prisoner—I guess that behavior was acceptable and normal under Army regulations.

"It's been decided that in everyone's best interest, the military and yours, that you leave the service." The words fell like a cinder block crashing to the floor in Captain Oliver's office.

"What?" I said astounded. "What do you mean, leave?"

"I've signed orders for your discharge effective tomorrow."

I was dumbfounded. I could not believe what I was hearing.

"But I don't want to leave."

"You can protest and ask for a hearing," Oliver offered. "It's your right, but I would not advise taking that route."

"But I don't want to leave."

"Look, son." Oliver leaned across the desk. "It would be a court martial and you'd never win. Do yourself, and all of us, a favor and just leave quietly."

"But I didn't do anything wrong."

"That's not how the system works."

Oliver explained that I would be given a General Discharge, not dishonorable, although I would not be entitled to benefits. Records would show that I had served in the military, but had been released. It would only become an issue if I chose to run for elected office in the future, where the terms of my dismissal could be made public. Other than that, I could claim I had been released for asthma.

"Asthma!"

"You want a better excuse?"

"What! Is asthma the new queer?" I said bitterly.

"Take what you can get, soldier. Be thankful you're not in the brig."

"For doing what you and all the other guys do? You're all such asshole hypocrites." I bolted for the door, then turned. "And I hope your next boy-toy gets your Camaro gassed up and washed with no water spots."

"You're dismissed, Halladay."

"I know." I saluted bitterly and stormed out the door.

CHAPTER NINETEEN
(November 22--November 23, 1967)

● ● ●

I packed my duffel bag with the few civilian clothes I had. Reveille sounded, blaring across Fort Eustis—the last time I would hear it. The other soldiers treated me as if I weren't there. News travels fast on an Army base. The MP yelled from the entrance to the barracks, "Halladay, you ready to move out?"

"In a minute," I answered, looking around the cubicle to make sure I'd left nothing behind, nothing to suggest I'd ever been there.

"Your final orders," the MP said, tossing me a manila folder. "Discharge papers and bus tickets are inside. Get a move on, kid. I'm taking you to the Greyhound station in Williamsburg. After that you're on your own…back to civilian life."

"Great," I mumbled.

"Fuck, a lot of us wish we had your ticket out of this hole," the MP said, moving toward the jeep.

"Right." I looked around the sad, empty room. Tommy Driscoll was nowhere in sight and had not slept on the lower bunk.

"You have time for breakfast," the MP said, looking at his watch. "If you eat quick."

"You hungry this morning?" the woman behind the counter asked, holding two serving spoons.

"Some scrambled eggs."

She scooped a glob of browned clotted eggs onto my plate. "Anything else?"

I looked at the slop on the plate, resisting the urge to hurl the tray onto the floor. "No. That's all." It wasn't her fault.

"How come you here so early by yourself?"

"I'm moving out," I said.

"On the day before Thanksgiving?"

"Yeah…a special assignment."

"Must be somethin' real special, 'cause nobody gets shipped out the day before Thanksgiving."

"High priority assignment."

"And I thought you and I was goin' to find the wishbone in the turkey and pull to see who gets a wish."

"Maybe next year." I faked a smile.

"No, honey. They won't be no next year. I know. I been here a long time. It don't happen that way," she said, slapping the spoons on the side of the metal food bin. "It don't happen that way."

I slid my tray off the ramp and took a seat at an empty table. I looked around the mess hall, knowing this would be the last time I'd be here. I poked at the scrambled eggs and took a sip of coffee.

"You ready, Halladay?" the MP hollered across the room.

"Ready to go." I pushed back from the table, dumping my uneaten breakfast into the plastic garbage can by the door.

"Happy Thanksgiving, kid, wherever you going," the woman called out behind the counter.

"You too." I waved, wondering what kind of Thanksgiving she would have.

The jeep was waiting. No send-off. No farewell. No good luck for the future—just a clear November morning.

"So how did you get off?" the driver asked as we cleared the entrance of the Army installation and turned onto the back road toward Williamsburg.

"Asthma," I said dismissively, hoping to end the conversation.

"Wish I was so lucky," the MP said, lighting a cigarette.

"Don't wish it on yourself," I said, looking out over the pastures of Lee Hall Farm and the railroad tracks separating the highway from the plantation. A lone cow stuck her head through the wood rail fence and gazed at me riding in the passenger seat of the jeep, looking at me with her sad brown eyes.

We drove without speaking. I remembered walking down the same country road a few weeks ago and Orleane, who gave me a ride in her pickup truck and offered a blowjob at the Texaco station. I laughed out loud thinking of that crazy experience.

"You okay, Halladay?" the driver asked, looking at me.

"I'm fine," I smiled, staring out the jeep. "Just fine."

"I'm taking you to the bus station. Then you're on your own," the MP said, taking a draw on his cigarette.

"I can handle myself. I know the area," I said as the capitol building at the end of Duke of Gloucester Street emerged through the treetops.

The jeep circled the historic district where no vehicles were allowed and pulled up in front of the bus station. "End of the line," the MP announced. "Hope that asthma clears up."

"Yeah," I said as the jeep pulled away from the curb. It was just after nine, and the Richmond local would not come for another hour. I was tempted to walk past the Wren Building and through the Sunken Garden on campus only a block away, but I was dressed in green fatigues, a symbol many students and professors held in contempt, so I decided to pass time in the dingy bus terminal.

I pulled out the travel documents: bus tickets from Williamsburg to Richmond, a transfer to DC and then on to the Port Authority in New York. There was a separate ticket connecting to New Haven where I'd begun this odyssey in July. I entered the waiting room and dropped my duffel bag on a broken pale blue plastic seat. The station was crowded with students sprawled out on the floor, leaning against rolled-up sleeping bags, waiting to leave for the Thanksgiving holiday.

I walked to the water fountain and twisted the metal faucet where a weak trickle oozed out of the spigot. The basin was slimy with mold. An old black man sitting nearby coughed and spat out a wad of chewing tobacco into a folded white handkerchief. I backed away, sensing the man's disdain, then looked up and noticed I'd been drinking from the water fountain labeled "Colored."

The bus hissed to a stop at the curb as people scrambled to collect their belongings. I stood in line, pretending to be invisible. The bus driver pulled my ticket and I boarded, taking a window seat in the rear. Although the bus was almost full, no one sat down next to me; I was the only soldier on board, the only one in a conspicuous green uniform.

The accordion door flapped shut, and the bus moved out of the station onto Richmond Road, heading north, passing the low brick walls defining the campus boundaries. Limbs of hundred-year-old magnolia trees sagged, dropping big elephant-ear leaves onto the mossy brick walkways. A line of students stood outside the Colonial

Deli, queuing up for coffee and bagels. Images slipped by like an unwinding roll of Kodak film as the bus chugged on. I fell back into the seat and closed my eyes, longing to be curled up on the back seat of my grandfather's Ford driving up Route 7 to the family farm in Vermont. Outside, the two-lane highway slipped by. Stuckey's roadside restaurant offering shakes, burgers and pecan pie faded into the distance as the bus took me farther away from the college campus and my short time at Fort Eustis.

An hour later the driver called out, "Richmond," as the bus lurched to a stop. "Transfer here for all points north."

The terminal was buzzing with people traveling for the Thanksgiving holiday. I checked the departure board and saw that the Washington/New York bus was leaving on schedule at noon, an hour away. I popped a quarter into a vending machine and retrieved a Coke, leaning against the wall outside the men's room, straddling my duffel bag between my feet. A well-dressed man in a pinstripe suit and bow tie approached. "I'm so proud what you're doing for our country."

"Thanks," I said automatically.

"God bless you, son. No matter what anybody says, we all have a lot to be thankful for…because of men like you." He turned and disappeared into the busy terminal.

I crumpled the soda can and tossed it into a trash container. Long lines of travelers, some sitting on suitcases, others resting against rolled-up sleeping bags, snaked around the entrance to the boarding gate.

A muffled announcement came across the intercom system, indicating the Northeaster Flyer, express service to Washington and New York, was ready for boarding. I inched forward along with other passengers and boarded the bus. I took a window seat and stowed my duffel bag in the overhead rack.

"Mind if I join you?"

I looked up to see the man in the pinstripe suit and bow tie preparing to settle into the aisle seat next to me.

"Sure," I answered inching toward the window.

"Looks like a full load," he said, removing his suit jacket, folding it neatly atop a small suitcase overhead. "The worst day of the year to travel," he commented, sitting down.

The bus pulled out of the terminal, wound its way through Richmond traffic before heading up the I-95 north onramp. The driver shifted into high gear and picked up speed on the busy thruway.

"Want a section of the paper?" the man asked, unfolding a copy of the *Richmond Times-Dispatch*.

"Thanks," I said, hoping if I got engrossed in the newspaper I wouldn't have to carry on a conversation.

"Hard to believe it's been four years," the man said referring to the front-page headline, *JFK Remembered*.

"My name is Ellis. John Ellis," the man said, handing me the sports and entertainment sections.

"I'm Tim Halladay," I said accepting the paper.

"Nice to meet you. How far you going?"

"New York and then up to Connecticut."

"I'm going to the city for Thanksgiving with my sister, her husband and the new baby. Ugh! A screaming six-month-old, and turkey dinner on the upper West Side," he laughed. "Why am I doing this?"

"I'm sure they'll be happy to see you."

"I'm thinking I should have stayed in Charlottesville," Ellis said, leaning back in his seat, folding the paper on his lap.

The bus inched along the highway in bumper-to-bumper traffic, jerking and braking, making it uncomfortable for any passenger who wanted to sleep or read.

"How long have you been in the Army?" Ellis broke the silence.

"Since July," I answered. "I was drafted right after I graduated."

"That's a bummer. Where did you go to school?"

"William & Mary," I volunteered, being more open than I intended.

"I teach at UVA. Freshman English."

"You look the part," I smiled. "I mean the bow tie and everything."

"Guess I'm pretty obvious," Ellis said, bumping his knee against my right leg in the cramped seat as the bus crawled on the slow-moving thruway.

"What's it like being in the Army?"

"I'd rather not talk about it." I withdrew, looking out the window at the endless stream of traffic on I-95. I pretended to doze off as the professor rattled pages of the newspaper, folding it in half, and then again in quarters, seeming to read every word.

It was late afternoon and the sun was setting behind the Virginia suburbs when John Ellis tapped me on the arm.

"Looks like we're coming into D.C."

I sat up in the seat and looked out the window. "Seems to be taking forever."

"Probably the worst day of the year to travel," Ellis repeated, eager to make contact again. The bus pulled into the Washington terminal and came to a jerking stop, brakes hissing as the front door unfolded.

"We have a half-hour stop here for you folks continuing on to New York," the bus driver announced. "You can get off, make a pit stop, stretch your legs and get something to eat, but be back at 5:30," the driver advised, looking at his watch. "Don't be late. We're moving out of here right on the dot. Traffic's gonna be a bitch and we're already running late."

"Getting off?" Ellis asked standing up in the aisle.

"I need to stretch," I said, easing my way out of the seat and brushing by the professor.

"After you," Ellis said following me and the other disembarking passengers.

"I need to hit the men's room." I broke away and headed toward the bathroom. Inside, I locked myself into a sleazy, graffiti-covered stall and sat on a broken plastic toilet seat, releasing a long, protracted stream of piss into the slimy toilet bowl. I stood up and kicked the flush lever with my boot and buttoned up my fatigues. Splashing a wave of cold water on my face, I looked into the cracked mirror over the sink to see the reflection of a young soldier in uniform. I thought I had done the right thing by accepting my fate and not resisting the draft. I wondered now if I had been just trying to fool myself—that being gay and being in the Army could actually work—telling myself I was as qualified to serve my country as the next guy.

In the deli concession off the waiting room, I bought a ham and cheese sandwich, a can of ginger ale and a bag of M&Ms—my dinner for the long bus ride to New York.

"Looks good," came a familiar voice as I turned around to see John Ellis standing behind me in line.

"Real gourmet," I laughed, handing the cashier a five-dollar bill.

"See you back on the bus," the professor smiled, holding a bag of ice cubes, some Styrofoam cups and a large bottle of club soda.

I settled back into the window seat I'd occupied from Richmond. A few minutes later John Ellis sat down next to me.

"This is the Express to Port Authority in New York City," the bus driver announced. "Anybody not going there better get off now, 'cause we ain't stopping along the way." The driver looked around, satisfied everyone on board was headed to the same destination. "Okay, folks, get comfortable. I'll get you there as soon as I can." He folded the door shut and switched off the cabin lights as the bus eased its way into the gnarl of Washington rush-hour traffic.

I unwrapped my deli sandwich and folded the paper bag across my lap. I bit open packets of mayonnaise and mustard, spreading condiments across the slabs of dry meat with a small white plastic knife that came with the paper napkin. I pressed the stale white bread across the mess and popped open the tab on the ginger ale.

"Looks like you could use some refreshment," Ellis smiled, looking at the dismal mess I had spread out on my lap.

"Not exactly what Mom would have fixed."

"Well, maybe some mother's milk will help," Ellis grinned, pulling a pint of Jack Daniels out of the brown bag he was cradling between his legs.

"Can we do this?" I asked looking around.

"What are they going to do? Put us off on the New Jersey Turnpike?" Ellis laughed. "Let me sweeten that." He leaned over, carefully pouring a swig from the pint into the opened soft drink. "Cheers!"

"Cheers," I returned, sipping the spiked ginger ale, then grimacing at the harsh taste.

Ellis smiled and handed me a plastic cup with ice. "Put it in here and it'll taste better."

I took the cup and poured my drink over the ice cubes.

"Let me top it off," the professor said, pouring another generous shot of Jack Daniels.

"That tastes better." I toasted my traveling companion.

I took a couple of bites of the tasteless sandwich, trying to balance it between the plastic cup in my other hand as the bus jerked and braked in the heavy traffic.

"Can you hold this for me?" I asked, handing Ellis my drink. "I'm through with this." I folded the half-eaten sandwich into the paper bag and rolled the mess into a ball. "Thanks," I said, stuffing the trash under the seat in front of me.

The bus rolled on, entering New Jersey Turnpike after crossing the Delaware Bridge. I looked out the window, watching white traffic lines on the pavement rhythmically disappear under the over-sized bus tires.

"You falling asleep on me?" The professor gently prodded my arm.

"It's been a long day," I responded, stretching in the cramped seat.

"Have a nightcap," Ellis offered, pouring another splash of Jack Daniels onto the melting ice cubes in my cup. "Should help you sleep."

I took a long sip of whiskey and settled back into the seat. I must have been sleeping a long time when the bus slammed to an abrupt stop, hurling me off the seat.

"What the fuck?' I said pulling myself off the floorboards, the melted ice cubes splattered over my pants.

"You okay?" John Ellis asked helping me back into the seat.

"What happened?"

"Sorry, folks," the bus driver turned around, switching on the cabin lights. "Had a loose German shepherd on the highway and didn't want to be the one to run him over. Not on Thanksgiving. Hope everyone's okay. We're just outside Newark, New Jersey…depending on traffic, about another hour to Port Authority," he said, looking at his watch. "But then there may be delays from all those balloons that'll be going through the tunnel."

"Balloons?" I asked.

"The Macy's Thanksgiving Day parade," Ellis said. "Most of the big balloons, like Snoopy and Mickey Mouse, are made out here in New Jersey, somewhere in Secaucus. They load them up on flatbeds, haul them into Manhattan through the tunnel in the middle of the night, and blow the things up near my sister's apartment on Amsterdam Avenue."

"You were right about it being the worst day to travel," I said, looking out into gridlock traffic. The bus passed Newark Airport and proceeded up an arching bridge over swamplands and railroad tracks, on its approach to the Lincoln Tunnel. The New York City skyline loomed on the horizon through a persistent rain.

"What time is it?" I asked the professor.

"Just after four," Ellis said looking at his watch.

"You've got to be kidding," I said, sitting up in my seat.

"You had a good sleep," Ellis commented. "Slept like a baby after that last drink. You must have been really tired."

"I thought we'd be in New York way before now."

"Accidents, traffic, dogs, rain…all kinds of problems on the turnpike," Ellis shrugged. "So much for home for the holidays."

I looked out the bus window at the Manhattan skyline, the Empire State Building illuminated in the middle of the island.

"Where you spending Thanksgiving?" Ellis asked.

"My family's in Connecticut," I answered vaguely. "But they don't know I'm coming. It's kind of last minute."

"You're welcome to come have Thanksgiving with my sister, brother-in-law, and a screaming six-month-old kid, on the upper West Side. We can watch the Macy's people blow up balloons in front of the entrance to the building."

"My mom would freak out if she knew I was in the city and didn't call."

"You said they didn't know you were coming," Ellis challenged.

"They'd find out some way."

"Whatever," he said letting the offer drift.

The moldy tiles of Lincoln Tunnel and the harsh fluorescent lights above blinked in cadence to the bus as we emerged from under the Hudson River and arrived at the Port Authority Terminal.

"You heading uptown?" Ellis asked as we moved with the crowd through the terminal.

"Walking over to Grand Central to catch a train to Connecticut." I had decided to dump the Army-issued bus ticket and instead take the commuter train to Westport.

"You're welcome for Thanksgiving with my sister. She would shit if I brought a hunk like you home."

"You're a nice person," I said, tapping John Ellis on the arm. "Have a fun stay with your family."

"You too, kid," he said, turning to descend worn tile stairs to the platform for the uptown local.

I slipped the duffel bag over my shoulder and passed through the turnstile to exit on 39th Street. It was raining lightly, and wooden police barricades had been erected along the parade route. Scores of people bundled in ski outfits and hand-knit mittens were lined up, waiting for the floats and balloons, waiting to clap for cheerleaders from Iowa in short skirts twirling batons, grinning glaciers of white teeth into TV cameras for their few minutes of fame.

I pulled out my flight jacket, wrapping it around me as I walked uptown on Ninth Avenue. I turned right at 45th Street and walked under a ladder with a man posting a sign over the Martin Beck Theatre—"Holiday Matinee Today." *Hallelujah, Baby*, starring Leslie Uggams, was playing. The wooden sign hanging from the marquee waved back and forth in the wind and intermittent rain.

I crossed Eighth Avenue, heading up 44th Street past the St. James Theatre and Sardi's restaurant, a handwritten sign taped on the door indicating reservations for Thanksgiving dinner were fully booked. I pushed past wooden police barricades lining Times Square where early crowds were gathered to watch the parade. Rain started pounding steadily as I passed the Algonquin Hotel and Harvard Club on my way to Grand Central Station. I was drenched by the time I reached the Vanderbilt Avenue entrance to the terminal. A gypsy woman sat cross-legged on a fake Oriental carpet, peeling limp petals off rose blossoms, offering stems for twenty-five cents. I pushed through window-paned glass doors, stopping at the marble stairs overlooking the waiting room below. A giant Kodak screen towered at the far end of the cavernous terminal, flashing brilliant color pictures of skiers sailing over moguls at Killington, horse-driven sleds of cozy families crossing wood-covered bridges in Vermont, hugging German shepherd puppies. I looked at the people in the color photos—they had no idea what was going on in the tunnels of Cu Chi halfway around the world.

The clock above the kiosk in the center of the terminal read a minute after seven o'clock. Long shafts of soft light, filtered by the rain, streamed in through upper windows of Grand Central, creating the feeling of a majestic cathedral—not a transient rail terminal. I stretched out on a wooden bench, resting on my duffel bag, looking up at the mural of constellations in the domed ceiling as I dozed off.

"You can't sleep here, soldier," the officer said prodding me with his wooden baton.

"What?" I sat up startled.

"You gotta move on," the officer said tapping my boots. "Can't hang out here all day."

"I'm just waiting for a train."

"Better get a move on," the officer said. "No reason for you to spend Thanksgiving in Grand Central."

The large watch-clock over the kiosk in the center of the terminal read ten past eight. I'd just missed the 8:07 local to New Haven stopping in Westport. The next train would not leave for another two hours due to a reduced schedule for the holiday.

There was a short line at the Chock full o' Nuts coffee concession where I waited, placing an order when my turn came up. "Small black coffee."

"Sure that's all you want, honey?" the young girl with large tits bulging out of the top of her apron flirted.

"That's it."

She returned, placing a plastic lid over the cup of steaming coffee. "No charge for you, baby," she winked. "You've already done enough."

"Thanks," I said, aware I was in uniform as I dropped a quarter into the tip jar on the counter. I returned to a bench in the waiting room and picked up a discarded copy of *The New York Times*. On the front page was a picture of the Eternal Flame in Arlington with a headline, "Four Years—Forever Remembered." I flipped through the paper while sipping the strong coffee. Full pages with photos of college students protesting the war faced the list of names of young men who'd been killed in action. I read the paper as hundreds of people brushed by loaded down with shopping bags from Balducci's and flowers wrapped in newspaper—all probably on their way to visit family and friends for the holiday.

A muffled announcement came across the cavernous waiting room—the 10:07 local for New Haven was boarding at gate seventeen. I folded the newspaper and squashed the Styrofoam coffee cup, stuffing everything into a garbage receptacle outside the boarding gate. I moved down the dark, piss-stained concrete ramp to the train and hopped onto the last car with a horde of other scrambling passengers. I settled into a seat facing backwards out of the terminal as the doors shut and the train inched forward, squealing and winding through the dark tunnel under the city streets, finally emerging into Harlem, stopping at 125th Street where frustrated passengers pushed onto the hot and crowded train. I removed my duffel bag from the seat next to me, and nodded to a heavyset woman struggling through the aisle, to sit down.

"Thank you, son," she said, parking her large body into the seat next to me. "You a real gentleman," she smiled.

I pulled up next to the window clutching the duffel bag resting on my lap.

"And serving your country too," she said, wiggling back and forth in the seat trying to get comfortable. The woman was dressed as if going to church: a small red pillbox hat perched on her tightly curled hair with a few streaks of gray; her maroon dress with large pearl buttons hugged her round body; nylon stockings rolled up just below her knees stretched from her clunky black shoes. She clutched a large patent-leather purse on her lap, and hummed back and forth with the rhythm of the train.

"You goin' home for Thanksgiving?" She turned to me, as the train crossed the trestle bridge over the East River.

"Yes," I answered.

"I'm gonna see my daughter in Bridgeport," the woman announced proudly. "And my new little baby granddaughter who's just three months old. Imagine me a grandma again," she beamed, closing her eyes and humming softly.

"All tickets," the conductor announced, pushing open the door between the rail cars. He maneuvered down the crowded aisle where people were sitting on suitcases and leaning against seats crammed with packages and luggage. He punched tickets with his small metal clicker and placed different colored stubs on the seat backs, indicating final destinations.

"Stamford will be the first stop. This train stops at all stations after that. Change in Norwalk for Wilton and Danbury," he called out as he edged down the aisle.

I looked out the dirty window streaked with small rain rivers. Abandoned factory buildings with broken windows and repair shops crammed with skeletons of mangled car frames next to mounds of old tires passed by as the train headed out of the city to suburbia. The train slowed to pass through Port Chester station; the Life Saver building with oversized metal rolls of multi-colored candy attached to the façade loomed alongside the tracks. It was across the railroad station parking lot, at Vahsan's Tavern, where I hung out with my buddies from Fairfield Prep, driving across the border from Connecticut on Friday nights to drink beer and Singapore Slings with our dates before heading back to park at Compo Beach and make out with willing Catholic girls.

We crossed into Connecticut, and I immediately sensed the change; the trees, Queen Anne's lace and poison sumac growing wild along the railroad tracks looked greener and more opulent. The train lurched to a stop at the Stamford station and crowds of people got off.

From there the train stopped at every station and rail crossing, even places like Noroton Heights. As the train left the South Norwalk station and crossed the bridge spanning Norwalk River, I could see the door to the fire escape on the three-story building of the Michael Richards Dance Studio. The door was open, but the space looked empty.

"Westport and Saugatuck, next stop," the conductor announced as he moved through the now half-empty compartment.

"My stop," I said standing up and stepping across the grandmother who had been humming to herself and clutching her large patent-leather purse since leaving the 125th Street Station.

"God bless you, son," she said touching my arm. "We so proud of you. And I know your mamma and poppy are real proud of you too."

"Right," I said, grabbing my duffel bag and stepping into the aisle to exit the train. "Have a happy Thanksgiving with your new grand-child."

"Bless you, young man," she smiled.

People got off and were met by relatives and friends in station wagons with barking dogs in the back. I crossed the tunnel under the tracks to the Westbound New York side, amazed to see lights on and people inside Mario's.

"You're open," I said, pushing through the storm door that had been erected over the two-step entrance in anticipation of nasty win-ter weather.

"Yeah," Tommy said, wiping a wet towel across the wooden bar. "We're kind of public service for people who got nowhere to go today. Like, I can watch football here or at home. What do I care?"

"Great," I smiled, slipping out of my flight jacket and draping it over a barstool.

"What'll it be, kid?" Tommy asked, sizing me up, taking note of the green fatigues.

"Bloody Mary," I said, turning to see who else was there: a couple smoking cigarettes and engrossed in an intimate conversation at the end of the bar—two upright martini glasses in front of them.

"You're Pete Halladay's kid," Tommy said, putting a tall Bloody Mary down on the bar in front of me.

"My dad and I used to come in here for lunch."

"I know," Tommy said. "Good man, your dad—one of the real down-to-earth Westporters. Not like a lot of the phonies who've moved into town."

"I guess," I said, sipping the spicy drink.

"Home for the holidays?" Tommy asked, continuing to wipe down the bar. "Bet your mom and dad will be happy to see you. They must be real proud."

The TV over the bar was on; Macy's parade was pressing on through the inclement weather, high-school baton twirlers from Indiana with plastic bags over teased hair were doing their best to stay in sync to the canned John Phillips Sousa music pumping out over Herald Square.

"Is there a pay phone?"

"In the back, by the restrooms," Tommy directed. "You need to make a call?"

"I probably should," I said. "You know if Nistico's is open today?"

"What? You like their food better than here?" Tommy raised his eyebrows.

"No. I just wondered. I went to school with Johnny and thought I might look him up while I'm home."

"I wouldn't," Tommy said. "You don't wanna go there."

"What do you mean?"

"Like I said...you don't wanna go there," Tommy stared at me, moving to pour another shaker of martinis for the couple sitting at the end of the bar. "Not sure you know, but Johnny got kicked out of the Air Force for some bad shit. Like. really perverted stuff, from what I hear," Tommy winked.

"I didn't know," I said feeling my stomach turn.

"When he got home," Tommy leaned forward and whispered, "some of the guys at Staples beat the shit out of Johnny one night when he was emptying garbage into the dumpster behind the restaurant. Beat the fuckin' shit out of him with a baseball bat."

"Why?" I ask horrified.

"Heard he got some other service guys into trouble trying to get himself off. Sounds like the fuckin' scumbag deserved it."

"Holy shit."

"He was in Norwalk Hospital with broken ribs, and I think they said he lost an eye. I don't know, but it was pretty bad," Tommy smirked as he wiped the bar.

"Did they catch the guys who did it?"

"Are you kidding?" Tommy said, leaning forward to whisper into my ear. "These guys did the town a fuckin' public service."

I took a sip of the Bloody Mary. "The phone in the back?"

"Next to the men's room," Tommy nodded. "Nistico said we could take in all the losers today who had nowhere to go, while those fat fuckheads sit home eatin' turkey and lasagna, watching football games. Ask me, I'd rather be here."

The TV over the bar was broadcasting the parade, the sound turned down low. Snoopy was entering Herald Square, an army of department-store employees struggling to keep the guy wires from ripping out of their hands and sending the giant beagle balloon into the stormy skies over Manhattan.

I stared at the pay phone outside the men's room. I pictured Mom in the kitchen chopping celery and onions, sautéing mushrooms in a swirling stick of butter before mixing in Pepperidge Farm stuffing crumbs, an eggnog sweetened with a shot of bourbon and a dash of nutmeg on the kitchen counter at arm's length. Every year she got up at dawn to prepare the turkey, sweet potato pudding, creamed onions, homemade cranberry sauce, deviled eggs and stuffed celery stalks—a lavish feast for the family. By the time everyone sat down at the dining room table late in the afternoon, Mom was in her wing-back chair, dozing off with her knitting bag at her feet, clutching the filmy eggnog glass that had become straight bourbon as the day wore on.

I slipped a dime into the coin slot and dialed the familiar number.

"Hello," Mom answered, clearing her throat.

"Hi, there. It's me."

"Tim! What a surprise. How nice of you to call on Thanksgiving."

"I'm here, mom," I said biting my lip.

"Here?" she said confused.

"I'm in Westport," I pressed on. "I'm at Mario's by the railroad station."

"What," she stammered not understanding. "You're here in Westport?"

"Yes."

"Why didn't you tell us you were coming home?"

"It was kind of sudden." I dogged the question. "Thought I'd surprise you."

"Well you certainly did. Your sister is here; she can come pick you up. We're having turkey at home. It was just going to be the three of us and now you're here. How wonderful! What a wonderful surprise!" she gushed.

"I'll be waiting outside Mario's," I said, fumbling with the coiled metal phone cord on the receiver.

"Did they give you leave?"

"Yeah, mom. They gave me leave."

I took a last sip of the Bloody Mary, looking up at the TV monitor over the bar.

"Another?" Tommy asked.

"No, I better not. My sister's coming to pick me up," I answered, sliding a ten-dollar bill across the bar.

"On the house," Tommy said.

I stood outside Mario's. Rain trickled down across my forehead while the TV monitor inside flashed images of a giant green Kermit Frog balloon. Cheerleaders from Teddy Roosevelt High School in Cleveland, plastic bags covering their heads, shook drenched green and white pom-poms that looked like sad kitchen mops, as the band following played "It Ain't Easy Being Green."

AFTERWORD

● ● ●

On February 28, 1994, the Department of Defense Directive 1,304.26 took effect.

The "Don't Ask, Don't Tell" (DADT) policy signed by President Bill Clinton became the official government policy dealing with gays, bisexuals and lesbians in the military. Transgendered people were not even on the radar screen, nor were they recognized as existing. The term "closet" took on a new meaning: you could be yourself and wear a military uniform, as long as you didn't tell anyone you wanted to suck every cock that passed you in the shower room. The irony of the President getting a blow job in the kitchen off the Oval Office with secret service men in sunglasses standing guard outside was an insult to every gay man and woman who risked their lives to serve their country in military service. Would the outcome have been different if the intern in the black dress and beret had been a young male page?

The wording of DADT prohibited people who *demonstrated a propensity*—an interesting term since it is defined in the dictionary as an inclination or natural tendency to behave in a particular way—*or intent to engage in homosexual acts from serving in the armed forces of the United States.* The ruling went on to state that the presence of homosexuals would create an unacceptable risk to the high standards, good order and discipline, and unit cohesion that are the essence of military capability. Whoever wrote that garbage had no understanding that I would have, in a heartbeat, thrown my body on a live grenade to save the life of my battle buddy. It had nothing to do with sucking cock.

In my freshman year at William & Mary, I was caught up in a scandal that rocked the campus. It was November 1963 when everyone was fixated on the assassination of President Kennedy, shocked and terrified that the civilized world was coming to an end. I found myself in a beer- and pot-fueled orgy at my English professor's apartment, only later that night to be picked up staggering down Jamestown Road in my Jockey shorts, according to the police report, disoriented and incoherent.

I was taken to the college infirmary, and my parents were called to meet with the Dean of Men. My English teacher, a visiting professor from Exeter, was sent back to England, and I was confined to the infirmary for observation. In 1963 homosexuality was treated as an illness, and under proper care, it was considered treatable and curable. Years later, Republican congresswoman Michele Bachmann and her Pillsbury Doughboy husband, Marcus, would continue the misdirected crusade to cure homosexuals through their Christian counseling practice in Minnesota. While reading an issue of the alumni magazine, I was shocked to find out in an interview with the congresswoman that she was a graduate of the William & Mary School of Law. How could Bachmann, John Stewart, Glenn Close, Thomas Jeffferson, James Comey and Tim Halladay all have been educated at the same venerable institution and turned out so different?

There was no "Don't ask, Don't tell" policy in effect when I was called into Captain Oliver's office to face charges from the Air Force officer that I had engaged in homosexual activity with another serviceman. It was a witch-hunt, and I was the victim of a fanatical hypocrite, keen on weeding out undesirables from the military. My grammar school friend Johnny Nistico was coerced into naming me in a harmless jerk-off session in a garage when we were both horny adolescents. Nistico was offered a deal to avoid a court martial.

The General Discharge, a classification created for servicemen who were not accused of any misconduct while in uniform but considered unfit for service, was a joke. It came with no benefits and was a stigma for anyone who ever wanted to run for public office. I knew as I stood in Mario's by the pay phone calling my family on Thanksgiving that I was coming home disgraced.

Years passed, and many lives would be shattered—men and women regardless of sexual orientation came home from Vietnam in boxes stuffed with rocks and photos instead of bones. Same-sex marriage would eventually become the law of the land, while redneck hypocrites acting under the pretense of God's law refused to issue legal marriage licenses. These same overweight fornicators in overalls, tricking the Pope into meeting with them to discus Christian values, were hugged by presidential candidates seeking the Evangelical vote.

At the end of the day I think most people want to hunker down under the covers, curl up next to their lover, maybe only in dreams or fantasies, snuggle with a warm hairy dog, or just cling to a lumpy pillow that doesn't talk back. I think that should be a right for everyone.

ABOUT THE AUTHOR

• • •

TOM BAKER is a graduate of the College of William & Mary. He enjoyed a successful career in the advertising world, winning many awards for the ads and commercials he produced. He now writes full-time. Baker lives in a tree house in Santa Monica Canyon.

CPSIA information can be obtained
at www.ICGtesting.com
Printed in the USA
FSOW01n0846260817
37886FS